PRAISE FOR THE
STEEL BROTHERS SAGA

"Hold onto the reins:
this red-hot Steel story is one wild ride."
~ A Love So True

"A spellbinding read from a
New York Times *bestselling author!"*
~ BookBub

"I'm in complete awe of this author. She has gone and delivered an epic, all-consuming, addicting, insanely intense story that's had me holding my breath, my heart pounding and my mind reeling."
~ The Sassy Nerd

"Absolutely UNPUTDOWNABLE!"
~ Bookalicious Babes

RAVENOUS

RAVENOUS

STEEL BROTHERS SAGA
BOOK ELEVEN

HELEN HARDT

This book is an original publication of Waterhouse Press.

Cover Design by Waterhouse Press, LLC
Cover Photographs: Shutterstock

ISBN: 978-1-64263-136-4

To my favorite cousins—
Carl, John (aka Yodel), and Chris (aka Tuna).

The psychiatric ward lives on!

PROLOGUE

Sometimes, when I'm watching, a memory haunts me. Torments me.

Reminds me why I'm watching.

Sometimes, when I'm watching, anger rages at me, pours out of me through my fists.

Reminds me why I'm watching.

Sometimes, when I'm watching, despair trickles through me, taking part of my soul.

Reminds me why I'm watching.

Most of the time, though...

I feel nothing.

CHAPTER ONE

Bryce

After staring at her for as long as I could and choking back a tear that threatened, I covered Marjorie's sleeping body.

I love you.

Had she meant to say the words aloud? They'd come out on a soft sigh during one of her many climaxes, and though I'd yearned to return them, I hadn't.

I couldn't go there. Not yet. Not until...

Not until I'd dealt with the demons that plagued me... including the long-buried secret from Joe's and my past that threatened us now.

I had to move on, make her understand that we couldn't ever be. I dressed quietly and then walked out to the desk in the kitchen. After finding a notepad and pen, I scribbled down some words.

Noxious words I didn't mean but had to say. She needed to move on, and I needed to help her. I walked back into the bedroom where my perfect angel still slept. I kissed her cheek lightly. She moved slightly but didn't wake up.

I wanted to remember her like this—soft and innocent and beautiful. So fucking beautiful.

I'm sorry, I said silently. *I'm sorry I can't be what you deserve.*

One more light kiss to her silky forehead.

Then I laid the note on the nightstand next to her.

I walked out of the bedroom.

Out of the guesthouse.

Out of Marjorie Steel's life.

I opened the door of the Mustang—I really needed to get rid of this damned car—sat down in the driver's seat, and pulled my phone out of my pocket.

Marjorie's text glared at me.

I need to talk to you.

We hadn't talked. I'd attacked her as soon as I got here. She hadn't resisted, but still...I should have asked her what she wanted to talk about. Instead, I'd chosen to be a selfish bastard and take from her body what I needed to stay sane.

Funny. The more I had of her, the less sane I became. The more I had of her, the more I wanted her, which was why I'd left. Why I'd written those hurtful words. Cold turkey was the only way to go with Marjorie Steel. Somehow, I'd have to find the willpower to leave her alone.

But she's in love with you.

She'd said the words in the throes of passion. I'd been thinking them myself but had held back. I wasn't even sure if she was aware she'd uttered them. If she could see inside my head, inside my dark soul, she'd see the truth.

I wasn't worth loving.

She was, though. She was so strong and so passionate. She deserved the world. I wanted to give it to her more than anything, but how could I? I was an empty shell—someone masquerading as a man but desolate inside.

I had such hatred for myself, and I hadn't thought I could hate myself any more.

But I did.

I did because I'd written those despicable words to the woman who meant more to me than anyone—other than my son—ever had.

I'd written them so she could see me for who I truly was—someone who could never give her what she deserved. The only way she'd stay away from me was if she thought I was a true louse.

I ruminated over the words I'd left on the page.

You can still sneak back in, destroy the note before she sees it...

I erased the thought from my mind. I'd done the only thing I could. She would hate me now, with good reason. I had to live with that.

I drove home, checked on a sleeping Henry, and then collapsed onto my bed for the last time.

Tomorrow we'd move to the guesthouse.

CHAPTER TWO

Marjorie

The note was callous.

The words were cruel.

Even the sheet of paper was crisp and unsympathetic.

Bryce Simpson was heartless.

I'd fallen in love with a heartless man.

My purse sat on a chair on the other side of the room. Still naked from our night of passion, I rose and grabbed it. Inside the hidden pocket was something I'd kept, even though I'd promised Mel I'd trashed it.

It was a reminder.

It was a security blanket.

Right now I needed it.

Stop.

I could walk to the kitchen. Open the refrigerator. Let the blast of cold air ease the unpleasantness from my mind.

Yes, it would be easier.

Much easier than...

I unzipped the pocket slowly and withdrew the sharp razor blade. I sat back down on the bed and regarded the scar on my upper thigh. It was still red, but it had healed. If I left it alone, it would eventually turn white and then gradually fade over the years.

Slowly, I lowered the blade to my flesh.

But the note caught my gaze once more. Why torture myself?

I couldn't help it. The words called to me like a gruesome accident I couldn't look away from, no matter how much I didn't want to see.

Because I *did* want to see. My rite of self-flagellation. Words would cut deeper than any blade ever could.

So I read them once more. Imagined his low and sexy voice uttering each one.

Marjorie,

I'm leaving, and I don't want you to pursue me. I can't deny our physical attraction, but I have no emotional ties to you. I'll be working on the ranch and living in the guesthouse, but I'll stay as far away from you as I possibly can. I need to be alone now. I can't have my attention diverted by my best friend's little sister. I need to give everything I have to my new position and to my son and mother. I don't need an extra distraction in my life. Nothing happened between us, and nothing more will ever happen. You are Joe's sister, nothing more.

Bryce

Such stilted words, as if he were addressing an audience of foreign dignitaries rather than a woman he'd just made love to.

A distraction? I was only a distraction?

Joe's sister? Nothing more?

Such coldness. No sorrow. No pleading with me to

understand. Nothing but hurtful and icy words.

Thank God I hadn't told him I loved him.

Oh, I'd been thinking it. Through all those orgasms, I'd been saying it over and over in my mind.

Once more I let the blade hover over my scarred flesh.

How easy it would be to slice into myself, allow the physical pain to overwhelm the emotional.

No. No. No.

I rose, still naked, and ran into the kitchen. The refrigerator loomed white and tall. My savior. I opened it and stood in the corner between the door and the shelves, letting the cold air waft over me.

My nipples puckered and goose bumps erupted on my skin.

Nothing went away, but at least the cool air eliminated the need—for the moment, at least—to cut myself. Mel would be proud of me. I should be proud of myself.

But I felt no pride. All I felt was devastation.

When I closed the refrigerator door, the scar on my upper thigh throbbed, taunting me.

Do it. Do it. Do it.

The cold air is gone. You know what will give you peace.

Do it. Do it. Do it.

"No!" I opened the refrigerator door once more. Inhaled the cold air.

Inhaled it again.

Again.

Again.

Again and again and again. I didn't stop when the urge to cut had escaped me. I continued to breathe in the cold air, ignoring the aromas of food, focusing only on the chill.

Finally, I closed the door once more, the scar still buzzing but no longer throbbing.

I could do this. I would be okay. For now, at least.

I tore the note into pieces and shoved it down the garbage disposal.

Not that it would do any good. I'd remember those words as long as I lived. Still, it gave me a sense of letting go of something I had no control over. Now to be proactive, as Mel said.

I'd get home to help Jade with the boys—anything to get my mind off Bryce and his cruelty. Jade had been ill last night after our talk with Colin. I dressed and hurried back to the main house to see how she was feeling.

The boys were still in bed, so I got them up and moving—Dale insisted he was fine to go back to school—and then I went to check on Jade.

I knocked softly. "Hey, it's me."

"Come on in." She was up and sitting in a recliner, clad in sweat pants and a T-shirt.

"Feeling okay?"

"Physically? Pretty good, actually. Emotionally? I'm a wreck."

I nodded. "Colin."

"Yup. What isn't he telling us?"

"I wish I knew. Where's Tal?"

"He got up before the butt crack of dawn. He told me why, I think, but I was half asleep and can't recall."

"He's probably in the orchard. The boys are up, and Dale says he wants to go to school today."

"Really? I should talk to him."

"Sure. I'll send him in to see you. Then I'm going to fix

breakfast for them. Do you want anything?"

"I don't think so. Not yet, anyway."

"Okay. Let me know if that changes."

Donny was already dressed and in the kitchen when I got there. Dale stumbled in a few minutes later while I was frying bacon.

"Dale, your mom wants to talk to you in her bedroom."

He nodded and left the kitchen. Dale still wasn't much of a talker, and since he'd freaked during recess over seeing someone he thought might be from his past, he'd clammed up even more. Talon was the best at getting through to him. Dale was still pretty distant with Jade, and I could tell it bothered her, but she was giving him the space he needed. She wasn't going to pressure him, I knew. She just wanted to make sure he was okay with going back to school.

A few minutes later he returned to the kitchen, and I set a plate of bacon, eggs, and toast in front of him.

"Still going to school?" I asked.

He nodded and started on his breakfast. Once the boys were off, I went back in to see Jade.

"Dale okay?" I asked.

"He seems to be. Thank God for Talon. I'd be lost handling Dale alone."

"You'd be fine, but Talon does seem to be able to reach him."

"I'm feeling kind of obsolete around here."

"You're being silly, and you know it. Those boys adore you."

"Well...Donny does."

"So does Dale. He's just quiet. Plus, he's scared everything is going to collapse around him again. All he needs is time."

"I know. It's frustrating, though. I've assured him time and again that Talon and I aren't going anywhere."

"He'll come around. What does Melanie say?"

"That he's healing and you can't put a time frame on these things."

I smiled. "Sounds a lot like what I just said."

"I know. Still, I'm worried, and Talon doesn't say so, but he is too."

"About the guy Dale saw at recess?"

She nodded.

"It could have been his imagination."

"I know that. But even if it's not someone he thinks he recognized, why is a guy in a hoodie hanging around a playground? It's creepy."

"Yeah, I know. The cops are on it. They'll be watching."

"Talon's calling in Mills and Johnson too."

"I figured he would."

"He'll do whatever he has to do to protect those boys," Jade said, "and so will I. That's why I think I need to go back to work."

"They need you here," I said.

"I know. But I'm pulling my hair out. I feel so useless. Gah! Let's talk about something else. And not about Colin, either. What were you doing at the guesthouse last night?"

Bam!

A two-ton rock crashed down on my head. Or so it felt, anyway.

Last night at the guesthouse.

I hadn't succeeded at forcing any of it from my mind, but at least I'd had something to do. Now? No way was I telling Jade any of this. I didn't need to add to her distress.

Plus...I'd never confided in her about the cutting. It was the only secret I'd ever kept from my best friend. I was just too ashamed. Only Mel knew, and I needed to call her. This morning had been a little too close for comfort.

"Just wanted to use the hot tub," I said, hating the acidic taste of the lie on my tongue.

"Marj, we have a perfectly good hot tub here."

"I know, but I needed a little alone time." Would she buy that?

"Oh. Yeah, I get it. It's kind of a three-ring circus around here. Sorry about that."

"I don't mean it that way. I love being here, and I love you and my brothers and those adorable boys."

"I know you didn't mean it badly. I'm just saying I understand."

I smiled—a forced smile, but a smile nonetheless. "If you ever need some alone time, just let me know."

"Are you kidding? I spend most days alone in this damned bedroom. The time I have with Talon, the boys, and you makes my days." She laughed. "Besides, no hot tub for me until I have this baby."

I loved hearing Jade laugh, and I especially loved hearing her talk about having the baby. After her scare at the hospital, she'd been nervous about losing the child.

"Once you give birth, you and I will have a girls' hot-tub date complete with bubbles—jacuzzi bubbles *and* Champagne."

"It's a date!"

I returned her smile as best I could. "I have something to take care of. Let me know if you need anything."

I walked to my own bedroom, grabbed my phone, and

pulled up my list of contacts.

CHAPTER THREE

Bryce

I woke to my phone vibrating on the nightstand. Joe.

"Yeah?" I said.

"Come outside."

I willed my brain to function. "Huh?"

"Come outside. Now."

"Yeah, sure. Okay." He didn't want to talk on the phone. I got it. I wiped the sleep out of my eyes and pulled on a pair of jeans, a T-shirt, and my slippers.

I walked out of the bedroom to find my mom feeding Henry in the kitchen.

"Hey," she said. "You were out late last night."

"Yeah. Joe and I had a lot of business to discuss." I kissed the top of my son's head. "Hey, buddy."

He gave me a sloppy smile, and I tousled his hair.

"Speaking of Joe, he's outside. I'll be back in a few."

"Tell him to come in. I just put on a pot of coffee."

I can't. Someone might be listening. A shiver skittered across my arm. At least we'd be out of the house today. "He says he's in a hurry, Mom. I won't be long." I walked out of the kitchen, through the small foyer, and out the door.

Joe stood across the street, next to his truck. He was dressed for work in jeans and cowboy boots. He even wore a black Stetson. I didn't own a cowboy hat. Not that I needed one. It wasn't a good look on me. At least I didn't think it would be.

And why I was ruminating over Joe's hat I had no idea. Anything to think about something other than what we were about to discuss.

Then a thought speared into my head. What if... What if Joe hadn't come over to discuss Justin and the Morses? What if Marjorie had called him? What if he was going to kick my ass for breaking his little sister's heart?

No matter. I deserved it.

I crossed the street. "Hey."

"Hey. Sorry to freak you out this morning."

Not Marjorie after all. I was relieved. A little.

"You didn't. I just didn't sleep well." A lie. I'd slept fine—after making love to his sister. Marjorie seemed to be my anti-nightmare drug. I just hadn't slept *enough*.

"I'm sorry. I haven't been sleeping great either. I hate keeping this from Melanie, but she's in her third trimester and I don't want to overload her."

"Good," I said, my tone a bit harsh. "Not just for Melanie, but we did agree to keep this solely between us."

"Easy," Joe said. "I haven't forgotten that. But she's my wife, and we don't have secrets. At least we didn't until now, and I don't like the feeling it gives me."

"I get it."

"You can trust me, Bryce. You know that."

"Yeah. Of course I do. What's up?"

"I found us a hacker."

"A hacker? What for?"

"To hack into the school system. To find Justin's last name."

I lifted my brow. "We just got done talking about keeping this between the two of us."

"I haven't told him anything."

"But you found him. Someone knows you're looking for a hacker."

"No one knows."

"How do you know that?"

He cleared his throat and adjusted his hat. "A friend of a friend."

"Who's the friend?"

He cleared his throat again. "I can't say."

"What do you mean you can't say? I thought we were in this together."

"We are. It's just..."

My heart slammed against my chest. "Joe, you didn't go surfing through the dark web, did you?"

"Are you fucking kidding me? You think I have a clue how to get on the dark web? Christ, Bryce."

"Then why can't you—"

"Because I can't. That's why."

"Sorry, Joe. Not good enough. This concerns us both equally."

"I know that. But there are other things involved here."

"What other things? Look, man, we've been friends our whole lives. I've got your back. You know that."

"Yeah, I know."

"Then be honest. I need to know what we're up against."

"We're not up against anything. Not from this, anyway."

"Then why can't you tell me more?"

"Look. You've got to trust me on this." He grabbed my arm—actually grabbed my arm.

I yanked it away. "Not cool."

"Sorry. If I tell you, you've got to promise me full confidentiality."

"That's a given, Joe. Christ."

"This friend of mine—I met him at a...club."

"The Future Lawmakers Club?" I blurted out.

Joe's eyes went wide.

"Sorry," I said. "Bad joke."

"Not a joke of any kind," Joe said.

"So what club, then?"

"A lifestyle club."

"Lifestyle? You mean swingers?"

"No." He shook his head. "I don't share. It's the...leather lifestyle."

BDSM? My best friend was into BDSM? Whoa. I'd dabbled a bit in the past myself, but never to the extent that I joined any kind of club.

"There's an underground community in the city," Joe continued. "I used to be a part of it."

"Okay. No offense, Joe, but TMI."

"Yeah? Don't knock it till you've tried it."

Did he and Melanie...? I so did not want to know. "Uh... okay. No judgment here."

"I'm not concerned about your judgment, Bryce, but there's an unspoken rule in the community. We don't talk about who or what we see there. Some of the people are pretty well-known, and if their names and involvement are revealed, it could hurt their business and everyday lives."

"I see. So you can't tell me who you got the name of the hacker from."

"That's right."

"Do I even know the guy?"

"Probably not."

"Then why—"

"Because I have integrity, damn it. That's why. I don't want people spreading word that I used to be a part of that club, and I won't do it either."

"All right. I respect you for that. Now tell me about this hacker."

"He comes highly recommended. He's damned expensive, but we need the information."

I swallowed. I didn't like the sound of any of this. "Why can't we just ask Jade for the information?"

"You know why. We'd have to tell her what information we want and why. You didn't want to use Mills and Johnson because you were afraid they'd put two and two together. Besides, we may need a good hacker for other stuff too."

"Good point." I shoved my hands into my pockets. "I wish I could help with the cost."

"Don't worry about that. You know I've got it covered."

"Should we meet with him in person?"

"He won't meet in person. He won't let anyone see his face."

Yeah. Not sounding good so far. "Okay... Then how do we get him the information?"

"I'll give him only what he requires. The year and the name. Tell him we need a last name and any other identifying information, address, whatever. I send it all in an encrypted file, and he gets back to me when and if he finds anything."

"Does this faceless hacker have a name?"

"He's called the Spider."

A chill swept the back of my neck. "That's a little creepy."

"Hey, if you have a better idea..."

I shook my head. "I don't. Go ahead and contact the Spider."

"I will. There's one other thing I've been thinking about."

"What's that?"

"I don't get how our memories are so fuzzy about that one camping trip. We were nine, Bryce, not three. We should be able to remember."

I'd been thinking and wondering about that myself. I had vivid memories from the time I was four. Finding a dead friend at age nine should have been traumatic for Joe and me, and it should have been imprinted on our long-term memories.

But it wasn't.

And I had come up with a plausible reason why.

CHAPTER FOUR

Marjorie

I sat with Melanie in her home office. "I'm glad you were free this morning. Thanks for squeezing me in."

"Anytime. You know that." She grabbed her notepad. "I've cut down my hours in the city so I can relax more at home. I've been seeing some patients via FaceTime. It's working well so far. Anyway, you caught me on a slow morning."

"I appreciate it."

"Marjorie, I'll always make time for you. How are you?"

How are you?

Three such innocent little words.

I'd come here for help, and Mel would help me. She always did.

So I would be truthful.

"Not good. Not good at all."

"Tell me what's going on."

That was Mel's way. Get straight to the point and then let me take the lead. She knew I'd tell her everything in my own time.

"I almost had a relapse this morning."

"Oh?"

"The razor blade."

"The same one?" she asked, her eyebrows arched.

I swallowed as I nodded. I'd told her I'd gotten rid of it. Instead, I'd tucked it in the inside zippered pocket hidden in the bottom of my purse.

"You still have it?"

I nodded again, pointing to my purse.

"First," she said, "don't beat yourself up about this. We all have setbacks. It's part of the healing process. You didn't *actually* cut yourself, right?"

This time I shook my head.

"Good. That's a win."

"I don't feel like I won anything."

"Life hasn't been the easiest for you, Marj. You've had to come to grips with your inadvertent role in Talon's abduction and the truth about your mother and father. Now you're taking care of Jade and the boys. That's a lot of responsibility."

"Responsibility I'm glad to take on."

"I know that. We all do. Doesn't make it easy. You're a young woman, Marj, and your life is out there. You're putting everything on hold. It's a very selfless thing for you to do."

"I thought..." I stared out the window at the ranch that was my home.

"You thought...what?"

"For about five minutes, I thought my life might be *here*."

"It is, of course. What I meant was—"

I held up my hand. "I know what you meant, Mel. I do. But something else happened, something I thought might keep me here in Snow Creek. Even here on the ranch."

"What are you talking about?"

I sighed. "Bryce Simpson."

Melanie's eyes widened slightly. She was trying to hide her surprise. Only Jade knew about my involvement with Bryce, and her word was as good as gold. Clearly he and I had kept our attraction under wraps. Melanie looked seriously astonished.

"What about him?" she asked.

Where to start? I stayed silent for a few seconds that seemed to stretch into hours.

Melanie didn't try to prod me. She always let me go at my own pace. Finally, I opened my mouth.

"I'm in love with him."

"I see. When did this happen?"

"I've had growing feelings for him for a while, and I've been attracted to him forever."

"He's going through a lot right now."

"I know that. And I get it."

"Does he have any idea how you feel?"

"That I love him? No. It doesn't matter anyway because he doesn't feel the same way."

"How do you know that?"

Words came tumbling out then. I told Mel everything. All of Bryce's and my encounters, our passion, how he told me I made him insane.

And our last encounter.

The note he'd left.

"It was devoid of even the slightest bit of emotion," I said, choking back a sob. "And I almost... I almost..."

"But you didn't, Marj. You didn't."

"Only because of Jade and the boys. They need me. I can't be broken right now. I have too much to do."

"The reason why doesn't matter. What matters is that you didn't succumb to the urge. You didn't harm yourself."

"He's moving into the guesthouse, Mel. He'll be living less than a half mile from me, and he'll be working here on the ranch.

How am I supposed to deal with any of that? The lovemaking was so amazing. He was so full of desire and passion. I swear the earth moved. How could he have been so passionate and loving but then turn so cold in the span of hours? How could it have meant nothing to him?"

"Have you considered that it *didn't* mean nothing to him?"

"But the note..."

"The note doesn't really matter. You've said already that he was honest with you from the outset that he wasn't in a place to have a relationship right now."

"I know. I just never expected him to be so cruel."

"I understand," Melanie said. "Bryce is not a cruel man, which makes me think something else might be going on here."

"He's not his father," I said. "None of us thinks he is."

"That's true. But have you considered that maybe *he* thinks he is? And he's trying to keep you at arm's length because he's afraid?"

I cocked my head. "You know, he's been letting his mother pretty much care for Henry twenty-four-seven since everything went down. He says it's because his mom needs Henry right now, but maybe..."

"Maybe Bryce is afraid to be close to Henry. Afraid of what he might become."

"That's silly."

"Is it? He's not the only one who's had thoughts like that."

I well knew my brother Ryan and his wife had both worried they'd turn out to be psychopathic like their biological mother and father, respectively.

"It's easy for me or anyone else to tell Bryce that it's unlikely," Mel went on, "but it's not so easy to get him to believe it."

"I know."

How well I knew. I'd had the same thoughts about my mother. She was far from a psychopath, but she was certifiably insane. She lived in her own reality where I was still a baby and Ryan didn't exist.

Which reminded me. I need to touch base with the other nurse who'd been assigned to her the day "my father" had visited. Icy spikes dug into the back of my neck. Nothing had shown up on the visitors' log, and it was certainly within the realm of possibility that my mother had imagined the whole thing.

Still, it niggled at me. With Dale having seen someone who spooked him, and with Colin Morse and his father acting strangely, I couldn't help but think some stranger might be lurking around my mother.

I didn't voice any of this to Mel. In fact, I'd neglected to tell my brothers. So much had happened in so few days that I'd actually let it float to the back of my mind.

I had to get in touch with Barry, the nurse, and I had to tell my brothers.

"Maybe you need to give him what he asks for. Give him the space. Don't seek him out."

"But I live in the main house!"

"I'm not saying you have to purposely avoid him. If that's what he wants, let *him* do the avoiding. My guess is he won't be able to stay away from you."

"Why?"

"Because he hasn't so far. He told you from the beginning that he couldn't be with you, yet you say he came back to you twice after that."

"What am I supposed to do if he comes to me, then?"

"That's up to you."

I stopped myself from rolling my eyes. "No offense, but that's no help at all."

"I can't make your decisions for you, Marj. You know that."

Yeah. Yeah. Yeah. I knew that. Therapy had helped me a lot, but sometimes it grated on my nerves. Sometimes I just wanted the easy way out.

"I don't know what to do. If he comes to me and wants me..." I couldn't finish the sentence. We both knew the answer.

I'd give in.

I'd give in to Bryce Simpson every time.

CHAPTER FIVE

Bryce

"I don't get it," Joe said again.

I cleared my throat. "Mathias roofied Ruby."

"Yeah. So?"

"And Talon only has fragmented memories of his time in captivity. He was probably drugged."

"Shit." Joe removed his hat and threaded his fingers through his hair. "You're not thinking..."

I scoffed. "Sure I am. They obviously had access to all kinds of drugs."

Joe's skin reddened, and his lips drew into a snarl I knew well. This was mad Joe. Hothead Joe. And I didn't blame him one bit.

"Your father *drugged* us?"

"We'll never know for sure, but what other explanation is there? We didn't remember for a long, long time, and even now the memories are fuzzy. But I have vivid memories of when I was younger than nine."

I couldn't say any more. I wasn't sure why the thought of my father drugging us was so foreign to me. Hell, drugging us was the least of his crimes.

"Rohypnol," Joe said, "can cause retrograde amnesia. Melanie told me."

"Exactly. Once this happened, my father had to effectively erase our memories. I can't think of any way to do that other than drugs."

"Fucking bastard," Joe said. Then, "Sorry, man."

"Are you kidding me? I wish there were a worse word for him. I wish I could pry every atom of his DNA out of me."

How true. I'd spent countless hours in the shower, scalding myself with hot water in a useless attempt to scrub and burn all of Tom Simpson out of my genes. Ridiculous, I knew.

I did it anyway.

"I suppose it's still only conjecture," Joe said.

"It's the most likely explanation. He told us it never happened. We were nine, not three. We weren't going to disbelieve something we'd seen with our own eyes."

"The kid was dead, though," Joe said. "I remember that much."

The image of Justin's limp, naked body cut into my mind. Had he been dead? Could he have been revived? His skin was... was...

"Damn!"

"What?" Joe asked.

"I can't remember what his skin looked like. Was it still pink? Or was it gray and pasty? Do you remember, Joe?"

"Are you saying what I think you're saying?"

"Yeah. Maybe. What if he wasn't *dead*?"

"Impossible. I mean... Where did he go, then? He never came back to school. His family must have left Snow Creek."

"If we knew his last name, we'd have a better chance of figuring this all out."

"Not if his name was Justin Smith or Jones."

"I guess it's up to the Spider now," I said.

"Do you really think Justin didn't die?" Joe asked.

I shook my head. "It's not likely, but we have to consider all angles, no matter how improbable they seem. Ted Morse knows about this forgotten blip on the radar of our lives, and he found out somehow."

"Yeah, but if— Oh, shit."

"What?"

Joe placed his hat back on his head. "Wendy, Mathias, Wade, and your father are all out of the picture now. That means if they were holding something over Justin's or someone else's head, it's no longer in effect."

"And Morse got to them."

"Or Morse *went* to them." Joe shook his head. "This is fucked up. So fucked up."

"This is our life now, Joe," I said. "It is what it is."

He grabbed his cell phone. "Time to coordinate with the Spider."

⋆ ⋆ ⋆

That afternoon, Henry, my mother, and I left our little house in town for the last time as inhabitants and moved into the guesthouse behind the main ranch house on Steel Acres. As I'd assumed would happen, my mother insisted I take the master suite. Good thing I hadn't made love to Marjorie in that room. The smallest room had been set up as Henry's nursery, and my mother chose another one, leaving the room where Marjorie and I had slept empty.

I wasn't sure if that was good or bad.

If the room were taken, I wouldn't be able to go in there and remember.

Of course, if my mother or my son were living in the room... Yeah, that would be worse.

We'd chosen to use the furniture already in the house, so only Henry's crib, our personals, and a few antiques of my mother's had been moved in.

My mother bustled around the kitchen, Henry on her hip. "It's stocked," she said. "I can't believe it."

"Believe it," I said.

"I'll whip us up some dinner." She set Henry in his high chair. "You hungry, doll?"

Henry gurgled happily.

"What do you feel like? They left us plenty of beef."

"I'm not that hungry, Mom. Just make whatever sounds good."

"Are you feeling okay?"

My mother had no idea what a loaded question that was. "I'm good. Just not hungry."

I hated lying to my mother.

Hell, I hated lying, period.

How could I possibly be my father's son? That man had perfected lying to an art.

The worst lie *I'd* ever told? That horrid note I'd left for Marjorie last night. I'd felt sick writing it, and I still felt sick. Between that and what I was recalling from my childhood, I might never feel physically good again.

Marjorie.

She'd said those three words I longed to hear.

I love you.

She'd said them in the middle of a climax, but so what? I had no doubt she'd meant them.

How I'd longed to return her sentiment, for I did love her.

I loved her so damned much.

And here I was, living on her ranch, and I had to stay as far away from her as I could.

I stepped outside the kitchen onto the patio. The hot tub whirred in the distance—the hot tub where I'd found Marjorie last night.

I grabbed my hair and pulled. How the hell was I supposed to live in this house?

You have to, Bryce. You just have to. You have to do this for your son and your mother. They need you.

If only I'd never initiated that first kiss.

But there'd been no stopping the kiss. There'd been no stopping the energy that sizzled between us.

Which was why—

Fuck.

Marjorie.

She was walking toward the guesthouse.

I went inside quickly, still watching her from the window of the French doors. When she was about a hundred yards away, she turned abruptly and headed back toward the main house.

Maybe she'd just been out on a stroll.

Or maybe she'd been coming to me and then changed her mind.

I thought again of the cruel words I'd written to her after our last night together. I didn't mean any of them, but I was determined to keep her away from me.

I was poison.

I couldn't infect her.

I was nothing but emptiness, and though she filled me beyond my wildest dreams, I was still nothing.

Nothing.

Nothing.

Nothing.

Talon had invited the three of us to dinner this evening to celebrate our move into the guesthouse, but I'd turned him down. I had to keep this business. Solely business. Eating dinner with Marjorie Steel would be too difficult. Too heart-wrenching.

She loved me. And God, if she truly loved me, my words had cut into her as much as writing them had cut into me.

I was a fucking piece of shit.

I thought about getting a drink, but alcohol wouldn't help me. Nothing would. Nothing ever would.

When you were nothing, the only constant in your life was...*nothing*.

CHAPTER SIX

Marjorie

I hadn't meant to walk to the guesthouse. I'd been outside with Donny and the pups, and my feet just started moving. Bryce had seen me and gone quickly inside, so I'd turned around.

He didn't want to see me.

He'd meant the words he'd so callously written.

But it didn't make sense. Our lovemaking could not have been one-sided. It just couldn't have been.

Give him space.

Mel's words echoed inside my head.

Walking to his home wasn't giving him space.

I went back inside to begin dinner. Donny would be clamoring for his supper before long. Dale was in his room, as usual, but had recovered somewhat from his scare on the playground at school a few days earlier.

I'd just put some chicken breasts under the broiler when Talon walked into the kitchen.

"Hey, Sis."

"Hey, yourself. Good day?"

"Decent. Hard to concentrate, though, with all this other stuff happening. How're Jade and the boys?"

"Jade's in the bedroom. She said she'll be in for dinner.

Donny's outside, and Dale's in his room."

Talon shook his head. "I worry about that boy."

"I do too. Maybe it'll get better after the adoption."

"It's been postponed until next week," Talon said.

"Oh?"

"Yeah. I got a call today. The judge had an emergency." He shoved his hands into his pockets. "And I'm not sure it will help. The kid needs time more than anything."

I simply nodded. If anyone knew what Dale needed, Talon did. He'd been through much of the same.

He continued, "You know, whatever Dale went through, it was worse than what I endured. I can't imagine watching my little brother suffer the same. It would have made it a thousand times harder."

I wasn't sure what to say. Talon so rarely mentioned anything specific about his time in captivity. I felt like a complete dolt for remaining silent.

"I'll go check on him." Talon left the kitchen.

Good job, Marj. Here I was concerned about a stupid note from Bryce, and the rest of my family was dealing with major abuse trauma.

I was in love with a man who could never love me back. So what? I'd taken up Melanie's valuable time today when she could have been helping people with real problems.

Jade was right. I needed to get back in the game. She didn't know about the cutting, but I'd stopped myself from doing it again after Bryce left me that hideous note. That had to mean something, right? Maybe I was okay.

Not okay exactly, but at least better. Good enough to date. I wouldn't fall in love, because I was already in love. Dating didn't have to lead to love. I was dead set against dating websites, so I'd have to do this the old-fashioned way. Back to the gym tomorrow, and I'd have a look around.

I removed the broiled chicken from the oven and seasoned it. By the time I was ready to call everyone for dinner, my phone buzzed. Not a number I recognized.

"Hello?"

"I'm looking for Marjorie Steel."

"You found her. Who is this, please?"

"This is Barry Wilson from Newhaven Center, returning your call."

"I don't recognize this number."

"Sorry. The center gave me your message, and I'm returning it from my personal cell. I wanted to wait until I got off work."

"Oh. Sure."

"What can I help you with?"

"I'm Daphne Steel's daughter, and I understand you were one of the nurses assigned to her a few days ago."

"I was."

"She mentioned that a gray-haired man had visited her. Do you recall?"

"Any visitor would be on the log."

"I've already checked the log, and no one is listed. And I know what you're going to say. My mother is mentally ill and probably made it up. Only it's not like her to make things up that aren't already in her head."

"I understand. I'd never assume she made anything up."

"Thank you. The other nurse in her wing that day wasn't quite as..."

He chuckled. "Lori. Yeah. She's a great nurse, but she's a little more seasoned, and she can be blunt."

"Got it. Anyway, do you remember seeing any strange men in the wing that day?"

He paused a moment. "I do, actually. I just assumed the person had logged in and was allowed to be there. I didn't specifically see anyone in Daphne's room, but I did see a man outside her room. He was only there a few seconds."

"So he could have been coming or going?"

"Right, or he could have been there for another patient."

"Then he'd still show up on the log, just not as a visitor to my mother."

"He should."

"You don't sound overly convinced."

"Let's just say it wouldn't be the first time someone got through without signing in."

"Are you serious? They're rabid about that log. I have to sign in every time I see my mother, and they all know me now."

He paused again. Then, "Some days are busier than others, and the front desk gets overwhelmed."

His tone didn't convince me. "Barry, this is serious."

"I'm being serious. I shouldn't have said anything."

"Yeah, you should have. My mother is a sick woman, as you know. My brothers and I don't want her to have unauthorized visitors."

"Like I said, I didn't see the guy go into her room."

"Can you describe him?"

"He was tall."

"Okay. Was his hair short? Long? Thick? Thin? Balding?"

"I don't know. I saw him by your mother's door for a minute at most, and I didn't really think anything of it."

"Had you ever seen him at the center before?"

"Hard to say. We get a lot of people some days."

I sighed. This wasn't helpful at all. "Did he speak to you?"

Another pause. "No. He didn't."

Damn. I wished I could see Barry's face. I got the distinct impression he was lying. I could easily set Talon and Joe on him. They could intimidate anyone into truthfulness.

"What about his clothes? Do you recall what he was wearing?"

"Not really. He was dressed normally."

"Jeans? A suit?"

"I really don't remember, Ms. Steel."

"All right. Let's attack this from another angle. What time did you see him?"

"I didn't check my watch, but it was shortly before I left for the day. I leave at four p.m."

"Okay. That's helpful. You say he was dressed normally. Can you elaborate?"

"How can I elaborate? If he'd been wearing bright purple, I'd have noticed. I didn't notice his clothes."

"And you really can't remember the length of his hair?"

"Nondescript. I would have remembered if he'd had really long hair, you know?"

"How tall was he?"

"Tall. Taller than me."

"Anything else?"

"Not that I can think of. I'm sorry I'm not more help."

"That's okay," I said sweetly. Best not to burn this bridge. "If I have more questions, I'll call you."

"Yeah. Of course."

"Thanks for your help."

"You're welcome."

Yeah, I was definitely bringing Joe and Talon in on this. I

began to text them when the phone buzzed again.

"Hello?"

"Marjorie, hello. Evelyn Simpson."

My heart dropped. Why was Bryce's mother calling me? "Hi, Evelyn."

"I'm so sorry to bother you, but Bryce went out, and can you believe this? We're out of diapers. I need to run into town and get some. I was sure I had another whole box, but they seem to have gotten lost in the move. Anyway, could you possibly come over and keep an eye on Henry while I'm gone? He's been fussy all day, and I don't want to drag him into town. He's cutting another tooth, poor thing."

Bryce had gone out. It was dinnertime, after all. Who had he gone out with?

None of my business.

None of my fucking business.

"I'm happy to, but I'm just putting dinner on the table for Talon, Jade, and the boys."

"Oh, goodness. I don't want to interrupt your dinner."

"No worries about that. I'm not hungry anyway." That was the God's honest truth. After Bryce's note, I might never eat again.

"You're welcome to anything here. The place is stocked." She chuckled, which sounded a bit forced. "With everything except diapers, that is."

"Thank you, but I'm fine. Give me about fifteen minutes. I'll get them fed, and then I'll walk over to the guesthouse."

"You're a gem, Marjorie."

"Call me Marj. Everyone does. I'll see you in a few."

"Thank you. Bye."

My heart sped as I got dinner on the table. Once everyone

was seated, I excused myself.

"You're not eating?" Jade asked.

"Not hungry right now. I'll eat later." I sped out the front door so no one would ask questions about why I was going to the guesthouse. I quickly walked around the sprawling ranch house to the pathway in back.

Bryce wasn't home. If he had been, Evelyn wouldn't need me. So why was my heart pounding? Evelyn would only be gone an hour or so. Still, setting foot in what was now Bryce's home gave me the chills—in both a good and a bad way.

I'd been in this house early this morning.

I'd read that horrible note here. In this house.

And now I was going back.

For Evelyn. For Henry. After all, a baby needed diapers.

Not for Bryce.

Not for Bryce at all. He wasn't even there.

I knocked softly on the front door.

"Hi, Marj," Evelyn said when she opened the door. "I can't thank you enough for this. Henry adores you, and since you're so close now—"

"It's no problem," I said, forcing a smile. "I'm happy to help with Henry anytime." I meant it. Bryce's son was such a sweetie.

"I can't believe the diapers disappeared." She sighed. "This move happened so quickly, and the movers took care of everything. At least I thought they had."

"Where's Henry?"

"In the kitchen in his high chair. He just finished his supper. Let's hope he doesn't start fussing again. I won't be long." She dodged past me and out the door.

I hurried into the kitchen. Henry wasn't fussing, but he

didn't smile at me either. Usually the kid was all happiness.

"Hey, sweetie. Let's get that face cleaned up, and then we'll find something fun to do. Would you like that?" I helped myself to a clean cloth out of a kitchen drawer, wet it with warm water, and cleaned Henry's adorable lips and cheeks. "That's better, huh?" I lifted him out of his chair and walked toward the bedrooms.

My skin tingled when I walked past the room where Bryce and I had made love. I peeked inside. That hadn't become the nursery, thank God. In fact, it appeared just as it had, nothing new. Evelyn had taken a different room.

The nursery was the next room, all white walls with no nursery décor. Only a crib, changing table, a rocking chair, a bookshelf, and a big toy box. I eyed the bookshelf. "How about *Goodnight, Moon*? That's always a good one." I grabbed the book and sat down in the rocker, settling Henry into my lap.

So much for not fussing. Henry couldn't get comfortable. I tried several different positions, but nothing worked. Finally I gave up on the book. I opened Henry's small mouth and took a look. Indeed, a lateral incisor was erupting into Henry's sore gums. Poor little guy. Something cold would help. With Henry still on my hip, I rooted through the toy box until I found some plastic teething keys. We walked to the kitchen, where I washed them with soapy water and then opened the freezer.

"Oh, Evelyn, bless you!" Another teething ring sat on the top shelf of the freezer. I replaced it with the keys and held the already cold ring against Henry's gums. He resisted at first, but once the ring warmed a little, he sucked at it gladly.

"How about that story now?" I said, walking out of the kitchen.

And right into Bryce.

CHAPTER SEVEN

Bryce

Such a perfect picture.

Marjorie holding my son, comforting him, helping him with his teething pain. For a moment I let myself imagine that she lived here, that Henry was her son as well as mine, and that I was coming home to my family.

My beautiful family.

She stared at me, wide-eyed, and then Henry reached his chubby little arms out to me. I smiled and took him from Marj.

Neither of us had spoken yet.

Finally, I said, "Where's Mom?"

Marjorie didn't meet my gaze. "She ran out to get diapers. I guess the movers lost them or something."

"Oh." Diapers. Man, I was a lousy father. My son was out of diapers, and I'd been clueless.

"I'm sorry she had to bother you. I'm home now, so—"

"So I can leave." Still not meeting my gaze. "I get it."

I ran back through that horrible note in my mind.

I'm leaving...

I have no emotional ties to you...

Nothing happened between us, and nothing more will ever happen...

You are Joe's sister, nothing more...

I wasn't staying away from her.

Of course my mother—not I—had invited her here. And why not? Mom had no idea what had gone on between Marj and me. It made perfect sense for her to call Marj if she needed a sitter. Marj was close, and she loved Henry. Henry loved her.

She finally looked up and met my gaze.

Hurt shone in her dark eyes. Those eyes, usually so warm and caring, were distant, devastated.

Devastation I had put there.

I was a jerk. A major fucking jerk.

She cleared her throat. "He's eaten. The cold teething ring seems to help his fussiness a little. We were just about to read a story."

"Da-da!" Henry said.

A grin split Marjorie's beautiful face. "He's talking?"

"Just 'Da-da' and 'Ga-ga,' for my mom."

She grabbed one of Henry's little hands. "Such a smart boy! Good for you, Henry."

"Ma-ma," Henry said.

Marj's cheeks pinked.

It was a fluke, of course. Henry made all kinds of silly sounds.

If only it were true. If only Marjorie were Henry's mama and she lived here with me.

If only...

I wasn't sure what to say. "Is that a new word, Henry? Did you say Marjorie?"

"Da-da," Henry said.

Yeah. A fluke.

"I haven't spent enough time with him for him to know my name," Marj said.

"Yeah. True."

"So...I guess I'll go."

"Thank you for watching him."

"I'm happy to help. Anytime." She turned away and walked toward the doorway.

Let her go. Do the right thing and let her go.

I kissed my son's rosy cheek. Then, "No. Wait. Don't go."

She turned, her expression a mixture of distress and hope. I'd offered her hope with just four words.

"Have you eaten?" I asked quickly. "The least we can do is feed you."

"I made dinner at home."

"Oh."

"But I didn't eat. I wasn't hungry."

I wasn't overly hungry myself. Rejecting the woman I loved had taken its toll. It was clearly taking its toll on her as well, a fact that made me feel like the lowest of the low. Which was true.

"Oh."

Great conversation, Bryce.

"Henry already ate. Your mom fed him before she left."

"Did she eat?"

"I have no idea."

"She usually waits for me. I'm sure she's planning something. Why don't you stay?"

She lifted her brow. "Seriously, Bryce? You want me to stay for dinner?"

For dinner. For the evening. For the rest of your life.

If only I could say the words.

"Sure. My mom would want you to stay. You know, for watching Henry and all."

"Your mom wants me to stay. Great. What do *you* want, Bryce?"

I want everything. Fucking everything.

Instead of saying anything, though, I stood like a zombie, my little son squirming in my arms.

"What I figured." Marjorie took Henry from me. "I promised him a story, and then I'll leave."

She walked away, taking Henry with her to the nursery. I loved how natural she looked with him. I loved how she commanded the house, which of course shouldn't surprise me. She'd been here many times before. I loved...

I just loved.

I loved everything about Marjorie Steel.

I *loved* Marjorie Steel.

I quietly made my way to the doorway of the nursery and stood against the wall. Marjorie's voice was soothing as she read the words of the classic children's book. I closed my eyes, seeing in my mind Marjorie in the rocking chair, my sweet son in her arms, as she held the book and read to him with care. With love. It wasn't a long book, so soon her voice petered out, and the soft sounds of her rising and placing Henry in his crib wafted to my ears.

When she strode out of the nursery, I couldn't help myself.

I grabbed her and kissed her. Hard.

Her lips remained closed, but I licked the seam, probing her to open.

When she did, I plunged inside.

It was a hard kiss, a kiss of need and urgency.

And no sooner had it begun than my mother returned, bustling through the entryway.

Marjorie pushed against me, breaking the kiss. She looked

away, wiping her mouth and hurrying toward my mother.

The wiping our kiss from her mouth got to me. She was wiping me away. Not that I could blame her.

"Good, you're still here," my mother said to her. "I saw Bryce's car and thought you might have left."

"He's only been home a few minutes. I was reading Henry a story and he dozed off. He's in his crib."

"Thank goodness. The poor thing's been so fussy with that tooth."

"The teething ring in the freezer helped."

"You found that? Good."

"I put another one in there to replace it."

"You think of everything, Marjorie. You're going to be an excellent mother someday."

I sucked in a breath at those words. She was right. Marjorie would be an amazing mother. She loved me, and I loved her. In a perfect world, Marj's children would also be mine.

If only...

But she deserved a husband and father to her children who wasn't a shadow of his former self. That would never be me.

"I've got dinner ready to go into the oven," my mother continued. "Green chile enchiladas. Please stay."

"It sounds delicious, but I can't."

"If you say so. Thank you so much for looking after Henry."

"Anytime. I adore him." She padded to the front door, avoiding looking toward the hallway where I still stood outside Henry's room, and she left.

Taking a big chunk of my heart with her.

CHAPTER EIGHT

Marjorie

Crying is for girls.

I'd lived by those words my whole life. Growing up on a ranch with a father and three brothers had made those words not only necessary but also a personal philosophy. Crying solved nothing. You have a problem? Find a solution. Don't wallow in tears. It's a waste of time.

I sniffed back the tears that wanted so badly to come pouring out of me.

I didn't just live with men anymore, though. I had Jade, my best friend in the world, and Mel, who argued that crying wasn't a waste of time. To the contrary, crying released toxins from the body and relieved stress.

It also left you swollen, red, and ugly.

I couldn't help a scoffing chuckle. Release toxins? My relationship—for lack of a better word—with Bryce was pretty darn toxic. Maybe I needed a good toxin release. Sounded a lot better than a good blubbering cry.

Where, though? If I went back to the house, Talon and the boys would be there. I'd have to hold my tears until I got to my bedroom.

Certainly not on the path to the guesthouse. Bryce could walk out back and see me.

Our ranch was huge. I could go anywhere, but we had hands working around the clock most of the time.

Biggest ranch in Colorado, and I couldn't find a place to be alone, really alone.

"Damn it!" I said aloud.

I didn't have my purse with me, just my phone. No tissues, and already the tears were streaming down my cheeks like tiny flowing rivers.

"Stop it," I said, again out loud. "Crying is for girls."

I had no choice. I had to go home to get a tissue.

Damn Bryce Simpson. Why had he kissed me? Why had I let him? If he couldn't give me anything, like he'd said in his letter, if nothing had happened between us, why had he kissed me?

Why?

Nothing could stop the crying now. Sobs racked my body, and I ran toward the main house. My vision was blurred from the tears, but I knew the way. No prob—

"Ow!" I screamed as I fell on the walkway. I'd tripped over something. Not that I could see anything at the moment.

My knee hurt a little, though the fabric of my jeans hadn't ripped. Nothing I couldn't handle. Growing up on a ranch, I'd had more than my share of cuts and bruises, and I'd learned how to walk it off the way my brothers did.

Not this time, though.

Not this time.

I cried. I crumpled on the walkway, and I cried and I cried and I cried.

Moments passed—how many? I didn't know—while I sat on the concrete walkway, hugging my knees to my body as the weeping continued. Did I truly have this many tears to give?

Would it ever stop?

I wiped my nose on my arm. Gross, but what other choice did I have? I sniffed back as much as I could, when—

"Hey." A hand clamped down on my shoulder.

I jerked and looked up. The face was blurry through my tears, but I'd recognize it anywhere.

I sniffled. "Go away, Bryce."

He didn't. Instead, he pulled a red bandana out of his pocket and handed it to me. I blew my nose unceremoniously into the soft cloth. Not ladylike at all, but it sure felt good to expel the watery snot. Embarrassment warmed my skin. Or heck, it could have been from my meltdown. Probably both.

With the only dry part left on the bandana, I wiped my eyes. Then I handed it back to Bryce. "Here."

"Keep it."

"I don't want it." I threw it at him. It landed on the grass next to his feet.

"Look, Marj—"

"Please, spare me your words. I've no more use for them. Not after..." I shook my head. I couldn't finish. Couldn't bring the words out of my throat.

Bryce sat down on the grass across from me. "Look at me," he said gently.

What the hell? I knew I was a disgusting mess. I met his blue gaze.

"I never meant to hurt you."

I scoffed.

"I mean it."

"The words you chose weren't hurtful at all," I said sarcastically. "And you couldn't even say them to my face. You left me a note, Bryce. A note!"

"I just—"

I held up a hand. "Don't even try to excuse it. It was cowardly, and you know it."

"I had to."

"Really? You couldn't have dumped me to my face?"

I regretted my word choice as soon as I spoke. Dumped implied we'd been in a relationship. We hadn't been. He'd been clear on that from the beginning.

"No, I couldn't."

"Because you're a coward."

"That's part of it. I won't deny it."

"*Part* of it? Come on." I rolled my eyes. "That's *all* of it. A real man would have said the words to my face."

"A real man?"

"Yeah. A real man. You're lacking there."

He shook his head. "You have no idea. A real man wouldn't start something he can't finish. A real man knows his limitations. A real man... Fuck."

"I grew up with three real men, Bryce. You don't have to educate me on what a real man is."

"A real man, Marjorie? Would a real man do this?" He cupped my cheeks and kissed me.

Again.

Hard.

This time I didn't start with my lips pressed shut.

CHAPTER NINE

Bryce

Her lips were salty from her tears—tears I had caused. But I didn't ruminate on that, not in this instant, when she opened for me so lovingly. How could I do this to her? Kiss her like this, when I'd leave her again? I had no control around this woman. These thoughts were jumbled in my mind until they became fragmented and shapeless. Feeling replaced them. Pure, raw feeling. Feeling like I'd never experienced, and I knew instinctively I never would again.

She kissed me back.

She was in love with me. She'd said the words. But she didn't know I was in love with her.

Had I really thought I could resist her? Had I really thought I could live half a mile away from her, work for her brothers, and still never see her?

I deepened the kiss, taking all her sweetness and goodness that I could. Our mouths molded together as though they were one. As if they've been made to produce the ultimate kiss.

I kissed her and I kissed her and I kissed her, sliding my lips against hers, my tongue against hers, exploring every crevice of her warm, sweet mouth. How I wished it could go on forever. My cock reminded me that it couldn't. If I didn't stop this kiss, I knew where it would head. To a place I'd been before, a place where I wanted more than anything to stay forever....

Still, I didn't stop the kiss.

I physically could not.

I didn't have to. Marjorie pushed hard at my chest, causing the suction of our mouths to break.

Her face was red and swollen with tears, the whites of her beautiful eyes bloodshot, her salty lips swollen from the kiss I'd given her.

She'd never looked more beautiful.

I sat like a zombie, no words coming to me. All I wanted in the world was to finish the kiss, to take it to its ultimate conclusion.

"You're not playing fair," she said solemnly.

What could I say? She was right.

"I'm going home." She turned away.

My hand automatically reached out to stop her.

She looked over her shoulder. "Don't."

I dropped my arms to my side. Then I watched her walk away from me, loathing myself for hurting her again.

★ ★ ★

After dinner, I drove to Grand Junction to meet Joe at the dive bar. He hadn't arrived yet, and I was sorry to see that Heidi—who I'd nearly had a one-nighter with—was working.

"Hey, Bob," she said.

I waved and took a seat at the bar to avoid her.

The elderly man named Mike sat at the other end of the bar. I waved to him as well. I didn't think it was an invitation to get off his stool and come talk to me, but apparently he disagreed.

"Good to see you. Bryce, is it?"

"Yeah. I'm just waiting for Joe."

"I don't mean to get too personal on you, Bryce, but you kind of look like you just lost your best friend."

"Not unless Joe doesn't show up. He's been my best friend for pretty much my whole life."

"Woman trouble, then?"

If you only knew. I didn't say anything.

"Heidi there seems to know you. *Bob.*"

"Nothing happened between Heidi and me."

"Did I say it did?"

Joe had described Mike to me as a kind of guardian angel to the Steel brothers. Frankly, I didn't see it. In fact, he was being a pain in my ass. But Joe liked him, so I wouldn't be rude.

"She calls me Bob because—"

"I didn't ask for any explanation."

"No, you didn't. Let me get your drink." I signaled the bartender. "I'll have a bourbon, and get my friend here whatever he's having."

"Obliged," Mike said. "Sorry if I got a little personal there."

"It's okay."

"None of my business, but something is definitely bothering you."

"Nothing I can't handle."

What a damned, damned lie. I couldn't handle anything. I couldn't handle what my father had been. What I might become because of him. And I sure as hell couldn't handle Marjorie Steel.

Joe walked in then, and not for the first time, I thought about what my best friend would do to me if he knew what had happened between his baby sister and me.

"Bryce," he said. "And Mike. Good to see you."

"Your friend here just got me a drink," Mike said. "I'll drink it at the other end of the bar. I get the feeling he needs to talk. I think it's a woman thing."

After Mike moved away, Joe said, "A woman thing?"

Damn. Yeah, partially. Nothing I could tell the older brother of the woman, though.

"Nah. He's wrong. I'm just a mess about all this shit."

Joe looked at me, his eyes serious. "What did you tell him?"

"Nothing. Why would you think I'd divulge anything we talked about?"

"Sorry, man. You know I trust you implicitly. I'm just so fucking on edge."

"I hear you. Did you contact the Spider?"

He nodded. "Now we wait."

"How long?"

"He didn't say."

"We're kind of in a hurry here, Joe."

"You think I don't know that? I can't sleep. I've got a pregnant wife at home who I can't share this with for many reasons. It's killing me."

"I know. Sorry."

"We've got to keep cool," he said. "We can't start fighting with each other, Bryce."

I nodded. He was right.

Joe ordered a drink, and we sat, silent, for a few moments. I nursed the rotgut bourbon slowly. It was every bit as harsh as I recalled. I was pretty sure it was leaving a trail of ashes down my esophagus.

"Hey, Bob." Heidi walked to the bar and laid her hand on

my shoulder. "Len, I need two raspberry margaritas and an amaretto sour."

"What the—"

Heidi laughed raucously. "Len, you know I'm joshing you. A rye and two Scotches."

Len poured the drinks, and Heidi ambled away.

"Bob?" Joe said to me.

"Don't ask."

"You and her?"

"No. Well...almost. But no."

"I've known you most of your life, Bryce, and I'd have bet my entire ranch that she's not your type."

"She's not."

"Then—"

"I was looking for a fuck, okay? Christ."

"But you just said—"

"Right. And I changed my mind. Obviously."

"She's got a hot body. I'll give her that."

"Yeah. But she smokes dope, and she's not..."

"Not what?"

Not your sister. Nope, couldn't say that.

"Not my type, like you said."

"How long has it been for you, man?"

"A while. I have a baby, remember? Wait until Melanie gives birth. The sex'll go way down."

"I doubt it."

"You'll have to stay away from her for six weeks after birth anyway."

"I know." He grinned. "We'll make do."

Oh, man. TMI again. I didn't want to think about the bondage things he did to his therapist wife.

Joe signaled the bartender—Len, apparently—and got us two more drinks. He looked down the bar. Mike had left, so we were free to talk.

"I talked to Melanie last night about Rohypnol and its effects."

"What? How did you bring that up without saying anything about this?"

"I said I'd read an article in the *Post* about date rape."

"She bought that?"

"Yeah, since it was true. I'd been looking it up."

"And she didn't wonder why you were researching date rape?"

"Bryce, come on. I said I stumbled across an article, and I easily could have."

"All right. All right. What did she say?"

"Pretty much what we already know. It can lead to retrograde amnesia for an hour or so before you take the drug. But more often than not, what it does is make you very malleable and suggestible."

"And we were nine years old, so we'd believe anything my father told us," I said quietly.

"Exactly. And while you can keep the memories, as we obviously have, they become so clouded that you never really think of them again. That's why rapists use it. They get what they want, and the woman essentially forgets about it."

"But the kid's family... He couldn't have roofied them into forgetting their kid."

"Remember that these guys got away with everything. Wendy Madigan escaped a criminal mental hospital."

"How?" I asked. "Seriously, how? How did my father do all of this while my mom and I had no fucking idea?"

Joe downed the rest of his second drink. "Money. You'd be amazed by what money can accomplish."

A thought pierced my brain with a sudden jolt. "I need to ask you something."

"Yeah?"

"Yeah. Did you pay off prison guards to beat up Larry Wade?"

He looked away, signaling Len for one more. Joe was a big guy, and he could hold his liquor, but that was three drinks in a pretty short time. Still, I didn't say anything.

"You going to answer me?"

"Where'd you hear that?"

"Ted Morse."

"That motherfucker."

"Look. I told him you wouldn't do that, that it was a lie. But I need to know. We need transparency here, man. Did you do it?"

"Does it matter if I did?"

"Hell no, Joe. You're my brother. I've always got your back."

He took a sip from the glass Len set in front of him. "I did. But I did *not* pay anyone off to have him killed. I sat through days of questioning with my lawyer to make that clear."

I said nothing.

"You can't clam up on me now," he said.

"I'm not exactly surprised. I know you, and the guy had it coming."

"Hell, yeah, he did. How the fuck does Morse know? I wasn't charged with anything, and part of the deal was that the records of my questioning were sealed."

"I have no idea. A friend in the DA's office maybe?"

"I doubt it. This goes way deeper. The guy found out about Justin. Damn, what was his last name?"

"It was a Spanish name."

"It was?"

"Yeah. I'm not sure why, but it just popped into my mind."

"The kid was blond, wasn't he?"

"No, he had dark hair. I think." I tried willing my mind to churn, but the rotgut bourbon had taken its toll. It was on the tip of my tongue. Rodriguez? No. Martinez? No. Velasquez? That sounded really close.

"We'll find out soon enough. The Spider'll come through."

"Yeah, but we're sitting on pins and needles until then. I'm a single dad, and you've got a kid on the way. How do you deal with this shit?"

"I keep busy. I've been working like a dog."

"I need to start my job."

"Monday will come soon. And trust me, you'll have plenty of work."

I still wished I'd be working outdoors on the ranch, but I'd make way more as the new CFO for the Steels. Money was important. I had a son, and I needed to do the best I could for him.

"Listen," Joe said. "I get why you wanted outdoor work. I'll make sure you get some. All of us work with the hands sometimes. We all need it. Talon probably does it more than Ry and I do, but lately, I've been seeing my share of our land. All this shit has been making me crazy."

I nodded. "It's got to be good for the head."

"It is. I mean, nothing goes away, but it helps."

Heidi strutted back up to the bar. "I'm off in ten minutes, Bob."

Joe stifled a chuckle.

I cleared my throat. “Busy tonight.”

“You think this guy is better than me?”

This time, Joe didn’t hold back. He laughed uproariously.

I gave him my best “fuck you” look.

“This is my best friend in the world. Heidi, meet John.”

Joe laughed again. “Yeah, John Smith. Good to meet you.”

“Are you free tonight, John?” Heidi asked with a smile. “Or both of you?”

“Sorry.” Joe held up his left hand. “Married.”

“With a baby on the way,” I added.

Heidi didn’t miss a beat. “So?”

Unbelievable. I was so glad I hadn’t done the deed with her. “I hate to be blunt, but we’re not interested.”

“No worries.” She placed the drinks Len set in front of her on her tray, turned, and then looked over her shoulder. “You two don’t know what you’re missing.”

“I feel like I need to scrub down after that,” Joe said when she was out of earshot.

“I hear you.”

“Man, you must have been desperate that night.”

I had been. Desperate to get his sister out of my head.

However, I was rapidly concluding that getting Marjorie Steel out of my head would never happen.

“I’ve got to admit,” Joe said. “It feels good to laugh a little.”

“I know,” I agreed. “There hasn’t been a lot to laugh about lately. I hate just sitting around waiting for the Spider. Isn’t there anything we can do in the meantime?”

“I honestly don’t know.” Joe swirled the brown liquid in his glass. “If we start snooping around or asking questions, people will begin to suspect we’re up to something. This isn’t anything I'm comfortable talking about to anyone."

I nodded.

"Nothing to be done about it." He pulled out his wallet. "I do have something for you. The Spider needed your information and mine. He wouldn't work without knowing everyone who was involved."

"Crap. Really?"

"My contact swears he's trustworthy, and I trust my contact. But because he has our info, I can give you his." Joe handed me a plain white business card with "The Spider" and an email address on it in plain black print. "I created a new email account for us. It's written on the back, and the password is in our code."

Our code. Wow. I hadn't thought about that in ages. Joe and I had used a secret code when we were kids. Did I even remember it? I turned the card over. The password stood out at me. Then I turned it upside down. Yup. I remembered.

"Just in case you lose the card, no one will know the password. But don't lose it. Memorize it, and then burn it."

"I will."

"We can both access that account, and that's how he'll communicate with us. It's on an encrypted server."

"Okay." This was freaking me out. I hoped I sounded more confident than I felt.

"I mean it. Memorize and destroy."

I cleared my throat, hoping to dislodge the lump that sat there, and simply nodded as I pushed the card safely into my wallet.

"We talk only here," Joe continued. "Not on our cells, and not anywhere else unless we're outside and alone."

"Got it."

"This is serious."

"I know it's serious. For God's sake, Joe."

"No, you don't understand," Joe said. "There's something I haven't told you. Something I'm going to tell you now."

CHAPTER TEN

Marjorie

I went straight to my bedroom. For Talon or the boys to see me after a meltdown would not be a good thing. Jade, finally feeling better, was taking more of a role in the household. She and Talon could handle the boys—at least for one night.

I needed to be alone, first, so my face could return to normal, but second, and more importantly, so I could figure out my next steps.

How to get Bryce Simpson out of my head and heart? I was in love. Completely and hopelessly in love.

With a man who wanted me—that much was clear—but who didn't love me. Would never love me.

Jade had suggested I get "out there." Myriad eligible men worked on this ranch every single day. Plus, there were the townies—the name we rurals had called the kids like Bryce, who lived in Snow Creek the town, when we were in school. I didn't keep up with who still lived around here, but I'd seen a few guys in the gym who might be interesting.

Okay. Tomorrow I'd go back to the gym. I needed to get in shape anyway. If that didn't work, I'd check out the guys on the ranch. Not a great idea to get involved with someone who technically worked for me, but I was desperate.

Not desperate to have sex, but desperate to get Bryce out

of my heart and head. Why not date, as Jade said? I didn't have to fall into bed with everyone I went out with. I had no desire to go to bed with anyone other than Bryce. Basically I needed a distraction.

What could distract me from a man better than another man?

Unfortunately, I knew already that no one would live up to Bryce, but I had to do something other than pine for him.

As I was contemplating starting to read a novel—anything to occupy my brain—my phone buzzed.

I recognized the number.

Colin Morse.

"What do you want, Colin?" I said, not nicely, into the phone.

"Hi, Marj."

"That's not answering my question," I said. I felt a little shitty, given what Colin had been through, but I had nothing to say to him.

"I want to talk to Jade, but I know she's probably not feeling real good."

I huffed. "What do you want from me, then? And don't ask me to set up another meeting with Jade. The last one ended with her sick in the bathroom."

"I have to tell her."

"Tell her what? I'm happy to take a message."

"I...can't. I can only relay this information to Jade."

"What information, Colin? You had the chance to tell her anything you wanted the last time you were here."

"I know. But...I couldn't."

"Why not?"

"You know why not."

"Actually, I don't. Enlighten me, please."

"Because you were there."

"Maybe you don't know how the concept of best friends works. Jade and I don't have secrets. Anything you say to her *will* get to me. Besides, neither Talon nor Jade wanted her alone with you."

"This is important, Marj."

Was it? Colin had been so vague the last time he spoke to us. He'd made it seem like his father had been behind his not showing up to his wedding with Jade. Perhaps we were reading into things. I had no idea. I knew one thing, though. We needed all the information we could get out of Colin.

None of the puzzle pieces fit together. Maybe Colin had answers.

"Fine," I said. "I'll see what I can do, but I'm not making any promises." I ended the call abruptly and then checked my face in the mirror. I still looked like crap, but at least the swelling in my eyes had gone down some. Hopefully I'd find Jade alone.

No such luck, though. She and Talon were out on the deck with the boys. Donny was running around with the dogs, and Dale appeared to be doing homework.

"Hey." I touched Jade's shoulder. "Can we talk for a few minutes?"

Talon, of course, missed nothing. "What about? And what happened to you?"

"Nothing," I lied. "I just need to talk to Jade."

"You look like you've been—"

"I haven't. I'm fine." I turned to Jade. "Just a few? In the kitchen, maybe?"

"Yeah, of course." She rose and followed me back into the

house. “What is it?”

“Colin just called. He wants to talk to you again.”

“Talon won’t like it.”

I bit my lower lip. “Which is why maybe we don’t tell him.”

“I can’t—”

“Until after the fact, I mean. Of course we’ll tell him everything. Colin must know that.”

“I don’t know if he does, Marj. If he asks me to keep it a secret...”

“Seriously? Jade, this is important to all of us.”

She nodded. “You’re right, of course. I just... I thought I loved him once, and he’s been through so much.”

“I have an idea, if you’re willing. You talk to him, but you have me on speakerphone while you’re doing it. That way, I hear everything.”

“Marj...”

“I know it’s underhanded, but I don’t want you alone with him. I mean, I realize you’d still be alone, but I’d be in the next room ready to rescue you if you need it.”

“He’s not going to hurt me.”

“I know, but he might use your past against you emotionally, and you’re hormonal right now.”

“Marj...”

“I just mean that... Oh, hell. There’s no PC way to say it. You’re pregnant, Jade. Pregnancy messes with you. But we need the information. We need it.”

“First of all, stop using my hormones against me. I’m fine.”

“You’re right. I’m sorry. But I can be recording the call as well. Then we can share it with the guys later.”

“It’ll have to be during the day, while Talon and the boys are gone.”

"Right, which means next week."

She sighed. "All right. Set it up, Marj. Tell him to come here."

"Done."

"I just wish we could all live in peace now, you know?"

"I hear you," I said. "Totally. But something's still going on, and we need to get every ounce of information we can." I pressed Colin's name on my phone.

He didn't answer.

CHAPTER ELEVEN

Bryce

My heart dropped into my gut. Had I heard Joe correctly? "Excuse me? You've been holding out on me?"

"Of course not. We're in this together."

"Then what the hell are you talking about?"

"New information." He looked away for a moment, seeming to focus on a spot above the bar. Then he turned to me, his eyes troubled. "I got a call today."

"From who?"

"I don't know. It was a number I didn't recognize."

"And...?"

"It was a guy. He didn't say his name. He just said, 'I'm watching.'"

Chills skittered down the center of my back. I took a sip of my bourbon, letting its fire dig spikes into my throat. Seemed almost like a premonition.

"Did you have the call traced?"

"No."

"Stupid question." Of course he hadn't. This was between the two of us. No one else knew about Justin. No one we knew of, anyway.

"I did some research on my own with the number. I found nothing."

"How about we give it to the Spider?"

"Yeah, I will. I'll send it through the account I set up." He downed the rest of his bourbon and set the glass back on the wooden bar with a clomp. "I don't scare easily, Bryce, but I'll tell you. That phone call freaked me out."

"It's freaking me out too." I finished my own drink and set the glass down.

Len raised his eyebrow at me, but I shook my head. I was done with alcohol for the evening. Maybe for a while. From here on, I needed to keep a clear head.

"Do you think it might've been Morse?" I asked.

"Didn't sound like him, and whoever it was didn't sound like he was disguising his voice in any way."

"He could have had someone else make the call. What area code was it from?"

"Somewhere in Iowa."

I lifted my brow. "Iowa? Why does that sound familiar?"

"Remember when Jade first met Mathias?"

"Yeah. He was dating her mother."

"He was posing as a guy named Nico Kostas, who was supposedly a state senator from Iowa. That's the only connection I can think of."

"Seems pretty farfetched. As I recall, he was *not* a state senator from Iowa."

"No, he wasn't. It was one of his many aliases."

"He's also dead."

"True enough."

"So I'm thinking this doesn't have anything to do with a fake name and the profession of a dead man."

"I don't know, Bryce. I can give this to the Spider, and I will, but he's a hacker. He isn't a PI."

"Fuck. We need a PI, don't we?"

"We do, and I know the best PIs in the business."

"Mills and Johnson." I looked at my feet hanging below the rung on the barstool. "But that means..."

"We have to tell them. Everything."

★ ★ ★

I woke up the next morning with a nasty stiff neck. Saturday dawned with the sun's rays streaming into the master suite at the guesthouse, but all I could think about was the pain in my neck—both literal and figurative.

Joe and I hadn't made a decision yet to involve Mills and Johnson in our dilemma. Neither of us was quite ready to tell them. They were the best, according to Joe, but they were also mercenaries. If someone offered them more than we did for any information on us, they'd probably bite.

So maybe we needed to find another PI—one who couldn't be bought.

The only problem was, as Joe had told me last night, everyone had his price. Everyone except his sister-in-law, Ruby Lee Steel.

But if we told Ruby...

So that was out of the question.

I had no idea where to even begin to look for a good PI, so Joe had taken that responsibility. My plan, for the time being, was to keep tabs on Ted Morse. Stay in the loop that way.

I walked out to the kitchen where Mom was feeding Henry.

"Da-da," he said happily.

I smiled. This little guy could always get a smile out of me, even when I was feeling like complete and total crap.

The secret Joe and I were keeping was weighing me down big-time. And then there was...

Marjorie.

Marjorie, whose tears I had caused yesterday. That only heightened my resolve to leave her alone. I had to for myself, but even more so, I had to for *her*. I wasn't being fair to her. As usual, I was being a selfish bastard.

No matter what, I had to keep her at a distance.

I couldn't hurt her. Her pain devastated me.

Today was Saturday, and I was determined to try to take my mind off all the troubles. No better way than spending some quality time with my child.

"How'd you like to go into town with Dad today?" I asked him. "We can go to Gymboree and then get some lunch and ice cream. We can go swing on the playground if it's warm enough."

Henry giggled, picked up a Cheerio from his tray, and stuffed it into his mouth.

"I think his tooth is feeling better," Mom said. "He slept really well last night."

Yeah, my son was sleeping, and I was out in a bar with Joe.

Something had to change.

"I wonder..."

"What?" my mom asked.

"What if you and Henry took a vacation? Somewhere nice where you could both relax."

"What? Who would take care of the house? Of you?"

"I'm thirty-eight years old, Mom. I don't need a caretaker. I'd just feel better if you and Henry were safe somewhere."

"Safe? From that man who showed up at the house? Ted Morse?"

"No, not Ted. I honestly think he's harmless. It's just..."

"What, Bryce? Just what? What aren't you telling me?"

Problem was, I didn't know myself. Maybe that was a wrong assumption. Maybe Mom and Henry needed to be right here. Where I could keep an eye on them.

"Never mind. Everything's fine. I'd miss you both too much anyway."

That was the truth of the matter. I missed my son now. I'd given my mom basically all the responsibility for him since the shit with my father had gone down. Henry had truly helped heal her, but because of that, he hadn't helped *me* heal. Not that it was a one-year-old kid's duty to heal anyone. That was a hell of a burden to put on a baby.

"Why would you bring that up?" she asked. "I don't understand."

"Nothing, Mom. Just forget I said anything." I pulled Henry out of his high chair. "Let's go check your diaper, buddy, and then we'll go out. Just you and me."

"That will be good for both of you." Mom smiled. "It will also give me some time to get this house in order."

I looked around. "This house is immaculate, Mom."

"It just needs Grandma's touch, I think. Henry has nothing but white walls in his room."

"Henry doesn't know a white wall from Noah's Ark," I said. "Don't bother. He'll be old enough to choose how he wants his room done soon enough."

"But it will be fun for me."

I nodded. "Okay, Mom. Whatever you want."

I quickly changed Henry and dressed him in some day clothes. Then I took his car seat out of my mother's car and placed it in the Mustang.

My father's car.

I so had to get rid of it.

We drove the half hour into town and stopped at the Gymboree playhouse. Henry was too young to do a lot of the activities, so I sat and watched him play in the toddler's ball pit. It kept him occupied for about forty-five minutes before he started to get fussy.

I picked him up and walked outside so he wouldn't bother the others, and—

"Ma-ma!" he exclaimed.

God. Marjorie Steel walked toward us dressed to kill in leggings, a tank, and a fleece jacket. She wore cross-trainers on her feet.

She smiled. "Hi there, Henry."

"Hi," I said as nonchalantly as I could. "What are you doing here?"

"I'm going to the gym," she said to Henry in a baby voice. "Not that it's any of your business."

Right. The gym was two buildings down.

Henry giggled and clasped his tiny hand around her first two fingers. Her red nails peeked out over his chubby fist.

"Did you go to Gymboree?" she cooed. "Are you having fun?"

"He played in the ball pit but got a little fussy, so we came out here for a few."

"His tooth again?"

"Probably."

"Did you bring a teething ring with you?"

I shook my head. I'd brought extra diapers, but other than that, I'd come hopelessly unprepared. That wasn't like me. I was usually on top of things where Henry was concerned.

"Oh. Well, maybe go get him a frozen banana at the smoothie shop. That might help."

The woman was a genius. The smoothie shop was next door, between the fitness club and Gymboree. Which meant she'd walk with us.

So much for keeping her at a distance. I'd had no idea she'd be in town this morning, but still... It was becoming increasingly clearer that staying away from Marjorie Steel would be impossible.

I wasn't sure why I'd thought I'd be able to accomplish it in the first place.

We walked along silently, Henry still clinging to Marj's hand. Within a minute, we'd reached the smoothie shop.

"See you," I said.

"Bye, sweetie." She pulled her fingers out of Henry's fist.

Nothing to me as she walked toward the gym. I watched her until she disappeared inside the building.

"Ma-ma," Henry said once more.

Damn.

CHAPTER TWELVE

Marjorie

Mama.

The third time Henry had called me Mama. My heart was at the same time filled with happiness and empty with sadness.

Was I never going to escape from Bryce? It was Saturday. What was he doing in town? He hadn't spent any quality time with Henry in weeks, and he picked today?

Nothing to be done. I slid my membership card through the entrance and headed toward the ladies' locker room. A few minutes later, I'd stashed my stuff and made my way to the gym. I checked the class schedule, but nothing appealed to me. Looked like the elliptical or maybe some free weights. I knew myself. If I started with weights, I wouldn't do my cardio. That was how much I hated it. So I found an empty machine and got set up.

I programmed what I wanted and then took a drink of my water and set it down. It tipped over and spilled all over the elliptical's dashboard.

"Here, let me help," a strange voice said.

I looked up to see a towel. Held by a man.

A very good-looking man.

"Thanks." I took the towel, wiped up the errant water, and handed it back to him.

"Not a problem." He held out his hand. "I'm Dominic. Dominic James."

"Marjorie Steel." I didn't take his hand.

"You don't look like you need to be working out," he said matter-of-factly. He could have easily sounded like he was coming on to me, but he didn't. It was an actual compliment.

"Thanks. Neither do you." No truer words. He was tall and muscular with tan skin and black hair.

"That's how it stays this way," he said.

I laughed. "True enough."

"Mind if I work out next to you?" He indicated the machine to my right that was unoccupied.

Well, heck. Jade had said the gym was a great place to meet men. Apparently, she'd been right.

"It's a free country." I smiled.

He placed the already wet towel around his neck and climbed onto the other machine.

I started my workout, and having Dominic next to me turned out to be a godsend. No way was I letting him see how out of shape I was. I kept at it, never succumbing to my desire to stop and go pass out somewhere. I stayed on the elliptical with the program I'd chosen for the full half hour, and to my surprise, I got it done.

I got it done!

I'd forgotten how great a decent workout felt. Though I was breathing rapidly, I could still talk when he asked me where I lived.

"You must be new around here," I replied. Everyone in Snow Creek knew the Steels.

"Yeah. Just moved here a couple of weeks ago. I'm looking for a house to rent. You know of any?"

I did, actually. Bryce's house. Bryce and Evelyn had been worried that they wouldn't be able to rent it to anyone in town because of who his father had turned out to be. Were they even interested in renting it? Or did they want to sell?

I didn't know.

"I might," I said. "I'd have to check with the owner first, though. They might want to sell."

"I could buy if it's the right property. I just want to get out of the hotel."

"What do you do?"

"I work here," he said. "I'm a personal trainer."

"Oh my God."

"What?"

"I just worked out next to a personal trainer? I'm a little embarrassed right now."

"Why? You did great."

"I haven't exactly been coming around regularly," I said.

"I can help you with getting back into shape," he said, smiling. "Of course, I'm not cheap."

That wasn't a problem, though it was clear he had no idea who the Steels were. He must have had his head down the few weeks he'd been in town.

"What do you charge?"

"If you go through the gym, it's one hundred dollars an hour. But I do take private clients."

"How can you do that if you work here?"

"I'm an independent contractor. I have a gym membership just like everyone else. I made sure I could still work privately when I took the job."

"How much for private clients?" I asked.

He smiled. His perfectly straight teeth were a beautiful

contrast to his tan skin. "Depends on the client."

He was going to play coy. I sure was out of practice. I hadn't dated in a while and not seriously since college.

Then there was Bryce.

Though we'd had panty-melting sex, we'd never actually had a date.

And we never would.

I smiled and touched his forearm lightly. His skin was warm. "For me?"

"How about lunch?"

"Sure. I'd be happy to buy you lunch."

"No," he said. "I'm a gentleman. A lady never pays when she goes out with me."

Damn. "How are you getting paid, then?"

"The company of a beautiful woman, of course."

Was he for real? I stopped myself from shaking my head.

What the heck? Jade had told me to get out there. To meet someone.

Dominic James was definitely someone.

"Okay. You've got yourself a client."

"Perfect," he said. "I have another client coming in ten minutes. After our half-hour session, I'll shower and change, and then it will be lunchtime. Meet me at the front desk at noon?"

"Well, I—"

"Treat yourself to a steam."

"A half hour in the steam room? I'd be a puddle," I said. "But I have some lifting to do. I'll do that, and then I'll steam and shower. I guess I'll see you at noon."

He smiled once more. "I'm looking forward to it."

★ ★ ★

Dominic James was even better looking in street clothes. Jeans, a T-shirt, and a black hoodie did a lot for him.

So he wasn't Bryce Simpson. He wasn't blond and beautiful.

But he was dark and handsome.

And he was here.

More importantly, he was interested.

"Hey," he said.

"Hey."

"Since I'm new around here, where's a good place for lunch?"

"Depends on what you're in the mood for. Jenny's is good for typical diner food. Then there's the Noodle. They serve Asian fusion and ramen. Sushi in the evening. There's the Bungalow that's run by Mrs. Pagliacci. She serves amazing pasta and other Italian stuff."

"They all sound wonderful. I'm sure we'll sample all of them while we work together. You choose."

I loved them all, but where was I least likely to run into Bryce? He and Henry could still be downtown. He'd most likely choose the diner, where Henry could have crackers and soup. Next to that, the Noodle. What kid didn't love noodles?

"Let's try the Bungalow," I said.

"Good enough." He gestured for me to walk ahead of him, and we left the gym.

The Bungalow was a block over, and we made it without running into Bryce and Henry. I was tense the whole way. We were seated quickly, and the server gave us water and menus.

"What do you recommend?"

"Everything's great. The lasagna is my favorite. She uses a special spice blend in the sausage that I've been trying to duplicate for about a decade. I haven't been successful yet."

"Are you a chef?"

"Not technically. I've taken a few classes, but it's still mostly a hobby."

"Ah. I love good food. I think we're going to get along just fine." He signaled to the server. "We'll both have the lasagna. I'll have an iced tea." He nodded to me.

"Two," I said.

"Two lasagnas, two iced teas. Got it."

Dominic turned to me. "If you're not a chef, what do you do?"

What did I do indeed? I was a live-in cook and nanny for my brother. That didn't sound very interesting. Not that I was embarrassed, but this was a first date.

God. A first date.

How long had it been since I'd had a first date?

"Have you heard of Steel Acres Ranch?"

He shook his head.

"I own a quarter of it."

"Steel. Marjorie Steel."

"That's the name."

"Tell me about your ranch."

"It's my brothers' ranch, really. They do all the work. I'm a silent partner. What I actually want to do is study at Le Cordon Bleu in Paris."

"What's stopping you?"

What *wasn't* stopping me? "Family obligations. For now."

"What type of obligations?"

I took a sip of water and then cleared my throat. "I'm

sorry, but we just met. I don't feel comfortable..."

"Telling me your family history?"

"Something like that."

"No problem. What do you want to know about me? I'm an open book."

"Where are you from?"

He laughed. "A tiny town in Iowa called Horse Fork. I'm not even kidding."

"Well, Snow Creek isn't exactly a thriving metropolis."

"That's why I'm here. I spent the last several years in California, but I like the small-town life. I like a place where everyone knows everyone and you feel safe leaving your doors unlocked."

"How did you learn about Snow Creek?"

"A fluke, actually. I was looking for a job as a trainer, and I focused on fitness centers in rural towns. I got several offers, and I chose here because Colorado is such a beautiful place to live."

I nodded. "It is. There's nothing like it. California can have its beaches. I'll take our mountains any day."

"I'm ready to experience four seasons again."

The server brought our iced teas, and I took a long sip. I was thirsty after the steam, and it also gave me something to do with my hands, which suddenly seemed overly big and gawky.

"Where did you study?" I asked.

"I did my undergrad and master's at UCLA. You?"

"University of Denver. I majored in Journalism, and I did a little work for the local paper here, but cooking is my first love."

"Why not go straight to culinary school then?"

"My father. He was adamant I go to a four-year program.

All three of my brothers had, and I felt I owed it to him."

"Owed it to him?"

I cleared my throat. "Yeah. He died right after I graduated high school."

I hadn't meant to lie. Until recently, that had been the truth as I knew it. My father had faked his own death after I turned eighteen, and I'd done the university thing because it was what he'd wanted.

No other reason, but I was glad I'd gone. I'd met Jade there.

"I'm sorry."

"It was a long time ago," I said. *Plus, it didn't even happen.*

"It's never too late. You look pretty young."

"I'm almost twenty-six."

"Ah, an older woman." He grinned. "I'm almost twenty-five."

Far cry from Bryce's thirty-eight. This guy wouldn't have a problem with my pink and yellow unicorns. He'd never even know about them.

The server brought our lunch, and again, I was happy to have something to do. We made a little small talk as we ate. When we were done and the server brought the check, he reached for it.

"I'd really like it if you'd let me pay," I said. "I can't take your training for nothing."

"I told you. It's not for nothing. It's for your company."

"I'd be happy to give you my company *and* pay for lunch."

"I wouldn't hear of it."

He was a gentleman for sure. He now knew I owned a ranch, so he must know I didn't have any financial issues. He couldn't know exactly how big the Steel operation was, though.

He paid quickly, and we left the restaurant. “I have another client in a half hour, so I need to get back.”

“I understand. When should we get together to train?”

He pulled a card out of his wallet and handed it to me. “Here’s my number. Give me a call”—he grinned—“anytime.”

He turned and walked back toward the gym. I stood, my mouth agape, holding the thick gray card. His photo was on it. His hair was longer in the picture, and if possible, he looked even better that way.

He was gorgeous. He was a gentleman. And he was ripped as all get-out.

But not so much as a spark.

Just being near Bryce made my skin tighten and tingle. This guy?

Nope.

But what did that matter? I wasn’t looking for a husband. I was looking for a date. And I got one. He was a good date. A damned good date.

I smiled to myself, still staring down at the card. When I finally looked up—

Bryce stood in front of me.

CHAPTER THIRTEEN

Bryce

Marjorie's cheeks were flushed, and her hair was damp. She looked fresh and relaxed after her workout.

That flush probably covered her entire body, from the swells of her plump breasts down her flat tummy to the tops of her perfect thighs.

My mind edged to the jagged scar on her left thigh. I'd meant to ask her about it, but I never had.

"Where's Henry?" she asked.

"Mom picked him up. He was getting fussy and he needed a nap."

"Why didn't you just take him home?"

Indeed, why hadn't I? I'd fibbed to Mom and said I had a few errands to run, but the truth? I'd been hoping to run into Marjorie again.

"I have some errands."

"Oh. I'll let you get to it, then." She turned.

"Wait." I gripped her shoulder. "You want to get some lunch?"

"What are you doing, Bryce?"

Nothing like getting right to the point. "I just thought... you might be hungry."

"I just had lasagna at the Bungalow, and you know how

big Mrs. Pagliacci's portions are. I'm not hungry, Bryce."

"Oh."

She bit her lower lip.

It was plump and firm. It had been against my lips, on my cock, and right now I wanted so badly to be the one doing the biting.

"Please stop doing this," she finally said.

Doing what? The words were on my tongue, but I couldn't say them. I knew damned well what she meant.

I grabbed her shoulders and pushed her against the brick of the building we stood next to. "I've tried, Marjorie. I've tried so hard to get you out of my head."

"According to your note, I basically mean nothing to you, so I don't see why it's that hard, Bryce. Now if you'll kindly let go—"

I couldn't help myself. I captured her lips with my own.

Usually she opened without prompting, but not this time. I slid my tongue over the tight seam of her beautiful mouth, coaxing, coaxing, coaxing...

Nothing.

Her lips remained tightly shut.

Not that I blamed her.

I kept at it a few seconds more until she finally pushed at my chest, breaking my grip. "Stop this!"

"I...can't."

"What is it, Bryce? What do you want? Because you can't have it both ways."

"I..."

"Spit it out, for God's sake. You push me away, say I mean nothing to you, that nothing happened between us, and then... we run into each other and you can't keep your hands off me?

It's not fair, damn it. It's not fucking fair."

She was right, of course. None of this was fair.

"If things were different..."

"If things were different...what?" she asked. "We'd be together? You'd want me in your life?"

I opened my mouth to respond, but she continued speaking.

"We are *all* going through this. All of us. Not just you. You're not even going through the worst of it."

"Marj—"

"Shut up! Just shut up. I'm not done yet. For once, I'm going to have my say, even if it's in the middle of town with everyone listening."

I scanned the area. Passersby looked our way.

"Can we go somewhere else?"

"Everyone knows, Bryce. There are no more secrets. They all know who your father was. Keeping quiet about it won't change it."

"But my mom..."

She closed her mouth. It was a cheap shot, but it worked. This affected my mother just as much as it affected anyone else. She was an older woman who didn't deserve any gossip—no more than she'd already put up with, anyway.

"You're right. I'm sorry."

"We can go somewhere else. You can keep yelling."

"Where? Where the hell do you think we can go? You don't want me at your house, and you won't come to mine. Where, Bryce?"

I eyed the Snow Creek Hotel across the street. "There." I pointed.

"Sure, that'll work. Bertie's at the desk, and of course she won't tell anyone that Bryce Simpson and Marjorie Steel went into the hotel together."

She had a point, but I no longer cared. I grabbed her arm and walked with her across the street to the hotel. I didn't have money to spend on a hotel room, but I would in two weeks. Until then, I had a credit card. I pulled it out of my wallet and laid it on the desk in front of the middle-aged blond woman. "A room please, Bertie."

"Sorry, Bryce. We're booked."

"Why isn't the no-vacancy sign on then?"

"It's burned out."

"Of all the— Fine." I grabbed Marjorie's arm and walked her out of the hotel. "So much for that."

"You just made a spectacle. Just because we didn't get a room doesn't mean Bertie won't spread the news all over town that we went into the hotel together."

"You know what, Marj? I don't give a flying fuck what Bertie and the whole town think. I really don't."

"Oh, yeah? Do you give a flying fuck what my brothers think?"

My mouth dropped open.

"Because they'll hear about this, and they'll want an explanation."

I'd been so worked up, so filled with passion and desire, that I hadn't thought about what the Steel brothers would think. Or do. I was a big, strong guy. Maybe I could take one Steel brother. Three? Not in a million years.

"You always say you're an adult and that it's none of your brothers' business what you do."

There. That should take care of her.

"I am. And it isn't." She huffed. "You know exactly what I mean, Bryce."

I didn't answer. Her lips were red from my attempt to kiss her before, and the warm flush crept up her chest. She stood with her hands on her hips, looking adorably angry and indignant.

My dick strained against my jeans. Nothing mattered except having her again.

One more time.

Just once more, and then I'd be able to leave her alone.

But I knew better.

I'd never get enough of this woman. No woman had ever excited me the way she did, had ever made exquisite love to me the way she did.

No woman ever would.

"Well?" she said. "May I go now?"

Only then did I notice she carried what looked like a business card. I glanced at it.

"Who's Dominic James?"

She hastily shoved the card into her handbag. "A trainer at the gym."

"Oh." That was innocent enough. None of my business anyway. "You hired a trainer?"

"Uh...yeah. Why else would I have his card?"

"Right."

"See you around, Bryce." She turned.

Everything in me screamed at me to grab her and never let her go. To take from her what we both desired. To make her mine wholly and completely right here in front of the hotel in Snow Creek.

I used every ounce of willpower to keep my feet glued to the sidewalk. Every fucking ounce.

Every.

Fucking.

Ounce.

* * *

After she was out of sight, I walked back into the hotel. "Bertie, I'd appreciate it if you didn't tell anyone Marjorie and I were here today."

"You *weren't* here today. We're full."

"You know what I mean."

"I'm not a gossip, Bryce."

I had to hold back an eye roll. "Please. It's important. We were going to have a business meeting. That's all. I'm working at the ranch now."

"I know." She smiled. "We all know. We think it's wonderful what the Steels are doing for your family."

"What do you mean?"

"You know. Taking you in as they have."

"Taking me in? I'm working for them, Bertie. I'm their new CFO."

"Of course you are. And it's wonderful for your mother and your little boy."

I pounded my fist on the desk, making Bertie jolt, and then I turned and walked out. The whole town thought the Simpsons were a fucking charity case. That was great. Just great.

Now what? I didn't have errands. I could go home and spend time with my son. And I would. After I made one stop.

My feet, of their own accord, took me to the gym. I wasn't a member, but we were a small town. Anyone could use the gym on a daily basis for a fee. I didn't have any workout clothes with me, but I wasn't exactly thinking clearly.

"Bryce," Todd, the guy working the front desk, said. "What's up?"

"Not much. Thinking about doing some training. You have a list of the trainers I could look at?"

"Sure." He pulled a flyer off a shelf. "Knock yourself out."

I quickly scanned the sheet of paper. No Dominic James. That didn't bode well. "I'm looking for some specific training. I heard you have a guy named Dominic who's really good."

"Dominic?"

"Yeah, Dominic James?"

"Doesn't ring a bell with me, but there is a new guy who started recently. We haven't updated our flyers in a while."

"Could you get me his number?"

"Why don't you just go upstairs to the office? You can talk to whoever you want."

"Perfect. Thanks, Todd."

CHAPTER FOURTEEN

Marjorie

Damn him. Damn Bryce Simpson.

It had taken everything in me not to respond to that kiss in the street.

Everything.

I'd wanted to open, feel his tongue against mine, taste him, lean into him and let my hard nipples scrape against his chest.

Then I remembered his words. The words that had shattered me to my core and led me to almost do something I'd have instantly regretted.

Then...*Mama*.

Little Henry...

His chubby little fingers squeezing at my heart...

Even now, the vein in my thigh throbbed along with my beating heart.

The scar.

I'd first cut myself when I found out Talon had been taken as a result of my own conception. Wendy Madigan, Ryan's birth mother, had been obsessed with my father, and when my mother turned up pregnant with me, Wendy had made him pay.

And she'd made Talon pay. My poor middle brother had been the real victim.

When I'd found out, I'd been distraught. Nothing helped the emotional pain.

Nothing...except self-harm.

I kept the cutting high on my thigh where no one would see. Bryce had brushed against it more than once but had never asked me about it.

I was thankful, for I had no idea what I'd tell him if he did.

It didn't matter at this point. We'd never be in the situation where he'd see it again.

And still the scar throbbed.

I'm here, it echoed. *I'm always here when you need me. I am what you can count on. Always. Always. Always.*

I drove into the driveway. Parked my car. Walked to the house.

Still my thigh throbbed in time with my heart.

I raced to the kitchen. It was empty, thank God. I opened the refrigerator and let the cold air whoosh over my body.

Breathe in. Breathe out. Breathe in. Breathe out.

Let the cold air saturate you. Let it consume you. Numb you.

You don't need to hurt yourself.

You don't need to hurt yourself.

You don't need to hurt.

Don't need to

Don't need—

I shut the refrigerator door quickly.

More. I needed more.

I raced to my room, closed and bolted the door. I yanked my purse off my shoulder and spilled the contents on to my bed. From there I could access the zippered pocket.

Home to my blade.

These are my friends...

The words to the song from *Sweeney Todd* echoed in my mind, a love song to his razors.

I understood all too well.

I held the sharp blade in my hand, regarded its shape against the light skin of my palm.

My friend.

Always could count on my friend for relief.

I shed my shoes and workout leggings quickly until I stood only in my green cotton panties.

The scar was still red and jagged. Yes, red and jagged...but healed. No scabbing. No oozing. It was totally healed.

These are my friends.

My friend.

I grasped the blade between my thumb and first two fingers and slowly lowered it to the scar.

I let the coolness of the silver blade sit against my flesh for a minute as I savored what was to come.

My friend...

Then I sliced into my flesh.

CHAPTER FIFTEEN

Bryce

The trainers' office was empty. I stood for a few minutes until a young woman entered.

"Sorry to keep you waiting. What can I help you with?"

"I'm looking for your new trainer."

"Dom? He's with a client right now. Are you interested in booking a session?"

"I'm not sure."

"Are you looking for something specific in a trainer?"

"Just want to get in shape."

"I can probably help you." She held out her hand. "I'm Amber."

"I'm sure you're great," I said, "but I'd feel comfortable working with a male trainer."

"I understand. Dom should be done in a few minutes if you want to wait. Or I can grab Sal or Mel for you."

Dom, Sal, and Mel. Sounded like the gym mafia. "I'll wait for Dom if that's okay."

"Sure enough. I'll send him in when he's done."

Amber walked out, her tight behind wiggling slightly. Yeah, she was cute and had a hot little body. Her auburn hair was attractive too. But like Heidi, she did nothing for me.

No woman—other than Marjorie Steel—would ever turn me on again.

I took a seat and pulled out my phone. Might as well check a few emails while I waited. I grabbed my wallet for the card Joe had given me last night. Time to see what the Spider was up to, if anything. I typed in the address and the password, and—

"Hi. You wanted to see me?"

I looked up. A tall guy with black hair and olive skin stood in the room. I rose and held out my hand. "Yeah, Bryce Simpson."

He shifted slightly. Probably just my imagination.

"Dominic James." He took my hand. "Amber says you're looking for a trainer."

"I am. Nothing major. Just need to get back in shape, you know?"

He glanced away from me for a second. "You look pretty good. I assume you just want to work on some definition?"

Why had he glanced away if he was assessing my physique?

"Yeah." I cleared my throat. "Right."

"You a member here?"

"No, I usually just pay the daily fee."

"If you want to buy a membership, I can give you a discount on training."

I didn't have the money or time for a membership, and I wasn't really interested in training. I was interested in learning more about this guy Marj was training with.

"Tell you what," I said. "Can we set up a trial session before I buy a membership?"

"Sure. Great idea. What's your schedule look like?"

Man, I really hadn't thought this through. As of Monday, I'd be knee-deep into Steel financials. I wouldn't have time to leave the ranch to work out. "Do you have weekend hours?"

"Sure. I'm here today, aren't I?"

Right. Today was Saturday. "Perfect. Do you mind if I ask you a few questions first?"

"Not at all. Shoot."

"Where did you study?"

"UCLA, bachelor's and master's in PE."

Funny, he didn't look like a California guy. He was about as far from a blond surfer as could be.

"And experience?"

"Three years personal training. Just moved here from Cali. I actually trained a few lesser-known celebrities. I don't have Beyoncé and Jay-Z as references, but I've worked with some great athletes and with some up-and-coming actors."

"Good. Good." What else? I didn't really give a rat's ass what kind of training the guy had. I wanted to know what he was doing with Marjorie Steel.

"I have an opening tomorrow if you want it. We can see if the chemistry's right."

"Great. I'll take it."

"It's early. Six a.m."

"On a Sunday?"

"Weekends are my busiest time, man. You know. Most people work during the week and all."

"Right. But six a.m.?"

"We can schedule another time, but you'll have to wait longer."

"No, it's fine. I'll take it." What the heck? I could always cancel.

"Perfect." He thrust a clipboard toward me. "Fill this out, and then I'll see you bright and early tomorrow. Leave it on the desk when you're through."

I nodded as he left the office.

I completed the paperwork quickly and then scanned the small room. I could snoop around, but someone would likely walk in, and what was I looking for anyway?

Fuck. I had Ted Morse on my back, the mystery surrounding Justin what's his name, and the legacy of my father...and here I was at the gym making an appointment for training I didn't want.

All because of Marjorie Steel.

Damn. Damn. Damn.

I walked out of the trainers' office, down the stairs, and out of the fitness center.

Time to go home to my son.

Time to be a father.

Time to be a man.

Except that my phone rang.

I didn't recognize the number.

"Yeah?" I said into the phone a little harshly.

"Bryce Simpson."

"You got him."

"I'm watching you."

★ ★ ★

"Different number," I told Joe at the bar that evening. "Still had an Iowa code."

"Did you send it to the Spider?"

"No, I haven't accessed that account yet. I was going to earlier—" I stopped, pulling my wallet out of my pocket. "Shit. Shit, shit, shit."

"What?" Joe asked.

"The card you gave me."

"Is destroyed, right? I told you to memorize it and destroy it."

"I was at the gym today, and I was looking at it, and then a trainer came in and shook my hand... Fuck."

"Don't even say what I think you're going to say to me."

"I must have dropped it. Fuck."

"Christ, Bryce."

"So we cancel the account and you set up a new one. No big deal."

"No big deal? The password is on that card."

"But it's in code."

"Right. Except it's nine-year-old-kid code. It won't take a genius to think of looking at it upside down." He punched into his phone. "I'm deleting the account right now and setting up a new one. The Spider is going to think we're idiots."

"Who cares? He's being well paid."

"Guys of his caliber don't waste time with idiots, no matter how rich they are. Idiots get you killed, Bryce."

He was right. I'd fucked up. Majorly.

"The gym's still open. We can go back to Snow Creek, go to the trainers' office."

"And tell them what?"

"That I lost something. It's probably not that uncommon, Joe."

"I'll ask you again. What the fuck were you thinking even looking at that card while you were in a public place?"

I'd been thinking about his sister, about her new trainer, about everything Marjorie and nothing about the potential trouble I could get myself into.

In other words, I hadn't been thinking.

I couldn't tell Joe any of that. Not if I wanted to live. He'd hate me being with Marjorie.

But you love her.

I silenced my inner voice.

I couldn't afford to love anyone right now, especially Marjorie Steel. She deserved a whole man, and I was so far from that.

"I'm sorry," was all I said.

Joe stared down at the wooden bar.

"I'm done apologizing now, man. So either get over it or take me outside and pummel me. I don't really give a fuck which one."

No truer words. My life was crap. Total crap. Even my beautiful little son wasn't giving me joy these days, which made me a crap father in addition to all the other crap that was my life.

"I'm tempted," Joe said.

"Nothing stopping you that I can see."

Instead, he grabbed a cocktail napkin and pen from across the bar. He hurriedly wrote some words on it and then handed it to me. "The new account and password, in code. Fucking memorize it right now, Bryce. Right fucking now."

I looked at it. Ironman908 was the account name. Easy enough. Then the password in our code. I quickly translated it and committed it to memory.

I wouldn't screw up again.

Which meant no six a.m. training session with Dominic James. If he was training Marj, so be it. I had to let go.

I had to fucking let it go.

No matter what it cost me.

And it might cost me dearly, for I'd just recalled something

I hadn't shared with my best friend.

I remembered where I'd learned our code.

CHAPTER SIXTEEN

Marjorie

People didn't appreciate the virtues of physical pain. The stabbing pain in my thigh didn't erase the emotional upheaval, but it dulled it, made it a little easier to bear.

The red trickle of my blood meandered out of the wound and across the fair skin of my thigh. I was always mesmerized by the slowness. It was a superficial wound, and I was in no danger. I was smart enough not to go deep, not to risk hitting an artery.

Soon, it would clot on its own as it always did. I'd add some antibiotic ointment to make sure I didn't get infected.

And that would be that.

Another cut.

Another emotional crisis averted.

So why did I feel like a complete failure?

Cutting myself was not a good thing. I knew that. Objectively anyway. I was always careful to do it in the same place—a place where no one would notice.

And no one did. Bryce hadn't. Or if he had, he didn't think it was anything unusual. No one else had seen that part of my thigh up close. When I wore a bikini, it was simply a little scratch. No one was the wiser.

The bleeding began to lessen, and I grabbed a tissue and

blotted it up. Then, as I always did, I applied pressure until it stopped.

Perfect first aid.

No one would ever know.

No one except me.

★ ★ ★

I woke in the middle of the night.

Why? Had I heard something? I was not a light sleeper, so this was unusual. Jade used to joke about me sleeping the sleep of death.

I went to the bathroom but still had a strange feeling, so I put my robe on and walked out the bedroom door.

Something jarred in the kitchen, and I flicked on the track lighting.

Dale sat at the table, squinting against the invasion to his eyes.

"Hey," I said. "What are you doing up?"

"Nothing."

The kid wasn't a big talker. I knew that.

"Are you hungry? Do you want me to fix you something?"

He shook his head.

"Okay," I said. "Mind if I sit with you?"

"It's a free country."

I couldn't help a smile. He'd heard that from me. I said it a lot. I sat down in the chair next to him. "So it is."

We sat in silence for a few minutes. I was hoping he'd start talking, but this was Dale, after all.

"You want a drink of water?" I finally said.

He shook his head.

I rose. "All right. You let me know if you need anything, okay? I'm going back to bed." I walked out of the kitchen.

Then, "Auntie Marj?"

I turned. Dale had never addressed me by "auntie" before. It was always Marj. I warmed a little. "Yeah?"

"Do you think I'll ever belong here?"

I sat back down next to him. His hand lay on the table, and I wanted to take it in my own to reassure him. Would that be too much for him? Mel had warned us to go slow with Dale, and since his issue at school recently, I'd taken that more to heart than ever.

I left his hand alone.

"You've always belonged here, Dale."

"Donny fits in better than I do."

"You're not Donny. You might be brothers, but you're two different people. Your dad, Uncle Joe, and Uncle Ryan are all very different, and they're brothers."

He nodded.

This time I touched his hand lightly but only for a few seconds. "How is school? Is everything okay?"

"Yeah."

"You haven't seen that strange guy again?"

"No. But I wasn't making it up. I swear."

"We all believe you, honey."

"Do you?"

"Of course we do."

"Did you ever tell Donny?"

"Well...no. Your mom and dad thought it best not to worry him."

"Yeah," Dale said. "He's just a little kid."

I smiled. Donny was only three years younger than Dale.

Then my smile dropped off. I suddenly understood what he meant. Dale had protected Donny from a lot of the abuse while they were in captivity. He'd taken the brunt to spare his little brother. Donny had told Talon and Jade.

"You want me to take you back to your room?" I asked.

"No. I want to stay here. Sometimes Talon gets up and sits here with me."

"Oh?" He'd been calling Talon "Dad" until he'd seen the stranger. He'd regressed a little, but Mel had assured us it was nothing to worry about.

"I mean Dad."

I smiled. "Whatever you're comfortable with. Do you and he talk during those times?"

"No. We mostly just sit here. I think he understands me."

More than Dale realized. The boys didn't know what Talon had been through, and they wouldn't until they were grown. Talon and Jade had already decided.

"You know, if you ever need someone to talk to, we're all here."

"I know. Sometimes I don't want to talk."

"That's okay too."

"But right now..." He stopped for a few seconds, and then went on. "Right now I have something I want to say."

"Okay. You want me to wake up your dad?"

"No. I want to say it to you."

I tried not to jerk in my chair from surprise. "Of course. You can tell me anything. I'll do my best to help."

"Okay," he said. More silence.

"Take your time," I finally said.

"I..."

I nodded, hoping to urge him forward but also give him time and space.

"Sometimes I miss my mom. My real mom."

Was that all? "Honey, that's okay. It's completely normal."

"I'm scared."

"Why?"

"Because. I miss her. But it's getting harder and harder to see her in my mind."

My heart hurt. We didn't have any photos of Cheri, the boys' biological mother. None had been found in her small home. Only a few portraits of the boys at different ages. No close relatives to shed light on her either, which at the time seemed like a godsend. Talon and Jade's petition for adoption had been simple and quick. But now... Of course the boys missed their mother. It was only natural, and a photo or two would have helped.

"Why don't you draw a picture of her?"

"I'm no good at drawing."

I sat silently for a few seconds, hoping some words of wisdom would come to me.

They didn't.

So I simply sat, my thigh still painful, and watched the tormented little boy who was my nephew.

And I realized how ridiculous I'd been.

I couldn't have Bryce Simpson. So what? This child had been through more in his ten years on earth than most face in a lifetime.

Time to stop feeling sorry for myself and take action.

Once the boys' adoption was final and Jade had given birth, I was out of here.

Paris and Le Cordon Bleu.

And for now? I had a prospect.

Dominic James. He wasn't Bryce, but maybe he could

help take my mind off the man I truly wanted until I could leave the ranch.

If not?

Nope. Not going there.

Bryce Simpson was not in control of my thoughts or my libido.

I was.

And I was taking back the reins.

CHAPTER SEVENTEEN

Bryce

Up at five a.m. to go to a training session I didn't want. I was still serious about backing off Marj by way of learning about Dominic James, but I wanted to take a look around the trainers' office to see if I could find the small card I'd inadvertently dropped there.

No luck. It was gone. Perhaps it had never been there. Or perhaps the janitorial staff had thrown it out when they cleaned.

Or perhaps someone had picked it up and cracked the code.

My father's code.

Maybe it was just a simple code to amuse his son. It was hardly difficult to break.

Maybe it was more.

I tried not to think about it during the half hour that Dominic kicked my ass. So far I wasn't feeling it, but I'd be sore as hell tomorrow.

Great. My first day as the CFO of the Steel Corporation.

When I returned, my mom was in the kitchen with Henry. He smiled when he saw me and then continued to shovel scrambled eggs into his mouth. Adorable.

I had to be more of a father to this little boy. More

importantly, though, I had to make sure he stayed safe. I'd been thinking about how to broach the subject of an extended vacation for my mom and Henry again.

She had a sister, Victoria Walker, who had moved to Florida with her husband, Chase. Their son, Luke, had been among my father's victims.

Florida would be good for Mom and Henry. As much as I'd miss both of them, I truly needed them out of harm's way. It was the only way I could function.

"So..." I began.

"What?" my mother asked.

"I know you didn't like my vacation idea, but what about you and Henry going to Florida to stay with Aunt Vicky and Uncle Chase for a few weeks? The sunshine and warmth will be good for you both."

"We've been through this, Bryce."

"I'm going to be so busy with this new position on the ranch."

"Which is why you need me here. You won't eat a decent meal if I don't fix it for you."

"I've lived on my own before, Mom." I wasn't much of a cook, but I managed.

"But—"

"No buts. You need to get away. Florida will be perfect. In fact, if you don't want to take Henry, I'll hire—"

"Stop right there. You're not leaving that baby with anyone other than me."

"I'm making good money now. I can get the best nanny."

"I won't hear of it. He's going with me."

"Does that mean you're going, then?"

"It means I'm thinking about it." She set a plate of eggs

and bacon in front of me. "Coffee?"

"Please." I took a bite of my breakfast. I'd miss this. My mother was a great cook.

I'd known she wouldn't go for the nanny idea, and truth be told, I wasn't really in favor of it either. I needed both of them, not just her, out of harm's way until Joe and I figured this whole thing out.

Best thing to do was let her mull this over without trying to convince her. The more I fought for the idea, the more she'd resist.

I'd already showered at the gym, so I figured a soak in the hot tub on the deck might be a good idea for my muscles. A preemptive strike against the pain that was sure to surface tomorrow could only be a good thing. I quickly dressed in my trunks, went out back, and lifted the cover off the tub.

It was a crisp morning, and steam rose from the hot water. I stepped in, letting it cocoon me slowly.

True relaxation was out of the question, but I could at least fake it. The soak would help me physically if not mentally. I closed my eyes and sank down, letting the steamy water cover my shoulders.

I inhaled. Exhaled. Again. Again. Again.

Still, my thoughts haunted me, and time flew backward.

★ ★ ★

"Justin?" I asked after Taylor Johns questioned me at lunch.

"Yeah, the little freak. What happened to him?"

Justin? Why didn't I remember? Then I did. Sort of. Our teacher had mentioned him. "Ms. Tucker said his family moved away suddenly."

Taylor Johns—for some reason, we always called him by both his first and last names—scoffed. "Good thing. We were going to run him out of here anyway. You and Steel wouldn't have been able to stop us."

What? Fragments of images peppered my mind. Right. Justin. I wasn't supposed to mention him. I wasn't sure why, but my father had said it was important. "I told you we'd crush your skulls if you bothered him again. He's gone now, and if you ever mention him again, you'll get that skull crushing, Taylor Johns."

Joe appeared at my side. "He's right. Don't mention Justin again."

We were both bigger than Taylor Johns. He shuddered slightly, trying to act cool.

"I got no beef with either of you. But Justin Valente better never show his face here again."

★ ★ ★

I jerked upward, the warm water splashing out of the tub. Valente. Justin's last name was Valente. I'd been thinking it was Spanish.

This was good. Italian surnames were less common than Spanish in Colorado. It was a long shot, but a lot better than if his name had been Smith.

Where had that memory come from?

As far as I could recall, Taylor Johns and his band of miscreants had never mentioned Justin to Joe or me again. Or to anyone else, for that matter.

Think, Bryce, think.

I closed my eyes again, hoping for more illumination. More memories. More recall.

Come on, I urged silently.

No use. I opened my eyes. I couldn't make it happen. But there was information buried in my subconscious. I was sure of it.

Joe had confided in me that Melanie's guided hypnosis had helped Talon a lot when he was dealing with his issues. I could ask for her help.

Except that would require telling her why I needed it, and she'd be there for the sessions, witness to whatever came out. Then she'd know Joe wasn't telling her something.

Nope. I couldn't come between my best friend and his wife. I wouldn't. I might not be able to have a relationship right now, but Joe deserved his happiness.

I couldn't help being a bit envious, though.

How had Justin Valente disappeared into thin air? He'd died, obviously, at my brute father's hand, but how had the entire memory of him in Snow Creek simply vanished?

My father was a lawyer then. He hadn't become mayor until much later. He had money. Money from his successful law practice and of course dirty money from his other life. But money didn't matter. He couldn't have erased the memories of a whole town. It wasn't possible.

Justin had been a quiet kid, an easy target for Taylor Johns and his cronies. That was the only thing memorable about him. If he hadn't been bullied, he'd have been easy to forget.

Perhaps he was easy to forget anyway.

We were all around nine years old. Our attention spans were hardly mature. Still, we were old enough to have memories.

Who else had been in our class that year? I hadn't kept in touch with anyone after school other than Joe, but surely some of them still lived in town. Another reason we needed that class information from the Spider.

Just thinking the name made me cringe a little. Then I laughed. The Spider was a hacker who didn't allow anyone to see his face. His name conjured images of a big man dressed in black, but in reality, he was probably a squirrelly computer geek who played video games when he wasn't hacking into high-profile systems.

I'd never know.

I was feeling a little warm, so I got out of the tub, wrapped a large bath towel around my shoulders, and went back into the house through the kitchen.

My mom was mopping the floor. "Hey! You're tracking in water."

"Sorry, Mom." Then, "Hey, do you remember anyone from my old fourth-grade class?"

"Your fourth-grade class? Where did that come from?"

"I was just wondering. You used to volunteer in the classroom. I thought you might remember who was there."

"Other than Jonah Steel, I have no idea. But I have an album of your old class photos around somewhere. I'm sure it's in one of the boxes sitting downstairs in the basement. I have no idea when I'm going to get through all of that stuff. Especially if I go on vacation."

"You decided to go?"

"It's not the best thing, but I *would* like to get away. I can't deny that. Even though we're out of the house now, I still feel the ghosts of the past."

"I understand." Boy, did I ever. The ghost of my father would haunt me until the day I died, it seemed.

"Henry would love the beach," she continued.

"He would. I'd come along if I could, but I think it's a little early to ask the Steels for a vacation."

"Of course it is. They've been so generous to us."

"Do you want me to make the arrangements?"

"I'm perfectly capable of doing that. I called Vicky this morning, and she's thrilled to have us."

"Good. I'll miss you both, but it's the best for everyone."

She nodded. "You're probably right."

She had no idea how right I was.

CHAPTER EIGHTEEN

Marjorie

Weekends were difficult. Dale and Donny didn't have school to keep them occupied, and Dale was usually moodier. Donny kept busy with the dogs, but sometimes he became restless.

Talon was good at keeping them occupied, but today he was busier than usual, meeting with Joe and Ryan to get everything up to speed for Bryce to begin his new position the next day.

The three of them were in Talon's office, and Ruby, Mel, and Jade were in the family room having a light lunch I'd prepared for them.

I'd decided not to join them for one reason and one reason only.

I couldn't face Mel. Not after I'd succumbed and cut myself. I'd tell her eventually. I had to. I needed her help. But I feared if she saw me, she'd see it written all over my face, and I couldn't risk that in front of Jade and Ruby.

Especially Jade. This was the one secret I kept from her.

I couldn't tell her. She'd be so disappointed in me, and I couldn't deal with that. Her friendship and respect meant everything to me.

Bryce was supposed to come by in an hour or so to talk with the guys, so I needed to make myself scarce. I could go into town and hit the gym—one of the few places open on Sundays in a small town—or I could drive to the city and do some shopping.

Or I could hole up in my room with a book.

Winner. I didn't feel like leaving the house.

I shouldn't have to. It was my home too. Jade and Talon reminded me of that on a daily basis.

But only Jade knew why I had to be scarce when Bryce was around.

Things like this were supposed to get easier, but that was a big crock of crap. I wanted Bryce more than ever, loved him more than ever, needed him more than ever.

When? Just when did it actually become easier?

I finished clearing the kitchen and looked down into the family room.

"Come join us, Marj," Jade said.

"Thanks, but I can't. I've got some stuff to do."

"It's Sunday," Melanie said. "What could you possibly have to do that can't wait until tomorrow?"

Avoiding Bryce. Nope, couldn't say that.

"I want to catch up on some reading," I lied.

"Oh? What are you reading?" Ruby asked. "I've been looking for a new novel to start."

Okay. Caught in a big-time lie. I wasn't reading a book. I'd been planning to stalk the bookshelves in the library next to Talon's office and find something. Or not. Maybe I just wanted to go to my room and wallow in my loneliness.

Yeah. That sounded good.

"I'm starting something new," I said. "I'll let you know if it's any good."

"Great," Ruby said. "I'd appreciate that. I have so little

time to read anymore. I miss it."

I'd had no idea Ruby was an avid reader. She and I weren't as close as Melanie and I were, but that was only because Mel was my therapist.

Now I had to go to the library. I walked past Talon's office and into the bedroom my father had converted to a library long ago. He had a great collection. Classics, mostly, and a lot of nonfiction about the ranching business. Over the years, though, we'd all added to it, and we had a good amount of commercial fiction as well.

Nothing screamed out at me. I definitely wasn't in the mood for a classic. They were slow and often dull. *Moby Dick*, anyone? A few romance novels sat on the shelf. Nope. Not in the mood for that, either. Happy endings? If I couldn't have my own happy ending with the man I loved, I didn't particularly want to read about anyone else's.

Ranching and farming? God, no. I truly was a silent partner here. I just wasn't interested.

I sighed. Nothing. I didn't want to read. I didn't want to go to town. I didn't want to go shopping.

I didn't want to do anything.

Was this what depression felt like? Losing interest in the things that usually made you happy? Even cooking had become a chore. I no longer pored over my recipe books to try new things for dinner. Last night we'd had pot roast and potatoes with winter vegetables. Ho-hum.

I sat down in one of the comfortable wingback chairs. Still, I perused the shelves.

Nothing.

Nothing stood out.

I rose and walked to the shelves, determined to take the

first book I found that sounded remotely interesting.

The Strange Case of Dr. Jekyll and Mr. Hyde by Robert Louis Stevenson. A classic, yes, but by an author who wasn't more intent on making his word-count than he was on telling a good story. That would work.

I grabbed the book and walked out of the library—

And met the blue gaze of Bryce Simpson.

Of all the...

I walked past him, determined to ignore him, but—

He grabbed my arm.

"Hey!" I said.

"You're going to ignore me?"

"It's what you want, isn't it? And you'd better lower your voice. My brothers are right there in the office."

He stood silently for a minute, and then he eyed my book. "Reading?"

"I thought it would be nice for a lazy Sunday afternoon." I held up the book.

And he turned white.

Of course. Dr. Jekyll and Mr. Hyde. A man who lived a double life with two distinct personalities.

Just like Bryce's father.

"Have you read it?" I asked.

"A long time ago."

"I wasn't..."

"I know. It's okay. I should read it again."

"Really?"

"Yeah. I can't just make the fact that he existed disappear, and I can't make everything that reminds me of him disappear."

I nodded. "Enjoy your meeting. Excuse me."

"Marj?"

I looked over my shoulder. "What?"

"I...uh..." Then he shook his head. "Nothing." He knocked on the door of the office.

"Bryce?" Joe's voice.

"Yeah."

"Come on in."

He walked inside and closed the door. I stood in the hall for a minute, thinking of listening in, but they'd be talking business. Bryce would certainly not be talking about me.

I took the book and went to my bedroom.

Dr. Jekyll and Mr. Hyde. Tom Simpson wasn't the only one. Bryce had two personalities. One where he wanted me, and one where he didn't.

Nothing I could do.

CHAPTER NINETEEN

Bryce

The meeting went nearly until dinnertime. "You want to stay?" Talon asked. "Joe and Ryan are staying. We're having grilled rib eye steaks. Jade's feeling better, so she and I are making dinner. Marj is getting the night off."

"She deserves it," Ryan said.

"I agree. She's been great. She was going to stay until Felicia returned, but I just got a call from her this morning. She's not coming back."

"Oh?" I said.

"Nope. She's happy being back with her family, and she already has a new job. I guess I'll be interviewing for a new housekeeper and cook. Probably a nanny too. We'll need someone to look after the boys and the baby once Jade goes back to work."

"Melanie and I just lined up a part-time nanny for the new baby," Joe said. "She's taking a part-time schedule after the baby comes."

"Jade and I haven't discussed it," Talon said, "but if she stays on as city attorney, that's a full-time job."

"She might want to stay home with the kids," Joe said. "Some women do."

"She might. We'll see. But we definitely need a

housekeeper and cook. Jade's repertoire is grilled cheese and tomato sandwiches, and I can't even boil water."

"So Marj is moving out?" I asked.

"She can stay here as long as she wants," Talon said. "She's determined to stay until the baby's born, and Jade needs her for that. But the guys and I want her to go to Paris to study cooking."

I cleared my throat as my heart fell into my gut. "Paris?"

"Yeah. She was excited about it before..."

He didn't have to finish the sentence. We all knew what he was talking about. Before the mess we were still all in. Before my father had shown his true colors. Before we'd found out Brad Steel was alive. Before he'd been killed by his lover, Wendy Madigan, who also almost killed her own son, Ryan.

Before I had fallen in love with the youngest Steel.

Marj.

Marj couldn't go to Paris.

She had to stay here. On the ranch.

With me.

Only she couldn't.

If she went to Paris, perhaps I could forget her. Out of sight, out of mind and all that.

But absence makes the heart grow fonder.

Stupid clichés.

"She won't leave until Jade has the baby," Talon continued. "She's made that clear."

That gave me about five months.

Five months of what? Pining for her? Trying to stay away from her? Ignoring her?

"Maybe she should go now," I said, the words hurting my heart. "Once you hire a housekeeper."

"Not doable. She absolutely won't leave until Jade has the baby," Talon said. "They're best friends, as close as you and Joe are."

I nodded. What could I say? I wanted to see the birth of Joe's child as much as Marj wanted to see the birth of Jade's.

"Are we done here? I have to make a phone call." I nodded slightly to Joe.

"I think so," Joe said. "Anything else, guys?"

Ryan and Talon both shook their heads.

"I have a call to make too." Joe stood and followed me out of the office and out of the house.

"What's up?" he asked me once we were outside.

"I got another call," I said. "Some unidentified number, and a male voice said, 'I'm watching.'"

"Shit." Joe spat on the ground, which wasn't like him. "Did you do a search for the number?"

"Not yet. But it's still on my phone." I grabbed my phone and pulled up the relevant call. "I'll text it to you."

"No, don't. We still don't know whether our phones are somehow being monitored. Just let me see it."

I handed the phone to Joe, and he wrote it down on a small pad of paper he pulled out of his pocket. "Man, this takes me back to elementary school days, before we did everything on computers. I haven't used handwriting so much in twenty-five years at least."

"That reminds me," I said. "I remembered Justin's last name. Valente."

He arched his eyebrows. "I'll be damned. That's it. How did you remember?"

"It came to me in the hot tub. No lie."

"Maybe you should take a soak more often."

"It was a fluke. I was trying to relax, and I kind of drifted into... I don't know. It wasn't sleep exactly."

"Self-hypnosis," Joe said. "Melanie told me how that happens."

"Yeah? Well, I tried to duplicate it, but I couldn't. I was thinking..."

"What?"

"Melanie used guided hypnosis to help Talon recover memories. Do you think—"

"No," Joe said adamantly. "We have to keep Melanie out of this. I hate lying to her, but this has to remain between the two of us."

"Yeah, I get that. What if I saw someone else? Another therapist?"

"No," he said again.

"But the memories are there, Joe. I know they are. I just can't access them. It's frustrating as hell."

"I get it. I have the same thing going on. But we're on our own with this. It's not safe to go talking to people—not until we know what we're dealing with."

"We're innocent, Joe. You and I both know that."

"Yeah, but others may not."

"A nine-year-old can't be held responsible for anything, especially when we didn't *do* anything."

"Bryce, you know the kind of people we're dealing with. They don't play by the rules, and they have access to loads of cash. Not a great combination."

"I know. It's just—"

"I get it. Believe me. I do. But the Spider is on it. He should have something soon, especially now that we have a last name. He can get an address."

"In the meantime, do you have any old school photos? Maybe we can find someone who remembers Justin."

"Anything we have would be in the crawl space of the main house. That's where we found my mother's and Marj's original birth certificates, the ones that had been tampered with. But seriously, if *we* don't remember Justin, who else would? He wasn't overly memorable."

"I don't know. It's like he just fell off the face of the earth. No one ever mentioned him again."

"I know. It's suspicious." He rubbed his chin. "When did the kids start going missing?"

"Good question."

"I have a file of news clippings about the disappearances. I'll find it, but Bryce, it might be hard for you to look at. I mean, there's one about..."

"Luke," I said quietly.

My cousin and I hadn't been close. He was a small kid, about three years my junior. I was the strong and athletic type. Luke? He was good prey.

Just like Justin Valente had been.

My fucking father. Luke had been his nephew! Nephew by marriage, but still.

Guilt pummeled me like pounding fists. Tom Simpson had left *me* alone. He'd been a good father. He'd taught me everything.

Everything.

I cleared my throat. "I can't hide from the past, Joe, any more than you can. We need to look at those clippings. My mom says she has my old school photos in an album somewhere. I'm sure it's in one of the million boxes that were brought over from the old house. I guess I'll get looking."

"I will too. Marj and Jade looked through some of the boxes in the crawl space already. Jade probably won't be up for it, but Marj can help me look for old school pics."

"What will you tell her?"

"That I'm looking for old school pictures. Maybe we have a reunion coming up or something."

"Our twentieth," I said. "Good ruse. Except that neither of us has ever had any interest in class reunions before now."

"True, and I wouldn't be the planning type. Maybe the committee is looking for old pictures, and someone contacted me because they...need funding."

I nodded. "That makes sense. It still doesn't explain the need for old photos, though."

"I won't bring Marj into it, then. I just thought she could help since she's looked through all those boxes before. She might be able to tell me where to look."

"Best keep her out of it," I said, wishing it weren't so.

"You're right, except for one thing."

"What's that?"

"I don't live there, so I'll need some excuse for pawing through those old boxes."

I sighed. "Use the reunion excuse."

"If Talon and Marj buy it."

"Then don't worry about it. I'm sure my mom kept every photo ever taken of me. Only child thing and all. I have the school photos somewhere."

"They could have gotten lost in the move."

He had a point. The movers had lost Henry's diapers, so old photos could definitely be goners.

My thoughts flew to my mother and father's wedding photo—the photo I'd hid in a book at my mother's request.

"My mom is taking Henry to visit her sister in Florida for a few weeks. Once she's gone, I'll have free rein of the house and can root through boxes without inviting questions."

"Sounds good." Joe shoved his notepad back into his pocket. "Keep me posted."

"How? How do we contact each other if we can't use any phones?"

"I've taken care of that. I had some people moved around in the office building. Your office will be right next to mine."

"Okay. That's good. What about nonwork hours, though?"

"We could text in code."

"Yeah, that's not suspicious at all," I said sarcastically.

"You got a better idea?"

Before I could answer, my cell phone buzzed.

CHAPTER TWENTY

Marjorie

I'd become engrossed in *Dr. Jekyll and Mr. Hyde.* Good versus evil was a classic trope in literature, but I wasn't sure I'd ever seen it more artfully crafted. I thought about so many people. Bryce's father, for sure, and my half uncle, Larry Wade.

But I also saw my own father, Brad Steel, in the mix.

He hadn't been an evil man, but he'd done evil things. He'd slept with Wendy Madigan, resulting in Ryan. I couldn't bring myself to regret that he'd been unfaithful to my mother, because if he hadn't, I wouldn't have Ryan as a brother. I adored all my brothers, but Ryan had always been special to me. He was so happy and joyful, a welcome respite when Joe and Talon had been brooding.

We were all a little evil in our own way.

But my father... I'd worshiped him. I'd mourned him when he "died" after I turned eighteen. I missed him still, even though I now knew he wasn't perfect. I'd been his baby girl. In fact, that was what he'd called me.

Baby girl.

He hadn't spoiled me. He'd tried a few times, but I hadn't let him. I'd learned the ranching business and had worked as hard around here as my brothers. I could run this business. I just had no interest in doing so. Silent partnership was great for me.

He'd taught all of us the value of a dollar and of a hard day's work. None of us took our money for granted. Oh, we treated ourselves for sure, but we were always grateful for our fortune.

Because of the Steel money, I could study cooking in Paris and not worry about funding.

Yes. I should do that.

But not until Jade had the baby. I couldn't leave my best friend, especially not since her pregnancy had been so difficult. Luckily, her spotting had stopped. Still, we all were walking on pins and needles, even though we tried not to mention it.

I scoffed to myself. Once the baby was born, would I be able to leave then? My best friend's baby. Plus, I'd already have a new nephew as well—Joe and Mel's son, who was due soon.

Plus Dale and Donny, who I'd grown very attached to and loved dearly.

And Bryce...

Would I ever leave?

Would I ever realize my dream to study in Paris? To become a world-class chef?

An epiphany struck me like a lightning bolt.

I had to go.

I had to go now.

There would always be something to keep me here at the ranch. Here in Colorado.

Jade's baby. Joe's baby. The boys. My brothers.

And Bryce Simpson.

He didn't want me. I had to accept that.

Perhaps getting away was the answer.

Yeah, things were still going on with Colin Morse and his father. Yeah, we were all still struggling with the past.

But the past was the past. I had an obligation to myself to

look to the future.

I had to go.

First, though, I'd talk to Jade. After I explained my reasoning, if she wanted me to stay until she gave birth, I'd stay. She was my best friend, and I owed her that much.

But if not?

I was out of here.

A smidge of guilt gnawed at me at the prospect of leaving my family. They needed me. But hired help could easily do what I'd been doing since Felicia had left.

My life wasn't on the ranch. I'd known that for a long time.

My life was in a big city somewhere, where I'd feed hungry people at a five-star restaurant. That was my dream.

It was time.

Time to do what was right for me.

★ ★ ★

"I understand," Jade said after I'd shared my revelation with her. "You have to go. I hate it, but you have to."

"It's killing me to think about missing your baby's birth."

"It's killing me too," she said. "But I get it. I really do get it."

Jade was the only person—other than Mel—who knew about Bryce and me. Who knew I was in love.

"One thing, though," Jade said. "You need to be doing this for the right reason."

"I am. It's what I want."

"I know it's what you want in the long-term," she said. "But think about it. If you're doing this to get away from Bryce, that's the wrong reason."

"I'm not."

"Marj..."

"Okay. Maybe. But it's not the only reason I want to go."

"Maybe it's time to make a list of pros and cons," she said. "They can be helpful."

"You sound like Melanie."

"Melanie's a very smart woman."

No disagreement there. A tinge of sharpness hit my upper thigh where my cut was healing. Jade, who knew me better than anyone, didn't know about that.

"Okay, fine. We'll make a pro and con list." I grabbed my phone and pulled up the notepad. "Pro. I get to do what I love in a place I love."

"You can even make that two pros." Jade smiled.

"Con. I miss your baby's birth."

"And Joe's baby."

"Okay. Two cons."

"Pro side. I get some distance from Bryce."

"I'm not going to give you two pros for that one."

"Fair enough," I said, though I thought it deserved about ten pros.

"What else?" Jade asked.

"The boys. I've grown to love them. I'll miss them a lot."

"Con," Jade said.

"Yeah. Two cons. One for each."

"Anything else?"

"My mother. She doesn't know who I am, but I feel I should be here for her. I read to her, and she enjoys that."

"So far the cons are winning, Marj."

"I know." I closed my eyes and drew in a deep breath. "I know."

"Let's get serious for a minute," Jade said. "This is something you want. Something you need, really, for your own well-being. Everyone should follow her dream."

I nodded.

"But you're young. You have all the time in the world to follow your dream. You can put it off if you want to."

"Believe me. I've been through all of this in my head, Jade. I know getting away from Bryce is a big reason I'm thinking about this, but look at it objectively for a minute. How many people in the world put off their dreams for valid reasons, and then those reasons turn into more valid reasons? It becomes a vicious circle, and before they know it, their lives are over and they never did the one thing they dreamed about all those years."

"Those people didn't have me for a best friend. I'm not going to let you give up on your dream, Marj. I promise."

I smiled. No, she wouldn't allow that. "You want me to stay, don't you?"

"Of course I want you to stay, but we're not talking about what I want here. We're talking about what you want. There are more cons for you going now than pros. That's just a fact."

She was right. No doubt about that. "I still want to go."

"Then I'll support you. I'll always support you, and so will Talon."

"I know. Thanks for that."

"Just don't make any hasty decisions for the wrong reasons, okay?"

"All right, all right. You've convinced me. I won't make any travel arrangements today."

"And tomorrow?"

"I'll think about everything. I promise."

"I'm not suggesting you *over*think it," she said.

"I won't." Though I would. I always did. "Thanks for the talk."

I walked out to the kitchen, but Talon shooed me away. "I told you you're getting the night off. I can handle steaks on the grill, and Jade says she'll throw together a salad."

"You can't just eat steak and salad."

"We're not. I put potatoes in the oven to bake."

"Did you fry some bacon?"

"What for?"

"For loaded baked potatoes."

"We'll have butter, salt, and pepper. We don't need them loaded."

"Yeah, you do. That's how the boys like them. I'll chop some chives for you."

"Get the hell out of here, Sis."

"You'll need some shredded cheese. And sour cream."

He laughed and actually pushed me out of the kitchen. "We'll make do. Go do something for yourself."

Something for myself? I'd read a good part of the afternoon, and then I'd debated going to Paris with Jade. What else could I do for myself?

I headed back to my room, fired up my laptop, and started researching cooking schools in Paris and other places.

Time for Marjorie Steel.

Time for me.

CHAPTER TWENTY-ONE

Bryce

"Hey, Mom," I said into the phone. "Everything all right?"

"We're fine, but I'd like you to come home."

"Why?"

"To spend some quality time with your son. We're leaving for Florida in the morning."

"Already? I didn't think you'd—"

"Vicky was ecstatic when I mentioned we might be coming. They're still struggling, Bryce, so I decided to make the arrangements. It's costing a lot at the last minute like this, but Vicky sounded distraught."

"Don't worry about money, Mom. I'll get my first paycheck soon enough."

"Anyway, come on home, please. I'll make a home-cooked meal for you and Henry."

"I'll be there as soon as I can." I ended the call and turned to Joe. "I've got to go. My mom and Henry are leaving for Florida tomorrow."

"Okay. That's good."

I rubbed my jawline, easing the stressful ache there. "Yeah. It's good. And it's not good. I'm going to miss my son like crazy, but I need him and Mom away from this mess until we know what's going on. He's just a baby, and if anything happened to him..."

"Nothing will happen," Joe reassured me. "He'll be safe with your mom in Florida. Believe me. I've thought many times of sending Melanie away somewhere since this all crept up again."

I couldn't help a chuckle. "I doubt she'd go quietly."

"If I told her it was important, she'd go," Joe said. "She would trust me."

"Why don't you, then?"

"Selfish reasons. I don't want to miss the birth of my child."

I nodded. "I get it. I do."

"If it gets worse, I'll send her off."

"Let's hope it doesn't get worse, then."

* * *

After we ate my mom's meat loaf and mashed potatoes and Henry and I played for an hour, I read him a book and tucked him into his crib. He was such a sweet little guy. I'd miss him so much, but he'd be better off in Florida—at least for now.

Not just because he'd be away from all the mess here, but also because I wasn't in any shape to be the father he deserved.

Not only would I figure the whole Justin Valente thing out, I also made another promise.

I was going to get the help I needed.

I owed that to my son. He deserved the best father out there, and by the time he returned, I'd be well on my way.

Rome wasn't built in a day, but I could at least lay a foundation.

I left the nursery and found my mother packing in her

bedroom. "Putting things from boxes into a suitcase," she said. "Unbelievable."

"Tell me about Aunt Vicky," I said. "What's going on?"

"She didn't get into specifics. Apparently she's okay, but now Chase is regressing. He stayed strong for her, and now that she's doing better, he's letting go."

"I'm sorry to hear that."

"I'm going for Vicky. She needs me. But honestly, Bryce, I'm not sure it will help Chase to have me there. I'm his son's murderer's widow." She winced.

I nodded. I didn't have to say anything. I was the devil's spawn. At least she didn't have any blood relation to him.

"We'll see. If it doesn't work out, Henry and I will come home, but I'm determined to give it at least a week. Vicky deserves that much. I just feel..."

"I know."

"...so responsible," she finished. "I had no control over your father, but still..."

"You don't have to explain anything to me," I said. "I get it. I get it more than you know."

"I know you do, Bryce. If I'd never married him—"

"Then I wouldn't exist, and neither would Henry. Don't go there, Mom."

"I try not to. You and Henry are everything to me. It's hard sometimes, though."

"I know." Boy, did I ever.

"I'll miss you, honey."

"I'll miss you too, Mom. And I'll miss Henry something fierce." Truth was, I'd been missing him already.

But this was for the best.

I left my mother to her packing, went back in the nursery

to kiss my sleeping son, and then walked out to the deck to enjoy the evening—as much as I could, anyway.

Joe and I hadn't finished our discussion. How were we going to communicate when we weren't at work? I had no idea. Maybe the Spider would know a way to do that.

Could I contact him? I pulled my phone out and logged in to the new account Joe had set up. Nothing was in the account, at least not that I could see offhand. On a whim, I checked the trash bin.

And I found a gold mine.

Joe and the Spider had emailed back and forth this evening...and he hadn't told me. It was in code—a code I didn't recognize. It wasn't like Joe to keep things from me. Could I wait until tomorrow at the office to confront him about this?

No. I couldn't.

I quickly told my mom I was going over to Joe's for a little while, got into the Mustang—tomorrow I was selling this damned car—and made my way to Joe's home on the ranch.

His and Melanie's house was smaller than the sprawling main ranch house, but not by much. I got out of the car quickly, and—

My heart jammed against my sternum.

Marjorie was walking out of the house.

I could get back in my car and drive away before our inevitable encounter. Yeah. That was what I should do.

Instead, though, I got out of the car and walked toward her.

She stopped suddenly when she met my gaze. "What are you doing here?"

"I could ask you the same," I said.

"I had to talk to Melanie."

"I have to talk to Joe."

She nodded. "He's out back on the deck. I'll get out of your way."

Let her go, I said to myself. *Just let her go.*

Instead, "Is everything okay?"

"Sure. Fine."

Her tone was anything but convincing. She and Jade were best friends, not she and Melanie. If she was speaking to Melanie, it was probably because...

None of my business.

Still, I loved this woman. She meant everything to me. Had she...? Had I...?

"Marjorie, I—"

"Not about you," she said abruptly, interrupting me. "Not everything is about you, Bryce."

"I didn't think—"

"Of course you did, and after my blubbering the other day, I can't blame you. But I'm over it. In fact, you won't see me around much longer."

"What do you mean?"

"I'm leaving."

"Leaving the ranch?"

She nodded. "The ranch. The state. The country."

My heart dropped to my stomach.

No. She wasn't leaving. She couldn't leave. "The country?"

"I'm going to Paris. If I can't get into Le Cordon Bleu, I'll find somewhere else to study."

"But...Jade. The baby."

"Jade understands."

"I'm sure she does, but—"

"No buts. The decision has been made. I leave next week."

"No. You can't."

"I assure you I can, and I will. Now if you'll excuse—"

I stalked toward her, closing the space between us. Already the heat was building. I could feel it, hear the inaudible drumbeat it produced in tandem with the rhythm of my heart. Even see it, a pulsing red that enclosed us.

She dropped her mouth open, and I gripped her shoulders and swept into her with a kiss.

Her lips were already parted, and I thrust my tongue into her mouth. She resisted at first, pushing against me, but I was determined. Determined that, if she insisted on leaving, she'd know what she was leaving behind.

No more thoughts about how I couldn't be with her. Only this kiss. This woman and this kiss.

She still felt resistant against me, but soon she melted, softly sighing into my mouth.

I kissed her and I kissed her and I kissed her, tasting her unique sweetness, letting it float on my tongue and infuse everything in me. If we had only this one last kiss, I'd make it count.

Oh, yes, she was responding. She was kissing me ba—

She pushed hard against my chest, breaking the kiss. "No! Damn it, Bryce."

All rational thoughts fled, and only feeling remained. Feeling, so much feeling coiled within me, building up pressure and ready to break.

"You're not leaving," I said calmly. "I can't lose everything. Henry, my mother, and now you."

"What? What's wrong with Henry?"

"Nothing. He's leaving. He and my mother. I'm sending them away."

"Why? Why would you do that?"

"I don't have a choice. I need them to be—"

Shit. I stopped. Here I was, standing in front of my best friend's home, and I was about to violate his trust.

"You need them to be what?"

I thought quickly. "My mom needs to get away, and I can't care for Henry with the new job starting tomorrow, so she's taking him with her."

"Oh."

Good. She seemed to buy it.

"You could get a nanny for Henry."

"My mom won't hear of it."

She nodded.

"Please. You can't leave too."

"I'm leaving. It was a hard decision, but I have to do it. I have to think of my future."

"Your future?"

"Yeah. I have a future. One without you, as you've made clear so many times."

"No."

She shook her head. "You've got to be kidding me."

"Do I look like I'm kidding?"

CHAPTER TWENTY-TWO

Marjorie

Fire laced his eyes. They burned the hot blue of a gas flame.

No. He wasn't kidding.

Didn't matter. I wasn't staying around for more of this. When he wanted me, he kissed me, touched me, made love to me. When he didn't want me? He tortured me with his poisonous words.

"None of this matters, Bryce. I can't stay here. It's too..."

"Too what?"

"Painful, damn it. Painful. You're breaking me, Bryce, and I don't deserve that. I thought I was strong enough to deal with everything, but I'm not. I need to get away, and I need to do it soon."

He gripped me again, his gaze burning into mine. "Please. Don't leave."

"Why not?"

"Just don't. I can't promise you anything, Marj. You know that. But you... You're the heart of this place. What would Steel Acres be without you?"

"Steel Acres functions just fine without me. I'm a silent partner, remember?"

"That's not what I mean."

"Then what do you mean? Because honestly, you're not

making a single bit of sen—"

His lips came down on mine once more.

Despite myself, I opened to the kiss. Here. Outside my oldest brother's home. Joe and Mel only a wall away.

I opened.

And I poured all my love for Bryce Simpson into this kiss—our last.

It was hard. It was wet. It was perfect.

The perfect kiss.

The perfect goodbye.

Finally, when I was no longer convinced I'd be able to hold back tears, I pushed him away, letting our mouths part.

"Goodbye, Bryce."

I walked to my car, not looking ba—

His arm yanked me back to him, and I let out an *oof* as I hit his hard chest. "No. I can't let you go."

"You have no say—"

Another kiss, this one even harder and more passionate than the last.

This was not a kiss goodbye.

This was a kiss of pent-up desire, pent-up passion, pent-up raw need for another person.

And this would not end with a kiss.

He broke the kiss quickly and pushed me into the passenger seat of his car.

"My car... Joe will wonder—"

"I don't fucking care." Bryce looked straight ahead as he started the engine and drove off.

"Where are we going?" We couldn't go to his place. His mother and Henry were there. His old place in town? No furniture.

He said nothing.

I cleared my throat, frantically searching for words that didn't materialize in my brain. There was a hotel in town, but whoever was manning the front desk would know us, and then the gossip would start.

Not that I cared about gossip. But my brothers didn't know about Bryce and me. We were adults, but still, there would be fallout.

Nuclear fallout.

I widened my eyes when Bryce turned off onto a different road than the one leading into Snow Creek. Where was he going?

Within a half hour, he pulled into a nearly invisible driveway where a small cabin stood.

"Here we are," he said.

"Where is here?"

"This cabin. Joe and I stayed here as kids with"—he paused a moment—"my father."

"Oh. Whose is it?"

"It's mine now, I guess. It belonged to my father, and my mother wasn't on the deed. My father left it to me in the will."

"Why didn't you ever say anything?"

"I wasn't sure I wanted it. I mean, this is where..."

"Where what?"

"Sometimes Joe and I stayed here with him during our camping trips. Other times we slept in tents."

"So you have memories," I said.

He nodded. "The thing is, the memories I have are mostly good."

"Then cherish them, Bryce."

"How can I? How can I when so many others have

horrible memories related to my father? Talon? Colin? My cousin Luke?" He shook his head. "Sometimes I think Luke was the lucky one. He doesn't have those horrible memories."

"He's dead, Bryce."

"Maybe that's a gift in itself."

"Are you kidding me? Talon is alive, and he found love and he's got two kids and one on the way. Do you really think he'd be better off dead?"

"Well...no."

"And Colin? This is new for Colin, but he's my age. He has his whole life ahead of him. He'll get the help he needs, and he'll have a life. I'm so sorry about Luke. I truly am. But neither Talon nor Colin would be better off dead."

"What about Ruby's friends? Juliet and Lisa? And Shayna?"

"First of all, Shayna escaped. She was traumatized, but she was never physically abused. She's doing well. And Ruby told me that Juliet and Lisa are in therapy. It's a struggle, yes, but they're both younger than Colin. They will be okay. According to Ruby, they're both happy to be alive."

He stared straight ahead, his headlights still on and focused on the small cabin.

"And Bryce," I said, "*you're* alive too. Don't ever forget that. Don't let the guilt eat you. It's not your fault that you *weren't* abused by your father."

He turned to me. "I know. Joe and I have talked about it."

"Have you talked to a professional?"

"No. Not yet, anyway. Melanie offered, but she's Joe's wife. It feels...weird."

"If it helps, I've talked to Melanie professionally. She's amazing."

"You?"

"Of course me. Do you think you're the only one who came out of this mess scathed?"

"I certainly don't think that. You know I don't think that. But you... You always seem so together. So whole."

I couldn't help a sarcastic laugh. The wound on my thigh was still healing. "Don't belittle what any one of us has gone through."

"I'm not. It's just—"

"It's just you feeling sorry for yourself, Bryce. That's all it is."

"You don't know everything, Marjorie."

"I never said I did. But we're all fighting our own battles, and none of them can be compared."

"Damn it!" He punched the steering wheel.

"Hey." I touched his forearm in an attempt to soothe him. "Let it go."

"Easy for you to say."

"None of this is easy for me to say. You know that. There comes a time, though, when you have to grow up and tell yourself that this isn't going to color the rest of your life. You have to decide what you want in life and go after it."

"And that's what you're doing? Leaving your family for Paris?"

I nodded past the lump in my throat. "Yes. That's what I'm doing."

"I call bullshit, Marj."

I said nothing for a few seconds, just digested his words.

I call bullshit.

"It's not bullshit," I finally said. "It's what I want."

That wasn't a lie. I *did* want cooking school. I *did* want

Paris. I wanted all of those things. Just because I wanted other things as well didn't negate them.

"You're running away."

"No. There's a difference between running away from something and running *toward* something. You know my dream is to study cooking."

"There are culinary schools here, Marj."

"Paris is the food capital of the world. Julia Child studied there."

"Okay, I'll meet you halfway. You're running toward something. But you're also running away. There's no reason why you can't wait to go to Paris. Say, until after Jade has her baby."

I swallowed down the lump. Nope, it was still there. He was right.

He was right.

"What do you think I'm running away from, then?" I asked, trying to sound light.

"This." He gripped my shoulders and pulled me in for a kiss.

As much as our previous kisses had been hard and passionate, this one was different. It reeked of desperation.

He was desperate for something.

But what?

I stopped thinking after a few seconds and melted into it, becoming one with it and sinking into all that was Bryce. His crisp masculine scent, the hardness of his muscles beneath my fingertips. The roughness of his light-brown stubble against my cheeks. The desperate sounds of his moans vibrating into me.

When he broke the kiss and inhaled a desperate breath,

I let myself go. I kissed his rough cheeks, his sweaty neck, inhaling more and more of him as I went. I nibbled the lobe of his ear and traced the shell. Then I thrust my tongue inside.

"My God." His voice was a low rasp.

His lips clamped on to my neck, and he sucked. Hard. He'd probably leave a mark, but I didn't care.

I wanted to be marked. Wanted to be branded.

Wanted to be *his*.

Breathless moans escaped my throat as my hunger increased.

Ravenous. I was ravenous.

Ravenous for this man I loved. Ravenous for his body inside mine.

Ravenous for everything Bryce Simpson.

He broke away, panting. "Inside. Now."

I could argue. This would make everything harder. I knew that.

But I didn't have it in me. I needed this. Needed him. Needed all of it.

I opened the passenger door of his car and exited.

CHAPTER TWENTY-THREE

Bryce

I'd vowed never to return to this cabin.

I hadn't been here in ages, not since college, at least. Once I became an adult, the camping and fishing adventures with my father had stopped. He'd told me I could use the cabin, but I never had.

Now, looking back, I wondered why. This place had been full of happy memories—memories that had only recently become tainted.

I jostled my keys until I found the right one. A key I'd had for a long time but hadn't used until now.

What would I find inside?

All these thoughts jumbled in my head, but one thing overshadowed them.

Marjorie Steel.

My aching need for Marjorie Steel.

Once the door was open, I grabbed her and pushed her inside. Darkness had already fallen, and the light switch didn't work. Within a few minutes, my eyes had adjusted. The cabin had one great room with furniture, a small kitchen area, and two bedrooms. One bathroom for the whole place.

There was a fireplace and matches and logs, but I couldn't be bothered to start a fire. Not yet. Not when my need was this great.

I dragged Marjorie to one of the bedrooms—the one Joe and I had used. Two twin beds still sat in the room, still covered in the same quilts I remembered. How old were those quilts? They might disintegrate if we so much as looked at them.

I didn't care. I pulled her to me and kissed her—deeply, passionately, emotionally. She tasted of sweetness and lust, of fresh berries and mint. Of Marjorie. Pure, sweet Marjorie.

This place was certainly no Paris, but it was an escape nonetheless. For me, at least, and probably for both of us.

I knew how much she wanted me. Loved me. Indeed, I'd heard her say the words. Even now, I wasn't sure she was aware she'd said them. She'd been in the midst of multiple climaxes, and I knew well what went through my mind when I shared an orgasm with her.

Many times I'd thought those three little words. Words so painless to utter yet so painful to deal with.

For I couldn't love anyone, not when I wasn't whole.

Marjorie deserved whole.

She melted against me, and I walked backward, leading her to one of the beds. I could go in the other room where a queen bed sat, but no. I wouldn't taint Marjorie with anything my father had touched.

I wanted so much to go slowly, to take my time and savor everything about her, but my dick had other ideas. I quickly unsnapped and unzipped my jeans to free my aching cock. Then I pulled off Marj's shoes, sweatpants, and underwear and shoved into her heat, her legs still hanging off the bed.

Sweet, sweet home.

"Bryce!" she cried out, her quivering walls encasing me with glorious suction.

"God, Marj. God, yes." I pumped into her again and again.

I wanted her to come. I wanted her to have as much pleasure as she was giving me. I wanted to take the time and make sure she climaxed.

But I was all about me at the moment. All about this place, about exorcising everything hellacious in my life.

Somehow, in my warped mind, I felt that if I made love to Marjorie here, it would burn away the rancid ash my father had left.

I pumped.

And I pumped.

And I pumped.

"Gone," I said through gritted teeth. "Gone. Be gone. Be gone."

If Marjorie was surprised by my words, she didn't indicate it. I closed my eyes, continuing my devilish chant.

Gone. Gone. Gone.

Until I erupted inside her tight heat, emptying into her beautiful body that so willingly accepted me for all I was.

And all I was not.

I squeezed my eyes shut, trying to prolong the intensity of the orgasm, holding on...

Holding on...

Holding on...

Until finally she squirmed beneath me. I moved off her, turning over in the darkness, my arm across my eyes.

I'd done it.

I'd fucked her in this cabin.

I'd wanted to, no doubt.

But it hadn't worked. It hadn't exorcised anything from me or from this place. All I'd accomplished was an even more intense desire for her.

Worse yet, she hadn't come. I'd truly been self-absorbed.

I needed her again, and I wanted her to come the way she had during our last time together—again and again, rolling from one orgasm into another.

That was when she'd said, "I love you."

Perhaps she'd say it again.

I longed to hear those three words in her soft voice. Even more, I longed to say them back. For I meant them. I meant them with every cell in my body, every beat of my heart, every tiny sliver of lightness and all the darkness in my soul.

With everything. I meant them with everything.

"You okay?" she finally said.

I nodded. Sort of.

"You sure? Because you kept saying 'gone' over and over again."

"It didn't mean anything."

"Okay," she said. "We'll play it your way for now. But you can talk to me, Bryce. Always."

If only I could. How could I show this beautiful woman my deepest weaknesses? How could I tell her the horrid things that haunted me?

And how could I do this when, even as I was tormented, nothing had actually happened to me?

"Maybe," I said. "Maybe someday."

"Better make it soon. I leave next week."

Was she still determined to run away?

"Fine," I said. "Go. But not before I show you exactly what you're leaving." I rose from the bed and knelt before her, spreading her legs. God, she was perfect. Even in the darkness, the glistening of her pink pussy was visible. Her thighs shone from her juices. I trailed my fingers over her smooth flesh...

until I came to the jagged scar.

It was scabbed over, which meant it had recently bled.

"What's this?" I asked.

She tensed and tried to close her legs, but I was between them. She squeezed my shoulders with her thighs.

"Marj?"

"Nothing. I scratched myself."

"Over a scar?"

She scooted backward on the bed, away from me. "Yes."

She was hiding something. Marjorie Steel, who I'd thought was an open book, had her own secrets. I couldn't bear the thought of her being in any kind of pain, but if she was? Then we had something in common.

Pain from something we had nothing to do with, through no fault of our own. Pain when neither of us had been abused as countless others had.

Pain.

Pain that seemed insurmountable sometimes. Pain that was, at its root, cloaked in self-absorption.

At least mine was.

Marjorie wasn't even close to self-absorbed. She'd stayed on at the house to help Talon and Jade with the boys when their housekeeper left.

The boys. She'd stayed with the boys, and she took care of them. And I couldn't take care of my own son.

Self-absorption versus selflessness had never been so clear.

And I'd never felt so low.

Marj had been determined to stay...until now.

Now she was going to Paris.

Was it self-absorbed to do something you wanted?

No. It was not.

She *did* want this. But she was also running.

From me.

This all had something to do with me.

Or did it? I shook off the self-absorption. This was about Marjorie, not about me. Something new rose within me—something I hadn't felt in a long time. I embraced it.

"Tell me," I said. "Tell me why you did this to yourself."

"Did what? I told you. It's a scratch. I can be clumsy sometimes."

I edged toward her and touched the smooth silk of her cheek. "Tell me, sweetheart. Please."

CHAPTER TWENTY-FOUR

Marjorie

My insides went frigid. All the heat Bryce had invoked in my body, the intensity between my legs, vanished as if it had never been.

Tell me, sweetheart.

Such innocuous words, but to me they spoke of endless danger. Only one person, Melanie, knew my secret.

My weakness.

My most cowardly thing.

Yet the thought of opening up to Bryce, of truly letting him see all that I was, felt...*good.*

What a strange idea—to let the man I loved more than anything actually *see* me.

It was a scary proposition, but it also gave me hope. Hope I hadn't felt in a long, long time.

Would he still want to be with me?

I held back a scoff. He didn't want to be with me now. Oh, we had an intense chemistry and attraction. That much was apparent. But he'd written me that note of poison, telling me that nothing had happened between us.

And every time we were together, he made it clear in no uncertain terms that it could never, never happen again.

"It's nothing," I finally said.

"I don't believe you."

"You don't have to believe me. You just have to accept my answer."

"Fine." He stood. "I guess we're done here."

He'd lost his erection, and he quickly zipped and snapped his jeans.

"I think we were done before we started," I said. Yeah, I could sling the shit too. It was about time I started doing it. Bryce wasn't the only one who could be purposely hurtful.

Hurting him gave me no pleasure, though. In fact, it made me feel worse. Did it do the same to him?

Why not ask?

"Did it feel good to write me that note, Bryce?"

"What?"

"You know very well what I'm talking about."

He looked away, and as he did, I took advantage of the time to put my clothes back on.

When he finally turned back to look at me, his eyes were heavy-lidded and almost...broken. "How can you even ask that?"

"How can I not? You wrote it, not me."

"I hated writing it," he finally said, his voice low. "It was one of the hardest things I've ever done."

"Then why, Bryce? Why did you do it?"

"I had to."

I scoffed. "I get it. Someone was holding a gun to your head and said either those words or your brains would be on that piece of paper."

He shook his head slowly. "Be serious."

"I *am* being serious. You said you had to write it. I'm telling you that you didn't have to, that it was your choice. No one but you made you do it."

He said nothing. Not that I expected him to. My logic had no argument.

After what seemed like an hour—but was only a few minutes—had passed, he said, "Don't go to Paris."

"Sorry."

"At least not now. Stay. Please. Jade needs you. I can't be responsible for your leaving."

"Who said you were responsible?"

"Marj..."

The look on his handsome face was one of so much sadness and pain, I had to choke back a sob. He was hurting too, and I hadn't let myself see that.

"It hurt you to write me that note," I said.

It wasn't a question. It was a statement. A statement of truth.

He nodded. "More than anything."

"Then why did you do it? And don't tell me you had to. Tell me the truth. The fucking truth. Why don't you want to be with me?"

"None of this has anything to do with what I want."

"So you want me. That much is obvious. No matter what you say, you can't stay away from me. I get it. I'm in the same predicament. The only difference is that I'm open to exploring, and you're not. Why, Bryce? For the love of God, tell me why."

He sat down on the bed and patted the spot next to him. "You want the truth?"

I joined him. "Of course I want the truth."

"Are you sure? The truth can be dark, Marjorie. You're so beautiful and full of light. I don't want to change that."

I was full of light? Me? The one who couldn't stop cutting herself open to relieve her emotional pain? Boy, there was a lot Bryce Simpson didn't know.

"I'm sure."

"Okay, here's the truth. I can't be with you because I'm a mess, Marj. I'm a big fucking mess, and I can't be with anyone. Especially you."

"Why especially me?"

"Because you're...fucking perfect. I'll screw you up."

"Bryce, come on."

"I'm serious. You're everything that's right in this world. You're giving everything to two little boys you just met, things I can't give to my own son right now."

"Bryce..."

He held up his hand. "No. Let me finish. You do everything for others. You're putting your life on hold—"

I interrupted him with a huff. "I'm not. I'm leaving."

"Would you let me finish?" He shook his head. "You're perfect, Marjorie. Absolutely perfect. Plus, you're Joe's baby sister. He'd never forgive me if I hurt you. Worse, I'd never forgive myself."

He'd already hurt me, but now wasn't the time to bring that up. He knew. It was written all over his face.

"This isn't making any sense. If this is about your fa—"

"I'd be lying if I said that's not a big part of it. But it's more. I have responsibilities to my mom and to Henry."

"I love Henry and your mom. You know that."

"That's not the issue. I've already let them down, and I feel like shit for it. I can't let you down as well."

"You haven't let your mom and Henry down."

He shook his head. "There are things you don't know. Things I can't tell you because of promises I've made."

“You just swore you’d tell me the truth.”

“And I have. But I can’t breach a confidence.”

Chills spiked the back of my neck. “Exactly what is going on here?”

“Marjorie, I can’t be with you because I’m an empty shell. I feel like the Tin Man.”

“You don’t have a heart?”

He sighed. “My heart is fine. I *feel*, Marjorie. I...”

“What?”

“I...” He shoveled his fingers through his mass of dark-blond hair. “I love you, damn it. I love you so fucking much.”

My heart leaped, and warmth surged into me, filling the holes. “I love you too.”

“I know. You said it once.”

“I did?”

“The last time at the guesthouse. You were having a lot of orgasms.”

Try as I might, I couldn’t make myself embarrassed over the words during a climax. “Well, I meant it then, and I mean it now.”

“I mean it too.”

“Then what’s the problem? When two people love each other, everything can be worked out.”

“Not when one of them is the Tin Man.”

“Stop it with that reference, already. Your heart is fine. You just said you love me.”

He touched my cheek then, caressed it carefully as if it were made of porcelain. “It’s not my heart that’s the problem, sweetheart. It’s my soul.”

CHAPTER TWENTY-FIVE

Bryce

My soul.

Yeah, my heart was fine. I wasn't lying. I loved my mother and I loved my son as much as I always had. And I loved the woman before me. So damned much.

But where my soul once was lay only a black hole. I felt used up, empty, as if my physical body no longer housed something full of light. Now, only blackness lived inside me. The blackness of my father and the guilt he'd left me.

Marjorie took my hand, entwining her fingers with mine. Her flesh was warm and inviting. Loving.

Marjorie had a soul, a beautiful soul full of love and light. I couldn't tarnish her. I just couldn't.

"You're being way too hard on yourself. You have a soul. You know you have a soul."

"It's an illusion," I said.

"Maybe all souls are illusions. Maybe it's something we're taught so we can believe something continues to exist after our bodies die. No one knows, Bryce."

"Semantics don't matter, Marj. Whatever I once had inside me that made me feel full and happy—it's gone now."

"You're feeling guilt," she said. "That's all."

"Oh, yeah. I feel guilt. But this goes beyond guilt. It's these memories of my father. They torture me. All the damned time."

"What memories?"

"From my childhood. All that time, he was doing horrible, awful things to innocent people. Young people, Marjorie. And at the same time, he was teaching me things."

"What things?"

"Things a father teaches a son. Things I'll teach Henry someday. How to camp, fish, shoot a gun. How to be a man." I raked my fingers through my hair. "I learned how to be a man from a monster."

Finally, my guilt poured out of me and into this lovely woman. She'd walk away for sure.

Hell, I wouldn't blame her if she ran away screaming bloody murder.

I was a fucked-up mess.

"That's not your fault," she said.

"But...he was a good father. To me. And at that same time..."

"Hey, it's okay."

"God. None of this is okay. Not even a tiny bit."

"Your father was a monster. You'll get no argument from anyone."

"How can I have happy memories of him? It feels wrong."

"You need to talk to someone."

"I'm talking to you."

"And I'm happy to listen, but I don't have any training in any of this. Melanie can—"

"She's too close. She's Joe's wife."

"She's also about ready to pop a kid. If you'd stop interrupting me, you'd know I was going to say that Melanie can recommend someone."

Of course. Not like I hadn't already thought of that. Problem was, a therapist couldn't help me with the new development Joe and I were dealing with.

No one could help me with that.

As much as I wanted to share everything with Marjorie at that moment, I owed Joe my confidence. He wasn't telling his wife, so I could hardly tell his sister.

"I'm just saying think about it," she said.

"I will."

It wasn't a lie. I'd already thought seriously about it. And I'd do it...after Joe and I took care of the Justin Valente situation.

Marjorie snuggled into my shoulder, and I kissed the top of her sweet-smelling head.

"You still going to Paris?" I asked.

"Depends."

"On what?"

"A lot of things. Are you willing to stop pushing me away?"

"I'm not ready for a relationship," I said. "That won't change."

"What if I like you the way you are?"

"Then you're nuts."

She chuckled. "Maybe I am."

"I was honest with you, as much as I could be without breaking a confidence."

"I'd never ask you to break a confidence. I hope you know that."

"I do now. So will you be honest with me?"

She sighed. "I'll try."

"All right, then. Tell me about that cut on your thigh."

She pulled away from me. "I did tell you. I scratched it."

"Sweetheart...please."

"It's nothing. It's under control."

"It's a new wound. It's scabbed over."

She rose from the bed and paced over the area rug covering the hardwood floor of the small bedroom. "This is hard, Bryce."

"I know."

"It's just that—" She lost her footing and tumbled to the floor.

I stood quickly and grabbed her. "Baby, are you okay?"

"Yeah, just clumsy. Seems to happen a lot when I'm trying to get away from you." She moved the corner of the rug out of the way. "Wait. What's this?"

CHAPTER TWENTY-SIX

Marjorie

Our eyes had long since adjusted to the darkness. One of the floorboards was loose, leaving a slight bump under the rug. That must have been what had caught on my foot and made me trip. Bryce threw the rug out of the way and knelt on the floor.

"What the hell?"

"It's loose," I said.

"I can see that." He tugged but couldn't pull the board up. "I'm going to need some tools."

"Are there any here?"

"There used to be. I'll be right back."

While he was gone, I looked around the room for anything we could use to jimmy up the floorboard. Nothing, and all I had in my purse was a nail file. That would hardly be strong enough.

Bryce returned with a small crowbar.

"Where'd you find that?"

"Out back. My dad kept some tools back there." Then he stopped.

"What?"

"What if I don't want to know what's under here? What if..."

Oh, no. He couldn't be thinking... "Babe, no. There'd be a smell."

"Not if it's been a long time."

"Then let's not look, okay? We can get someone else out here to—"

"I have to know," he said. "I have to know." The second time more to himself than to me. He stuck the crowbar between the seams of the wood.

Within minutes, the board had loosened and Bryce pulled it up.

"What is it?" I asked.

He picked up some manila folders. "Looks like documents."

"We'll need more light," I said.

"Yeah, definitely. I'm just going to grab everything out of here, and then we'll take it... Shit. Where can we take it?"

"The guesthouse? You said your mom and Henry are leaving for Florida tomorrow."

"I suppose. I'd prefer a safer place."

"Then maybe we leave them here. If no one's found them by now, they're not looking. Plus, these could be nothing."

"Marj, things hidden underneath floorboards aren't usually nothing."

He had a valid point. "Anything else down there?"

"Yeah, hold on. It's like a box or something. I may need to remove another board." He jammed the crowbar back into a seam to remove the hidden staples, and soon another board sat next to the first one on the floor. "Oh my God."

"What?"

"Do you have a handkerchief or something?"

"I've never carried a handkerchief in my life, Bryce."

"A tissue. Anything."

I grabbed my purse and pulled out a small package of tissues. "Here."

He removed one and then pulled a gun out of the floor. "I don't want my prints on anything here," he said. Then he pulled out another gun. And another.

"Three?" I gasped.

"That I've found so far." He pulled out a metal box secured with a combination lock. "I'm guessing there are more in here."

"Is that all?"

"Joe and I used to sleep in this room." His voice sounded like an echo.

"I know. It's okay."

"All this time..."

"We don't know what's in those files, what's in that box."

"We sure as hell know these are guns."

I said nothing. I certainly couldn't dispute him. "That's not really anything, though, right? You and Joe used to shoot with your dad."

"Yeah. But we didn't hide our guns under floorboards."

I exhaled slowly. "If you don't think the stuff is safe at the guesthouse, we can still leave it here."

"And risk someone getting in here and taking it?" He shook his head. "No way."

"Bryce, the case is closed. Your father and the other two are dead. The compound in the Caribbean is shut down. The victims were freed. It's over. If they were looking at this cabin, they'd have already found this stuff."

He looked above me, as if staring into some distance that wasn't actually there in this small room.

"Bryce?"

"It's not over, Marjorie. Not by a long shot."

"If you're talking about Colin and Ted Morse—"

"I'm not talking about them. At least not *just* about them."

I gulped. "What are you talking about, then?"

"I can't say any more."

"You can't just—"

"I made a promise. You have no idea how much I want to be able to talk to you. To anyone. But I can't."

"Is this why Henry and your mom are leaving?"

"We need to get out of here. I'm going to put this stuff in the trunk of my car until I figure out what to do with all of it."

"Bryce, we have—"

"This is over. I... I didn't mean anything I said. You should go to Paris. I want you to go."

"Oh, no. You're not going there again. You need some paper? Want to write me another note? Why not send an emotionless text? That's easier these days. Do what you want. Say what you want. I don't believe a fucking word of it now."

"Don't you see? I can't protect you."

"Who says I need protection? Exactly what are you talking about, Bryce?"

"I made a prom—"

"That ship has sailed. I'm in this now. If you think my safety's at stake, I need to know what's going on."

CHAPTER TWENTY-SEVEN

Bryce

She was right.

She was in this now, and all because I'd brought her here. Because I'd wanted her so badly and had nowhere else to go. Because I couldn't control my need and desire—my love—for this woman.

So I'd brought her to this place—this place where I'd had so many happy memories, memories that were now stained by my father's sickness.

Only to find more secrets—more secrets I now had to deal with.

"I'm serious," she said. "Tell me what's going on."

Was this place bugged? I hadn't given that possibility a thought when I'd come here with Marjorie. Joe and I were so careful about everywhere we went, yet I'd been completely blinded by lust. This cabin had been my father's, so of course the FBI would be watching it.

And if they were watching it, they would have searched it.

And if they'd searched it, they'd have found...

Something wasn't adding up.

Ted Morse was right. This was far from over.

"Bryce, come on," she said again.

"Joe will kill me."

"My brother? My brother's in this? You need to be straight with me. Now."

How could I? How could I bring her goodness and light into this dark world that had become my existence?

Thank God my mom and Henry would be safe in Florida. Now, if I could convince Marj to keep her plans to go to Paris, she'd be safe as well. The Steel ranch without Marj would be like a Colorado day without sunlight, but her safety was more important than anything.

I cleared my throat. "When are you leaving again?"

"For Paris? You just spent an hour convincing me not to go."

"I changed my mind."

"This is a crock," she said. "You're going to level with me. Right. Now."

I said nothing.

"Fine. I'll go to Joe, then. He'll tell me."

"No!" If she went to Joe, he'd know I let something slip. He'd also know about Marj and me.

"Sorry." She stood. "I'm out of here."

"Do you even know where we are?"

She plunked back down on the bed. "Fine. You're in charge, but you still owe me an explanation. Quite frankly, you're scaring the hell out of me. What exactly are you and Joe involved in?"

I sighed. "More than you can imagine."

She took my hand and pulled me onto the bed to sit beside her. "Start talking. I'm here for you."

Where to start? How could I put memories that had just resurfaced into words? And I'd be violating Joe's trust.

Should I call him first? Did I even have service out here?

"If I tell you," I said, "you have to promise never to tell another living soul. Especially not Joe."

"I can't do that. If you tell me, you have to tell Joe that you did. And what if I feel you're in danger or something? I can't promise not to say anything."

"Then I can't tell you."

"Not an option. I'm in this now."

He nodded, his brow wrinkled. "Tell you what. I'll make you a deal."

"What kind of deal?"

"I'll tell you, in confidence, what's going on with Joe and me, and you tell me about that cut on your leg."

She bit her bottom lip.

Even in the darkness of the cabin, she was beautiful and enticing. Even when she was troubled. Especially when she was troubled. All I wanted to do was take away everything hurting her and banish it so she'd never be unhappy again.

Finally, she cleared her throat softly. "Deal."

"You go first," I said.

"We'll go in shifts," she said. "You're right. The wound is self-inflicted. Now...you."

I couldn't fault the fairness of her idea. "Something happened about thirty years ago, while Joe and I were camping with my dad. Something we'd both forgotten until recently."

"Oh my God!" She clamped her hand to her mouth. "He didn't—"

"No, no, no. Joe and I are fine. He didn't do anything to us."

"Thank God." She rubbed her forehead. "I don't know what I'd do. This has all been so awful."

"Honey, you weren't born yet when this happened, and I

promise it has nothing to do with you."

"I wasn't born yet when Talon was taken. Rather, I was born while he was gone, and—"

"Look." I gripped her shoulders. "If this is too much for you, trust me. You're safer not knowing."

She shook her head vehemently. "No. I'm in this now. Tell me."

"You owe me a sentence first."

"Are you kidding me? What you're hiding is so much bigger than me cutting myself, Bryce. I fucked up. I let the guilt get to me. Talon was taken because my mother got pregnant with me. No me, no Talon being taken. It's that simple. And yeah, I had issues. I tormented myself to the point where I needed a release, and physical pain gave me that. I only cut myself in one place, and I thought I had it under control until..."

Her gaze shifted away from me.

The words she didn't say echoed around me as clear as if she'd uttered them.

Until you, Bryce.

I'd driven her to this.

"I'm sorry," I said.

"It's not you. It's me. I'm responsible for my own actions, no matter how much pain I'm in. Melanie taught me that."

"Melanie."

"She's the only person who knows."

"Not Jade."

"Only Mel. And now you."

"Your secret is safe with me."

"I know it is. Please give me the same benefit of the doubt. Anything you tell me is safe with me."

"I just hate to think of you hurting yourself."

"Is it really anything worse than what you've done to yourself? You wallow in the guilt about your father when you had nothing to do with anything he did."

"It's not that," I said truthfully.

"What is it, then?"

"It's that...he spared me. He never touched me. I remember him as"—I winced before saying the words—"a *good* father."

"Is that so horrible?"

"Of course it is! He was a monster. A demon. He raped and murdered children. He tortured your brother. He killed my cousin. He wasn't *human*."

"He was a sick man."

"He was so far beyond a sick man, Marj. You and I both know that."

She nodded. "I know."

"I never physically injured myself."

"I don't recommend it."

"I never even thought about it. Maybe it would help."

"For God's sake, Bryce. Self-mutilation isn't the answer. Please don't go there."

"You did, and you said it helped."

"It only transferred the pain. Pain is pain."

I squeezed her hand. "I'm so sorry you were in that much pain."

"I'm sorry you were too. Still are. Let me help. Let me take some of the burden from you. Please."

I'm sorry, Joe. I'm sorry.

I grabbed her hand and pulled her out of the room, out of the cabin.

Then words tumbled from my mouth.

CHAPTER TWENTY-EIGHT

Marjorie

I sat, numb. Bryce's voice almost became monotone, as if it were coming from somewhere in the woods. Was he throwing his voice? No. It was both of us. The words were hard for him to say, and they were equally hard for me to hear.

A young boy. A friend. Justin had been his name. Justin Valente.

"You think your father drugged you?"

"It's the only thing that makes sense," Bryce said. "And if we know anything, we know Tom Simpson was capable of far worse."

"Capable of drugging his own son?"

"How else does this make sense? How could Joe and I nearly forget that a kid died on our watch?"

"It wasn't your watch. You were children. You weren't responsible."

He shook his head. "Still..."

"I know."

How well I knew. I was merely an embryo when Talon was taken, and still I felt responsible. It was silly but no less real.

"Then he just seemed to disappear. No one talked about him. His family moved away. It's creepy."

Creepy was too tame of a word, but I understood what

Bryce meant.

"You and Joe have been keeping this to yourselves all this time?"

"Yeah. We don't talk anywhere that might be bugged. That's why I brought you outside."

"But the cabin..."

"I know. It's unlikely, especially since no one found the stuff hidden in the bedroom, but Joe and I aren't taking any chances. That's why I need your promise that this stays between us."

"You have to tell Joe that you told me."

"I can't. Then he'll know..."

"That you and I are..."

What were we? I paused, hoping he'd fill in the words.

He didn't.

"We've slept together," I said as nonchalantly as I could. "So what?"

"You're his little sister."

"Who used to have pink and yellow unicorns on the walls of her room. We've been through that, Bryce."

"Yeah, but he can't know that I... You know... Without..."

"You're making no sense at all."

"That I fucked you, Marj. That we fucked without any commitment."

"You're not the first man I fucked without a commitment." Though his words hurt. After all this time, I still wanted a commitment from him. I loved him so much.

"It's not even that. It's that..."

"For God's sake, spit it out!"

I was immediately sorry for my harshness.

Then again, I wasn't. I felt for what Bryce and Joe had

rediscovered, but how much was I supposed to take?

He raked his fingers through his disheveled blond hair. "I love you, goddamnit! I love you, Marjorie Steel. I love you with everything I am!"

I froze, my skin going numb while my heart thundered. "I know," I said softly.

"You're everything to me. Every fucking thing."

Then his lips were on mine, and I opened for him. The kiss was so powerful and so full of love.

Our tongues twirled together in perfect harmony like the strings of a violin and then clashed like cymbals.

My nipples tightened and my pussy pulsed.

He loves me. He loves me. He loves me.

He broke the kiss and gazed into my eyes, his own eyes burning. "Inside. Now."

I wasn't about to argue as he pulled me back inside. We didn't make it to the bedroom. We ditched our clothes in the entryway, and then he lifted me, pushing my back against the rough wall. I might get a splinter in my back, but I didn't care. All I cared about was Bryce inside me, filling me, leaving every last crevice of emptiness a distant memory.

Then he was inside me, pumping, his lips on mine.

Perfection. All perfection.

My clit rubbed against his rough pubic hair, and soon an orgasm was imminent. I groaned into his mouth as the tickle in my pussy intensified, shooting out to my limbs, stars exploding around me. Still we kissed, and his groan told me he knew I was coming.

Coming for him.

He thrust again, again, again...

Once more...

Until—

He embedded himself so deeply inside me, we became one.

Every pulse of his cock radiated through my body, my heart.

My very soul.

Finally we broke our kiss, both of us panting, and he released me. My feet hit the floor, and I melted against him, his chest slick with perspiration.

"My God," he rasped.

I nodded into his chest.

"I love you so fucking much." He kissed the top of my head.

"I love you too, Bryce. Always."

He pulled away slightly and met my gaze. "I was so afraid. I...still am."

"It's okay."

"But it's not. You deserve a whole man."

"You *are* a whole man, Bryce."

"I don't feel whole."

I couldn't help a short laugh. "Who among us does? Do you think I'd have cut myself if I felt whole?"

"But—"

I pressed my fingers against his lips. "Stop. I'm not making light of anything either of us has been through. But you are as whole as anyone else is. Believe it. I do."

"I have so many other responsibilities. Henry. My mom."

"Who says I'm going to be your responsibility?"

"I do. I want you to be. I want to take care of you."

"I love you for that. I do. But I'm not looking for someone to take care of me. If we're in a relationship, we're partners.

We'll have equal responsibility to care for each other. That's how it works."

"How do you know so much about relationships?"

Good question. I'd had very few in my life. "Honestly? From my parents, I think."

"Oh?"

"Yeah. I know they weren't perfect. I hated my father for lying to us, but look how he took care of my mother, always did what was best for her. And if she'd been able to, she'd have cared for him as well. I truly believe it."

"I wish I'd had that kind of example."

"You did," I said, "or you wouldn't feel so strongly about not getting into a relationship before you're ready."

He cocked his head. "You're right, but that's exactly what I'm fighting. Those good memories of my father. They're killing me."

"It's okay to have good memories of a bad person."

"No, it's not. It can't be."

"But it is. That's something else I learned from Melanie. I wanted to hate my father, but he was a good father to me until he"—air quotes—"*died* when I was eighteen. I was his baby girl. I have no memories at all of my mother, so everything I learned in life I learned from him. Well, him and my brothers. You don't have to forget the good stuff just because there's bad stuff."

"You're so strong."

"No stronger than anyone else. I've obviously had my own issues." I pointed to the scar on my thigh.

He touched it gently. "Does it hurt?"

"No. Not anymore."

"Can you promise me you'll never hurt yourself again?"

I swallowed, trying to think of the right words to say. They didn't come.

"Please, sweetheart? I can't stand the thought of you harming yourself in any way."

"I'll try," I said. "I've made that promise to myself before, only to break it. I made the promise to Mel, only to break it. I don't want to ever break a promise to you."

"Then don't."

"Which is why I can't make that promise. I will try. That's the best I can do."

He nodded. "That's good enough. For now."

I touched his cheek, his stubble scraping against my smooth fingertips. "I love you."

He smiled. "I love you too. I've wanted to say that so many times."

"Have you?"

He nodded. "Writing you that letter was torture. Pure torture."

"Good. Because it was pure torture to read it. Believe me."

"I'm so sorry."

"I forgive you."

"Do you? Really?"

I nodded. "Really."

He looked around. "I really want to make love to you. Slowly and completely. But I don't want to do it here. Not in either of those bedrooms, and not in this room either. It has to be perfect, and anything in this old cabin, where God only knows what went on, won't be perfect."

"The place doesn't matter, Bryce."

"It does to me."

His eyes held such torment that I wanted to cradle him

like a child and tell him everything would be all right.

But everything wasn't all right.

We loved each other. We were going to do this.

But everything was far from all right.

Bryce had confided in me. Someone was watching him.

I flashed back to the night Jade and I had met with Colin at the main house. His obscure words.

I'm sorry for what I did. For what I allowed to happen. And for what's to come.

CHAPTER TWENTY-NINE

Bryce

She was in it now. I'd brought Marjorie Steel into the ugliness of my life. I'd broken my promise to Joe. I'd told our secret, and he hadn't even told his own wife.

I hoped I hadn't just ended a lifetime friendship. Joe meant so much to me, and now that I was with his sister, we might be family someday.

Wow. Family. I could marry this woman. Have more kids with her, brothers and sisters for Henry.

I was getting ahead of myself, but the thought filled me with something I hadn't felt in a long time.

Joy.

"We can go," she said. "I understand. This place kind of gives me the creeps."

I grabbed my jeans and began to dress, and she followed suit.

"What do you want to do with the stuff we found under the floor?"

"Put it in the trunk of my car for now." The trunk of the car that had been my father's. Why hadn't I gotten rid of it yet? I thought about it every time I saw the damned thing, yet I still hadn't dumped it. It was a cherried-out Mustang. I could easily sell it and buy my own cherried-out Mustang if I wanted to.

Better yet, I could start a college fund for my son and buy a Prius.

Which reminded me that I started my new position at the Steel Corporation in the morning.

Once we were dressed, we headed to the bedroom. "Don't touch the guns," I warned Marjorie. "Use a tissue or something. In fact, don't touch them at all. I'll take care of them."

She nodded, grabbed the manila folders, and pointed to the metal box. "I wonder what's in there."

"It's a gun case. Probably more guns."

"Okay to touch the box?"

"No one's going to arrest you because your prints are on a box," I said.

She smiled and grabbed the handle— "Oh!" The box fell open, and its contents spilled to the floor. "I'm sorry."

"No worries. Let's have a look."

No more guns. I gaped at the contents spread on the area rug that had hidden the floorboards.

"Jewelry?" Marjorie gasped.

Jewelry. A lot of it. Pearls and rubies and diamonds. I had no idea what the quality was or what any of it was worth.

My father had hidden fine jewelry in a gun case.

Only Tom Simpson.

"I thought you said it was locked," she said.

"I thought it was." I inspected the metal. "It's rusted out here. It just gave way."

"Whose is this?"

"It must have belonged to my father."

"Which means it now belongs to your mother. And you."

"Not necessarily. Not if it was bought with dirty money. Then it belongs to the Feds."

"How can we possibly know?"

"Hell if I know." Several velvet pouches sat among the necklaces and rings. I picked one up and poured the contents into my hand. "Diamonds?"

Marj grabbed her phone and turned on the flashlight. "No. They're not clear. They're yellow. Could be citrine, a semiprecious stone."

"Why would he keep a semiprecious stone locked up?"

"The color's not right either. They're too light. Maybe they are— I mean, if they are..."

"What?"

"They could be fancy yellow canary diamonds. Those are rarer than clear diamonds."

"How do you know— Never mind." She was a Steel heiress. Of course she knew about jewels.

"Some of these are three carats at least. Maybe four or five."

The gems sparkled in the light from her phone. She picked up what appeared to be a large pendant with a pink stone.

"This is gorgeous! I've never seen a pink sapphire so big."

"Shouldn't it be on a chain?" I asked.

Marjorie laughed. "It's a brooch, silly. A pin to wear on your collar or lapel."

"Sorry. I'm not a jewelry expert."

"I wouldn't expect you to be." She smiled.

"There are several other pouches," I said, quickly putting the yellow gems back in their pouch. "What am I going to do with all this?"

"I guess first we need to figure out if they're stolen or if they were bought with dirty money," she said.

"And how are we going to do that?"

"We go home, and we go through these files," she said. "Maybe there's something in there."

I placed my finger over my lips, signaling her to be quiet. We'd both forgotten that we shouldn't be talking in here.

"Let's just get this out to the car," I said quietly.

She nodded.

Once everything was safely ensconced in my trunk, I led Marjorie away from the cabin and the car. The moon shone above in the clear night sky. I pressed my lips to hers in a soft kiss and then pulled away. "I hope I didn't just make a terrible mistake."

"Oh, no." She shook her head. "You said you love me."

I laughed. "Not about that. I broke Joe's confidence. In over thirty years, I've never done that."

"I won't tell a soul, Bryce. I promise."

"I made that same promise to Joe."

"You really don't think he told Mel?"

"He swore he hasn't."

"But he might have. They're really close, and they've both been through a lot of crap. Melanie was left tied up in a garage with a running car. Remember?"

I nodded. I remembered everything. "But Joe—"

"Joe will do what he has to do," she said. "I doubt he's keeping this from the most important person in his life, but even if he is, I won't say a thing to him. I swear it, Bryce. You can trust me. Love isn't anything without trust."

I smiled. She was wonderful. Truly wonderful. I kissed her again, this time harder and with tongue. When my cock reacted, I broke the kiss. "We need to get out of here. Somewhere with a bed, or I'll be doing you right here in the moonlight."

"Anything wrong with that?" she teased.

"Only that it's winter."

"It's a beautiful night. We'll keep each other warm."

"Hold that thought for when it warms up," I said. "I have to get home, and so do you. I have an early day tomorrow, and I want to get up even earlier to spend time with Henry before he leaves with my mom."

"I understand." She touched my cheek, sending a shiver through me. "Thank you."

"For what?"

"For trusting me."

"No thanks needed."

"And for loving me."

"Really, no thanks needed. I should be thanking you for loving an empty shell like me."

"You're not so empty," she said. "If you were, there wouldn't be anything for me to love."

I moved my head and kissed the satiny palm of her hand. "Your love will fill me. I only hope I can do the same for you."

"You already have."

We kissed again, a soft kiss with a promise of things to come.

A kiss under the moonlight, a kiss for all time.

★ ★ ★

My time in the morning with Henry was too short. He dealt with the separation much better than I did. When the car came to pick up him and my mother for the airport, I didn't want to let him go. After he gave me several sloppy kisses, I finally gave him up to my mother's arms.

"Do a good job for the Steels," my mother said.

"I will."

"I know." She smiled. "We'll miss you."

Then she was in the car with my son, driving away.

His absence left an emptiness in me, but I couldn't dwell on it. I needed to get my head in the game. Work started today. I already had a good idea of what I'd be doing, thanks to my previous meetings with Joe and his brothers. More good news... I didn't have to wear a suit. It was strictly casual in the office building, so jeans and a button-down it would be.

I took a few more sips of my coffee, grabbed my briefcase and laptop, and headed for the car to drive to the office building. Everything was on Steel property, but the ranch was huge. It was nearly a half-hour drive from the guesthouse to the office building, which was located between the cattle ranch and the orchard. Ryan's vineyards were farther east, on the actual slopes of the Rockies.

Joe was waiting for me outside the building.

"Hey," I said. "I didn't expect an escort."

"Unfortunately, this isn't business. I need to talk to you."

My heart fell. This couldn't be good. I already felt like a shithead for telling Marj our secret. Why had I burdened her with it? She certainly didn't deserve that, and Joe didn't deserve having his trust broken.

Then again, he had some explaining to do. I'd found encrypted emails in the trash bin of our account with the Spider. I'd been on my way to confront him when I'd been waylaid by Marjorie.

I sighed. "Yeah. I need to talk to you too."

"Shit. Did you get another call too?"

"No. Did you?"

He nodded. "I couldn't tell if it was the same voice or not.

It was muffled this time. Like he was talking through a rag or something. Or maybe using some voice-scrambling software. I have no idea."

"It was a man, though?"

"I think so. I couldn't actually tell. The first one was a man, or maybe a woman with a really deep voice."

"What did he say?"

"The same, that he was watching, but then he said something really disturbing."

"What?"

"He said to watch my back."

"Okay. That's weird. If he's watching, you're obviously already watching your back."

"It was the way he said it, Bryce. Almost like he meant someone close to me was betraying me."

"Who would do that? No one but us knows about this."

But chills rippled up my spine. Had this person somehow heard my conversation with Marjorie at the cabin?

No. Couldn't have happened. The outside couldn't be bugged. Could it?

If it could be done, it would require a huge level of sophistication that I couldn't even begin to fathom.

But there was an easier way to eavesdrop.

Someone could have been in the woods with us.

More chills.

"I always have your back, Joe."

In my heart, I knew it wasn't a lie. I'd confided in the woman I loved, as he probably had as well. Marj had said she couldn't imagine him keeping this from Melanie.

Then again, Melanie was pregnant. She didn't need any extra stress.

I had to come clean, and I had to do it now. Coming clean also meant telling Joe about Marjorie and me.

It was time.

Joe and I were about the same size. I could fight him off if he decided to take me out. But he was a hothead.

"I have something to tell you."

"Fuck. Are you telling me—"

"No. I mean, yes. I told someone."

"Damn it, Bryce. Goddamnit all to hell!"

He didn't advance on me. Instead he paced in the grass, the heels of his boots digging in.

"I could say I'm sorry, but I'm not. I trust this person completely, and when you find out who it is, you'll agree.

"Not your mother."

"God, no. Not my mother. I couldn't burden her with this."

"Yeah? Who *could* you burden, then?"

His baby sister. The person he was most protective of in the world, other than his pregnant wife. I hadn't thought this through. Too late now.

Joe continued, "One of my brothers."

"You're getting closer."

"Who, then? Who else is there? One of their wives?"

"I hardly know Jade and Ruby."

"Then who, Bryce? Christ."

Marj wasn't even in the running, as far as Joe was concerned.

I was in deep shit.

"I'll tell you, but first you have to know something else, which, when you get over your shock, I hope you'll consider good news."

"I'm really not in the mood for your evasive language, Simpson."

He never called me by my last name. We were always Bryce and Joe. Never Simpson and Steel, like some of the other guys in school had called us.

"Calm down. This isn't easy for me to say."

"I ought to fucking knock your lights out."

In truth, I was surprised he hadn't tried already. The Joe I knew would have come at me as soon as he found out I'd broken our trust. "If it'll make you feel better."

"I'm angry as shit right now."

"I know. I get it."

"You've pissed me off before, Bryce. You know you have, and even though I've wanted to smash your face into the ground more than once, I never have. You know why? Because you're my brother, man. As much as my brothers by blood. So you'd better start talking." Then, "Wait. Let's move farther away from the building."

When we'd walked several hundred feet more, he turned to me, his dark eyes angry. "Now."

I shoved my hands into my pockets. This was Joe. The guy who'd been at my side for nearly forty years. Jonah Bradford Steel, oldest heir to the Steel fortune. The ultimate hothead—but also the ultimate good guy.

"I'm in love, Joe."

His facial features softened. A little. He said nothing.

"Did you hear me?"

"Do I look deaf to you?"

"So you have no comment on that?"

"You haven't left town without me knowing about it since your father died. How the hell could you have met anyone?"

"It's someone you know. Someone you're close to."

Confusion marred his features, and then—

His eyes changed. He'd figured it out.

"You brought *her* into this?" Joe curled his hands into fists.

"I love her, man. I fucking love her."

"Fuck!" He punched the air. "Fuck, fuck, fuck!"

"I didn't want to—"

"Then why did you? Why? Damn! Now there're four of us who know."

"She's strong, Joe. She's strong, and we love each oth— Excuse me? Four of us?"

Finally I knew why Joe hadn't thrown a punch when I started this conversation.

"Don't even get on me now. You knew I couldn't keep this from my wife."

"So it's okay for—"

"No, damn it. None of this is okay. Fucking none of it." He punched the air again and then unclenched one fist and rubbed his forehead, his eyes squinting as though the sunlight was bothering him.

"Joe..."

"Don't even. Don't even talk to me."

"You want to be mad at me? Fine. But be mad for a good reason, not for something you're just as guilty of."

"Melanie is my wife."

"She is. But you made the same promise I did. You said no one knows. Not Melanie. Not anyone."

"And sure as fuck not Marjorie."

"I'm sorry. I love her, man."

"She's just a baby."

"She's almost twenty-six. She's Jade's age, and Jade is Talon's wife." I paused a few seconds. "These are all things I've been over and over again in my mind. I remember when she was born. I'd just turned thirteen. I remember all of it. Believe me, I didn't expect this."

"How am I supposed to protect her if—"

"You don't have to protect her. That's my job now. Your job is to protect Melanie."

"Protecting my baby sister will always be my job, Bryce."

At least he was back to calling me Bryce.

"How the hell did this happen, anyway?"

"We started to get close when she babysat Henry. Turns out she's had feelings for me since she was a kid."

"That was puppy love."

"Yeah, that's what I told her. But it turned into something real. For both of us."

"Have you..."

"None of your business, man."

He huffed. "You just answered my question."

"Hey, I don't ask what you and your wife do."

"My wife and I are married."

"Okay. Play that card if you want to, but I'm willing to bet you were engaging in stuff well before your marriage." I could have thrown in his membership at the BDSM club for good measure. You didn't go to a club like that to be celibate. But I kept my mouth shut.

He said nothing, just gave me a "fuck you" look.

I'd seen that look before. I was actually happy to see it now. It meant he was cooling down.

"It's the real thing, Joe."

"You know she decided to go to Paris?"

I nodded. "I actually want her to go."

"You do?"

“She’ll be safe there. We’ll hire a bodyguard, just in case.”

“I was going to anyway.”

“I figured you were.”

“She won’t want to go now. You know that, right? She’ll want to stay with you and help you.”

“I know. I’m going to insist. She’s going if I have to carry her onto the plane and buckle her in myself.”

That got a laugh out of him. “I see you don’t know her that well yet.”

I returned his smile. “Actually, I do.”

“Then you know she’s not going anywhere. At least not now.”

I sighed. What could I say? He was right. And though I wanted more than anything for Marjorie to be half a world away where she’d be safe, I couldn’t bring myself to be unhappy that she wasn’t going.

“There’s one more thing,” I said.

“What?”

“I found some encrypted emails on our account. In the trash.”

“What?” Joe hurriedly fumbled with his phone.

“Have you been contacting the Spider without telling me?”

“Hell, no!” He pulled up the account. “Shit, I don’t know—”

Joe’s phone dinged with a text. He raised his brows when he looked at the screen.

“What?” I asked.

“The Spider. He says he has news. Maybe he can explain the emails.”

CHAPTER THIRTY

Marjorie

My emotions were tangled. I put them on hold long enough to get the boys off to school and fix a light breakfast for Jade.

Then I couldn't put it off any longer.

Was there a name for this feeling? This feeling of complete happiness and love mixed with dread?

Bryce loved me. He really loved me, and I'd finally broken through the wall of armor he'd built around himself after discovering the truth about his father. I should be over the moon, and I was.

But I also wasn't.

Our hell wasn't over, not by a long shot. Someone was stalking Bryce and my oldest brother, who'd been witness to another heinous crime Tom Simpson had perpetrated.

Now it was coming back to haunt them.

Bryce wasn't safe. Joe wasn't safe.

I could escape all of this. I could go forward with my plans for Paris. Indeed, Bryce had told me to go because I'd be safe there.

But he loved me.

And that changed everything.

No way was I leaving him. Not when he needed me. He'd sent his mother and son away, but Evelyn was a senior citizen and Henry a baby. They needed protecting.

I didn't.

I was a sister to three older brothers, daughter to a father who'd resisted at first but had succumbed to my determination and taught me everything he'd taught my brothers. I could run this ranch as well as any of them. I simply didn't want to. It wasn't my interest. It wasn't in my soul the way it was in theirs.

But I'd done all the chores, learned all the ropes, and I'd built a lot of tenacity along the way.

I could hold my own.

I needed to hold my own.

I needed to be here for the man I loved.

Not to mention my best friend and my brothers. And, though she didn't recognize me, my mother.

They all needed me, and I would not desert them.

Paris would still be there tomorrow. Next week. Next year. Next decade, even. I was young.

Besides, another brain helping to figure out what was going on now would be an asset.

Bryce had sworn me to secrecy about Justin Valente, and I would keep his confidence. He'd tell Joe, I knew. My brother would be angry, but in the end, he'd be okay. He was Bryce's best friend. He of all people knew what a good man Bryce was.

Bryce would take care of me, and I would take care of him. We'd take care of each other as equal partners.

Oh, he'd get all Alpha on me sometimes. He'd grown up around my brothers, after all. But I'd also grown up around my brothers. I knew my way around a Steel man, and Bryce was an honorary Steel man. He always had been.

What to do?

First, I'd tell Jade about Bryce and me. As she was the

only person who knew how I felt about him, she'd be thrilled.

She'd expect me to be ecstatic. Indeed, I was.

I was also freaked out and frightened.

This wasn't over. Colin had been right. There was more to come.

I'd already showered, so I went to Jade's bedroom. I knocked quietly and then entered. The whoosh of the shower wafted toward me. She was busy, so I went back to the kitchen and drank a glass of water.

I needed to take the edge off, expend some energy. Bryce was at work for his first day at his new job, so I couldn't bother him.

The gym. I was already dressed in leggings and a tank. I hurriedly put on my cross-trainers and set out.

I didn't have a session booked with Dominic this morning, but maybe he'd be available. If not, I'd do my own workout. Maybe try some of the circuits Ruby had put together for me. I drove the half hour into Snow Creek, parked, and walked inside the fitness center.

Dominic wasn't in the trainers' office, so I took off for an elliptical machine. That thing always kicked my ass, and what I needed this morning was a good ass kicking. Something to punch the tension out of my body.

I grabbed an extra towel and my water bottle and started to set up a program on the machine.

"Hey, stranger."

I turned, dropping the towel with my locker key pinned on it on the floor next to the machine. Dominic James stood beside me.

"I didn't know you were here," I said.

"Yeah. I'm not on duty. I had an early morning baseball practice."

"You play?"

"Not anymore. I help coach the high school kids."

"Oh? That's cool."

"I love the game. I was all state in high school and had a scholarship for college, but I couldn't finish because of an injury. I'd love a real coaching job, but for now I make more doing training part-time. The school job pays a little."

"That's good." I wasn't sure what else to say. I hardly knew the guy.

"I think so. Sure, I'd have loved a chance at the majors, but it is what it is."

"True enough." If only he knew.

"You just starting? Or can I interest you in a breakfast smoothie?"

I cleared my throat. A breakfast smoothie sounded great, but I was off the market now that Bryce and I had declared our love for each other. "I have to pass."

He reached toward me. "Let me twist your arm a little."

I jerked away from him. "I know we had a deal for my training. Lunches and stuff. But I feel I should tell you. I'm in a relationship now."

"In two days?"

"Well...yeah. I didn't think it could happen, but it did." I couldn't help smiling.

"I can't say I'm not disappointed," he said, "but we can still be friends. And I can still buy you a smoothie, right?"

I laughed. "I'll take the smoothie, but I'll buy my own. After my workout, okay?"

"Perfect. Meet me down by the spa. An hour?"

I nodded. "Sounds good."

I watched his perfect ass as he walked off. He was built like a male model, but then, so was Bryce. And I much preferred a male ass in regular jeans than in workout spandex. Still, I was flattered. No reason existed that I could see why I shouldn't still train with Dominic. I'd pay him, of course. Ruby didn't have time to work with me, so I needed a good trainer.

Now I had one.

I set the timer and started my workout.

★ ★ ★

I guzzled from my water bottle and wiped my face with one of my towels as I made my way down to the women's locker room. I'd pinned the key to a towel, so I—

"Shit," I said aloud.

My locker key was gone. It must have fallen off. I retraced my steps back to the machine I'd been using. No key.

No biggie. I stopped at the front desk, and a clerk with a master key walked with me to the locker room and opened my locker. After she left, I checked my purse and wallet. Everything was still there, and nothing seemed amiss. Clearly I just hadn't pinned the key securely to the towel. I checked my watch. Fifteen minutes until I was supposed to meet Dominic downstairs. Time enough for a quick steam and shower.

The steam room was my favorite. I loved inhaling the steam perfumed with spearmint and eucalyptus, even when I didn't need to clear my sinuses. After five minutes, I felt relaxed—as relaxed as I was going to get, anyway—so I took a quick shower and dressed in some jeans and a cardigan I'd brought along.

Dominic was waiting at the front desk, as he'd promised. My hair was wet, and I'd pulled it up in a sloppy bun on top of my head. I wasn't out to impress any man except Bryce Simpson.

Still, Dominic said, "You look amazing."

I laughed. "Wet hair and all. Thanks, I guess."

"Just telling the truth."

Should I mention my relationship again? I didn't want to seem repetitive. I kept quiet as we headed to the smoothie shop.

I'd eaten breakfast, but I was always ready to eat after a workout. He didn't try to touch me again as we walked the few buildings to the shop.

"I'll have the vanilla raspberry," I told the clerk.

She looked to Dominic.

"These are separate," I said.

"Oh, sorry."

I paid quickly and found a small table by the front window. Bryce was on the ranch at his first day of work, but why should I hide anyway? This was completely innocent.

Dominic finished ordering and sat down across from me. "What are you up to today?" he asked.

Good question. What was I up to? So many things swirled in my mind, none of which I could tell the man sitting with me. Before I could think of something to say, our smoothies were ready. Dominic went to get them and then brought them to the table.

I sucked the fruity goodness through the straw.

"I'm working this afternoon," he said.

I nodded. Was I supposed to react to that?

Unease swept over me. Something didn't feel right about being here, and it went beyond the fact that I was now committed to Bryce.

Dominic was as affable as I remembered, and nothing seemed out of place at the shop. Yet I couldn't shake the niggling like little insects underneath the skin of my neck. It was creeping me out.

"I lost the key to my locker," I heard myself saying without knowing why.

"Oh? Did you find it?"

"No. The desk clerk had a master key and opened it for me."

"Was anything stolen?"

"No."

"That's good. It probably just fell out of a pocket or something."

I shook my head. "I pinned it to the towel I was using. It was sitting on the floor next to my machine the whole time. It should have been, anyway."

He sipped his smoothie. "That's strange."

"I know."

"This is such a small town. I'm guessing you don't have a lot of crime. People probably leave their doors unlocked." Dominic's phone buzzed on the table. He picked it up.

"Some do. We're a little more careful these days."

"Oh? Why?"

Yeah, I'd said a little too much. I really wasn't in the mood to go through the entire saga of our esteemed mayor being exposed as a psychopathic rapist and murderer—who was also the father of the man I was in love with.

"Just some stuff happened here recently." And might still be going on, though I couldn't say anything more.

"Uh...okay. You want to elaborate? I mean, I just got here, and I've got jobs I love. Are you telling me to leave?"

“No. Of course not. It’s just... Our mayor, who’s dead now, was involved in some pretty illegal stuff. I don’t really want to talk about it. I’m sure you can get the whole story somewhere else.”

“Sure. I understand.” He went back to his phone as if I’d said something as simple as the sun was shining.

Which I found extremely odd.

CHAPTER THIRTY-ONE

Bryce

Chills traveled down my spine at light speed. "News." A statement.

"Yeah."

"What is it?"

"He doesn't say. He'll send it in a different document."

"Okay. When?"

"He didn't say."

"Great."

"Ease up, Bryce. We'll just wait here until he sends it. In the meantime, I'll ask about the stuff in the bin."

I nodded, trying not to hyperventilate. We wouldn't get through this if one or both of us lost it.

"Anything yet?" I asked after a few seconds.

"Nope."

I shoved my hands into the pockets of my jeans. "Now?"

"Ease up, I said."

Five more minutes—that seemed like hours—passed. "What the hell is taking him so long?"

"I don't know." Joe stared at his phone. "Nothing's coming through on the account."

"Maybe he has to type it up."

Joe didn't reply.

"Or maybe something came up that he had to attend to. A sick kid or something."

Again, no answer.

"I mean, we don't know anything about this guy."

Finally, Joe regarded me. "We don't know him, but I do know the guy who recommended him, and I trust him."

"A guy you met at a BDSM club? Really?" I paced a few steps.

"You don't know what you're talking about."

"Do you?"

"Yeah, I do, damn it. If you'd ever been a part of that community, you'd know how trustworthy they are. I met senators there, Bryce, and others. People whose careers would be ruined if the general public knew how they spent some of their free time. We all trust each other to keep quiet. No one in Snow Creek knows I've been there, do they?"

"Not that I know of. Sorry."

"It's okay. I'd probably be thinking the same thing. But the guy is trustworthy, and if he says the Spider is trustworthy, he is."

"For the record, man, no judgment here."

"I know that. I wouldn't have told you otherwise."

"And it's safe with me."

"I know that too."

"I'm sorry I told Marj about the other stuff."

"I know. I'm sorry I told Melanie. Except that I'm not."

"Me neither."

"You better treat my sister right. I've never laid a hand on you in my whole life, but I will if she sheds a single tear over you."

She'd already shed many, but Joe didn't need to know

that. I simply nodded. I'd felt like kicking the shit out of myself for making Marjorie feel even a morsel of sadness.

It wouldn't happen again.

"Still nothing," Joe said.

"He must have gotten sidetracked."

"I don't like this." Joe shoved his phone back into his pocket.

"Me neither. Nothing we can do about it now. I should get to work."

"There's plenty of it. I'll check in with you later."

I nodded and walked back to the office building, leaving Joe staring at the ground.

* * *

Joe wasn't kidding. Plenty of work awaited me, and it kept my mind occupied, thank God, until my cell phone chimed midafternoon. My mother.

"We're here at Vicky's, safe and sound," she said.

"Good news. Can I speak to Henry?"

"Sure. Come here, honey. Daddy wants to say hi."

"Hi, buddy," I said, already missing him terribly. "Did you have fun on the airplane with Ga-ga?"

He gurgled into the phone.

"Daddy misses you," I said.

"Da-da."

I smiled. I had a Henry-sized hole in my heart, but I was happy he was safe in Florida and away from the mess my life had become.

My mom got back on the phone. "He's still teething badly. Fussy. Vicky got him some of those large plastic beads..."

She went on, but I was struck by the word "beads." The jewelry from the cabin popped into my head.

"Mom, I have a question."

"Yeah?"

"Did Dad ever give you any jewelry?"

"Jewelry? Nothing other than my engagement and wedding rings. Why do you ask?"

"It's just... I was at the old cabin, and I found some stuff. A lot of jewelry, actually."

Silence for a few seconds.

Then, "What kind of jewelry, Bryce?"

"Some pendants. Some loose gems. I found a bunch of stuff hidden in the cabin."

Silence again.

"Mom?"

"Unbelievable," she finally said softly.

"What's unbelievable?"

"I haven't thought about this in years."

My skin tightened. "Thought about *what* in years?"

"You were just a kid at the time, but about thirty years ago, our house was robbed."

I lifted my eyebrows. Total news to me. "Robbed? In Snow Creek? Was this before or after..."

Even I had trouble saying the words sometimes.

"Before Luke disappeared," she said. "You would have been seven or eight at the time."

Crime was almost unheard of in Snow Creek until Luke disappeared, so a robbery would have been very unusual.

"Did we even have anything to steal?" I asked.

"At that time, yes. An old great-aunt had died and left some things to Vicky and me."

"What kind of things?"

"Jewelry. And some loose gems." Her voice was icy.

My neck chilled. "Was it worth anything?"

"A lot, actually. Our great-aunt had married into money but hadn't had any kids. Most of her assets went to charity, but her jewelry went to Vicky and me. It was a pretty big haul. Vicky and I were both thrilled."

"So what happened?"

"Since we were both living in Snow Creek, the stuff was shipped to me. We never had the chance to divide it up. We were robbed a day later, and they took everything."

"Someone knew you had the stuff in the house."

"Yeah. Someone." My mother paused a moment. "Damn him."

My mother almost never cursed.

"I hadn't looked through everything," she continued. "It all happened so fast. Aunt Esther was fond of diamonds, and her husband bought her anything she wanted."

I cleared my throat. "Yellow diamonds?"

"Probably. Like I said, I didn't get the chance to go through everything."

"Would you recognize any of the jewelry if you saw it again?"

"Bryce, it's been thirty years."

"Think back. Would you recognize any of them?"

"It's been forever. I think there was a ruby pendant and matching earrings. Several diamond rings. Pouches of loose stones. Maybe some emeralds. Oh! There was this gorgeous brooch with a large pink stone. I never knew what it was, but it was going to be my first pick when Vicky and I divided it."

Big pink stone. In a brooch.

A pink sapphire, according to Marjorie.

Unbelievable, as my mother had said.

My father had robbed my mother. Perhaps he'd used some of the stones to finance his other life, though I doubted it. From all accounts, he'd been very well paid for his work. Still... he had the safe house where Joe had found him and Colin, the place where Melanie had nearly been killed, and who knew what other properties? Whether he'd used the jewelry or not, much of it clearly remained.

It belonged to my mother and Aunt Vicky.

This was good news for them. Good news for all of us. This wasn't dirty money. It was stolen property that belonged to our family.

"Looks like you and Aunt Vicky can still go through your inheritance," I said. "I'll get it into a safe-deposit box as soon as I can."

The only problem was...I was being watched.

Someone was watching me.

No one else could know about the jewels, or they'd have leverage to extort from me. My father had left us with next to nothing, and he'd left my aunt childless. I was going to make sure my mother and aunt got their inheritance, even if it was thirty years late.

"I have to go, Mom. First day of work and all. Give Henry a kiss, and I'll call him this evening to say good night."

"Okay. Remember that we're two hours later here, so don't call too late."

"I won't."

I had to get the stuff appraised and insured as soon as I could. But how could I do that without anyone knowing? Everything was still in the trunk of my father's Mustang, which was parked outside the building.

Was it safer there than in the guesthouse? Here in the office building? How could I get it to a safe-deposit box?

I rose and went to the next office to see Joe. The door was open. "Hey."

He looked up from his computer screen. "What's up?"

"I need to talk to you." I cocked my head to indicate outside.

He nodded and rose.

"Do you guys have a safe or something?" I asked after telling him about my find.

"We have many, but no safe is foolproof."

"Have you checked them lately?"

"Are you kidding? I don't have time to go around checking every safe on this property. But I've checked the ones here in the office building and in my home. Also the ones at the main house. Everything's good."

"What about the guesthouse?"

"I haven't checked it, but there's one in the master bedroom behind the Monet copy."

"What do you keep at the guesthouse?"

"Ryan used to use it for personal stuff. I assume he moved all his stuff to the new house. I'm not sure what's in there now. Probably nothing."

"Would the jewels be safe there?"

"Depends. If there's nothing in there now, we can't know if it's been tampered with. And no one's lived there for a few months. Someone could have easily broken in."

"Do you know the combination?"

"I have access to all of them, yeah."

"All right. Come over after we're done for the day, and

we'll check the guesthouse safe."

He nodded. "Where's the stuff now?"

"In the trunk of my car."

"Are you nuts?"

"Where else was I going to put it? Leave it in the cabin? Along with the guns?"

"You didn't—"

"No. We used tissues. Neither Marj nor I got our prints on the guns."

"Crazy." He shook his head. "We need to read the files."

"I meant to look at them last night, but I got a little spooked. I didn't want disgusting stuff on my mind right before my first day of work here."

"I'm not looking forward to it either, but armed *with* information is better than not."

I nodded. He was right.

I just hated the idea of discovering more horrendous secrets about my father.

"Did you hear back from the Spider?"

He shook his head. "He disappeared."

My stomach flopped. "What?"

"I got in touch with my friend who recommended him. Said he'd tried to reach him earlier today and couldn't."

"He disappeared right after he sent you an email saying he had information?"

"Looks that way," he said gruffly.

An invisible black cloud surrounded me. Something was coming.

Something big.

And something bad.

Joe pulled his phone out of his pocket. It must have

buzzed. I was too freaked to hear it.

"Hey, Sis," he said into it.

CHAPTER THIRTY-TWO

Marjorie

After making sure Jade was okay to get the boys from the bus stop after school, I drove into the city to see my mother.

I tried to get there every week. I wanted to tell her about Bryce and me. She wouldn't know who either of us were, but still, she was my mother, and I needed to tell her my good news.

Having a little good news in the wake of what was happening seemingly all over again was a gift. A gift I intended to let myself revel in. I deserved that much, and so did Bryce.

The cut on my thigh still ached a little when I walked, reminding me of what I'd done. It had numbed up pretty good during my time on the elliptical this morning, but at the moment, it was pounding with my heart.

I erased it from my mind as best I could and signed the visitors' log. Then I walked to my mother's wing.

Her door was closed, so I knocked gently and opened it. "Mom?"

She wasn't in bed or in her chair, not in itself unusual. She was probably in the common area. I found her there sometimes, cradling the doll she imagined was me and talking to other patients. I strode toward the end of the hallway, smiling at nurses and orderlies along the way, until I reached the large room where patients congregated to watch television and play board games.

The TV was turned to a talk show. I looked around the room. No mom. Strange. Maybe she had an appointment with one of her physicians.

I walked back toward her room and grabbed the first caregiver I found. His name tag read Barry. "Barry, hi. I'm Marjorie Steel. We spoke on the phone about the man who visited my mother. Daphne Steel?"

"Yes, hi. I've seen you around here."

"Where is she? I came to visit, and she's usually in her room around this time of the day."

"Your brother came and took her out for a while."

My heart dropped. "What?"

"Your brother. Didn't he tell you?"

"My brothers work during the day. They only visit Mom on weekends."

"He must have taken some time off."

Okay. That could very well be. We owned the ranch, after all, and Talon and Joe could come and go as they pleased. Both took their work very seriously, though, and were definitely hands-on. And neither had ever taken our mother away from the facility.

"Which brother?"

"Joe Steel, I believe. He should be on the visitors' log."

I hadn't noticed either of my brothers' names on the log when I'd signed in, but then I hadn't been looking either.

Plus, today was Bryce's first day at the new job. It was unlikely either Joe or Talon would leave the ranch.

Wasn't it?

Something smelled rotten.

"I'm going to check the visitors' log." I walked as casually as I could muster back to the front and glanced over the log. Sure enough, Joe Steel was signed in.

The problem? Joe always used his given name, Jonah, when he wrote and signed his name.

Panic welled in me. Where was my mother? She lived in her own cloud of fantasy. She wasn't safe outside this place unless she was with one of us. And clearly she wasn't.

I frantically called Joe.

"Hey, Sis," he said into the phone.

"Joe, I'm trying to visit Mom, and she's gone."

"What?" His voice was loud and panicked.

"Yeah. And the nurse says *you* signed her out earlier."

"Fuck."

"Your name's in the log, but I knew it wasn't you. Someone wrote Joe Steel, and you always write Jonah Steel."

"Damn right it wasn't me. Call the cops. I'm on my way."

I quickly dialed 9-1-1 and explained the situation. Then I turned to the clerk at the front desk. "You people have a lot to answer for. You let my mother walk out of here with a stranger this morning."

"Ma'am, I assure you—"

"My brother Joe is on his way here. He was *not* here this morning, and he did *not* sign our mother out. You let a stranger take our mother!"

My heart beat like galloping wildebeests. My mother—my mentally deficient, innocent mother. Where was she? And who had taken her? What could anyone want with—

Dollar signs clouded my head. Money. This had to be about money. If Talon or Joe had received a ransom demand, I'd know about it, and Joe would have mentioned it when we talked a minute ago.

"Listen," I said. "You need to tell me everything you remember about the man who took my mother out of here. What did he look like?"

The clerk reddened, clearly flustered. "I don't know. I don't really look at everyone who comes in."

"He had to have shown you ID. I show my ID every time I come here. Are you telling me you don't bother looking at everyone's ID?"

"I... I..."

"I want to see the surveillance videos."

"A private security company handles them. I'll call them." He looked to his computer screen. "I just have to find the right number."

Red anger—or was it fear for my poor mother?—pulsed through me. "You're completely useless. I hope you're ready to lose your job over this. I want you to call Barry right now and get him out here. I have a lot of questions for him."

He didn't speak to me but did as I asked. In a few minutes, Barry appeared.

"The person who took my mother today was *not* my brother. I need you to tell me everything you remember about him."

"What?" He reddened.

"You heard me. What did the guy look like?"

"I barely saw him. He had dark hair. I'm pretty sure I only saw him from behind."

"You've seen my brothers before, right?"

"Not that I can recall."

"Don't you work on weekends?"

"Not usually."

"Shit. How the hell is a stranger just able to come in here

and take a mentally ill woman? What kind of system are you people running? I want to see the manager now."

"He's in a—"

"I don't give a rat's ass where he is. One of his patients is missing. Get him now!" I balled my hands into fists, frustration and fear overwhelming me. My poor mother. My innocent mother. Anything could be happening to her right now.

God. I couldn't go there. But the people we were probably dealing with...

I had to get a grip. Had to. For my mother.

The police arrived and took my statement through my angry and scared tears. They questioned everything, and the manager, who finally appeared, was thoroughly questioned, though I wasn't allowed to witness it.

Joe and Talon arrived while the manager was being questioned, and behind them...

"Bryce!" I ran into his arms.

Talon lifted his brow.

Joe cleared his throat. "I guess they're together now."

Talon didn't look thrilled, but we all had something more important to focus on.

"Where's Ryan?" I asked.

"We didn't tell him," Joe said.

"But he'd want to be here for us."

"I know, but why put him through this? He's been through enough."

"Haven't we all?" I turned to Bryce. "What are you doing here?"

"I came for you, of course. Do you really think I'd let you go through this alone?"

I burrowed into his chest. If it were possible to love him

more than I already did, this deed made it happen.

"I'm sorry. This is your first day, and—"

"Shh. I know what your mother means to you and to Joe and Talon. Of course I'm here."

The manager came out of the room with two officers, and Joe and Talon pounced. Bryce led me to a chair in the waiting area.

"They'll take care of this," he said. "You sit down and relax for a minute."

Relax? Right. Still, I sat. Bryce sat next to me and held my hand tightly.

"Joe knows? About us?"

He nodded. "I told him today."

"And?"

"He's grudgingly happy. He'll be okay."

"And Tal?"

"He knows now, but he's more concerned about your mom, as he should be."

"Who would do this? Who would take a mentally unstable woman away from her safe place?" I let out a sarcastic laugh. "Safe place. What a crock."

"We'll find her, sweetheart."

"What if we don't?"

"We *will*. Your brothers will put the best people on this. You know that."

"I just got her back, Bryce. I just got her back."

Daphne Steel was hardly normal, but she was my mother. I'd never had a mother, and now I did. A broken one, but still, she was mine. I loved her, and I couldn't bear the thought of anyone hurting her.

"You'll have her again. This is most likely a ploy for money."

"But what if it's all related to...everything else?" I didn't say the words. Bryce had sworn me to secrecy.

"If it is, we'll figure it out."

I looked into his blue eyes. He looked at me with so much love that I believed him, if only for a few seconds.

He kissed my forehead.

"I love you," I said softly.

"I love you too."

★ ★ ★

Back at the ranch, everything was in turmoil. We'd gathered at the main house, wives included. Joe and Talon moved the table on the deck well into the yard, and we sat outside. Donny played with the dogs while Dale sat on the deck doing homework.

The police and PIs had been called, and though we were all worried, we now had to deliver more upsetting news to the rest of the family.

"We honestly didn't remember any of this," Joe said after telling the story of Justin Valente. "We wanted to keep it to ourselves until we figured it out, but Ted Morse seems to know about it somehow."

"You really think Tom drugged you?" Ryan asked.

"It's the only thing that makes sense. How else would two nine-year-olds forget the death or disappearance of a classmate? It wouldn't happen."

"I can find their last-known address in the school system database," Jade said. "I'm technically still the city attorney."

"We thought about asking you," Bryce said, "but we didn't want to drag any of you into this. Especially with you expecting and all."

"Women have been having babies forever," Jade said. "This is family. I'm here for you guys."

"They were just protecting you, blue eyes," Talon said. "You've had a difficult time."

"Time to stop protecting me," Jade said, her blue eyes on fire. "This is my family. I want to help."

"That would be a big help," Joe said. "The hacker we hired seems to have disappeared."

"Disappeared?" Talon shook his head. "I don't want Jade in any danger. If they can take Mom—"

"Tal," Jade said. "No one is going to take me anywhere. Unlike your mother, I'm fully aware of my surroundings and won't put myself in danger. Besides, with the safeties I've had installed in all the databases, no one will even know I was there."

"These guys can hack into anything," Ryan said. "They changed Mom's and Marj's birth certificates. Remember?"

"Which is exactly why I had additional security installed," Jade said. "Besides, I'm not going to change anything. I'm just doing research."

"I don't like this," Talon said.

"This is something I can do to help," Jade countered. "And I intend to do it."

I silently rejoiced at Jade's chutzpah. I loved all my brothers dearly, but they took the Alpha male thing to a new level.

"We also need to go through the boxes in the crawl space," Joe said. "There might be some information."

"And I found old files at my father's cabin," Bryce said. "Joe and I are going to go through them later tonight."

Ruby sighed. "Here we go again."

"I know," Ryan said. "I'm sorry, baby."

"Don't be. And by the way, you all seem to be forgetting something important. I was a *detective*. I'll be happy to look through boxes, files, or help Jade. She's right. This is family. And Daphne may not be your natural mother, Ryan, but she did raise you for seven years."

Ryan nodded, an absent look in his eyes.

"Just so we're all clear," Joe said, "no one speaks of any of this inside our homes."

"This is crazy," Melanie said. "If our homes are bugged, we need to take care of it. Now. It's a total violation. It's like mental rape."

"I agree," Ruby said. "I'll check our homes myself. Why haven't you told me about this before now? I'll say it again. I was a detective, for God's sake."

Ruby had a good point, but I didn't listen to my brothers' replies. I sat, saying mostly nothing. My mother was foremost on my mind. I hadn't known her long, but she was mine, and I wanted her safe. Safe and back where she belonged, which wouldn't be at that same facility. Their security was shit.

Only their security *wasn't* shit. That's what worried me most of all. This had Wendy Madigan and the rest of the Future Lawmakers Club written all over it.

Except they were all dead.

Bryce sat next to me, his strength emanating from him. Empty shell? No way. He sold himself way short. His look of determination made him all the more magnificent.

If only we could escape for a little while, forget about all this other stuff and celebrate our love.

If only...

We'd already eaten dinner, but our plates were still mostly

full. No one had an appetite tonight.

Just worry and torment. You'd think we'd be used to it.

CHAPTER THIRTY-THREE

Bryce

After I'd called to say good night to my mother and Henry, Joe and I sat in the guesthouse office, the manila files I'd found in my father's cabin on the desk in front of me. We could finally talk. Ruby had gone over the house and hadn't found evidence of any auditory surveillance. She made no guarantees until she had the proper tools, but she was pretty confident.

"I'm afraid to look," I said.

"I hear you." He grabbed a folder. "But we have to."

I opened the file in front of me. Nothing to get excited about. It was the deed to the cabin. Odd, though. It wasn't in my father's name. Some company called Tamajor Corporation owned it. Another corporation? The Future Lawmakers had put together a dummy corporation called the Fleming Corporation, which held their assets, including the safe houses.

"Check this out." I handed the deed to Joe.

He lifted his brow as he perused the document. "Hmm. Doesn't ring a bell?"

"Nope."

"Isn't Tamajor a village or something in Nepal?"

"I have no clue. How would you even know that?"

"Read it somewhere."

"You're saying some Nepali corporation owns my dad's cabin?"

"I'm not saying anything. God only knows what Tamajor Corporation is. Keep digging. The property could have been transferred again."

I nodded and went through the rest of the file. Mostly sales invoices and receipts for various stuff, including firearms. I'd have to check them against the guns I'd found. The invoices were all in my father's name.

Next I found the police reports on my mother's stolen jewelry. Why he'd kept them, I had no idea. He'd stolen the shit himself.

I slammed the folder down on the desk. "I'm so fucking sick of this shit!"

Joe laughed. Actually laughed. "You think you could possibly be sicker of it than I am? And now my mother."

"They won't hurt her. They want something from us, and she's their leverage."

"I know," he said.

"But you're still worried. I get it. I am too." I sighed and looked to the ceiling.

The smoke alarm flashed a blue light at me in a hypnotizing rhythm.

I'm watching you. I'm watching you.

No way. I was making things up, letting the little imp in my mind go wild.

Ruby had swept the place.

But Ruby had swept for auditory devices...

"Joe," I said softly. "Let's go outside."

He raised one eyebrow and nodded. We walked out of the office, through the house, and onto the deck.

"What is it?"

"I have a weird feeling that I'm being watched."

“You’re spooked from the calls.”

“That’s probably part of it, but I tell you. It’s like I can feel a hidden camera on my skin.”

I expected him to tell me I was nuts.

Instead, he said, “I got the same feeling in my office today. Not so much that someone could hear me, but that someone could *see* me.

“Then I’m not crazy?”

“You probably are. We both probably are. Ruby looked the place over pretty closely.”

“Yeah, but all she said was she didn’t see any evidence of tampering. She couldn’t do a full sweep without the right tools.”

“True.”

“Those phone calls. They specifically said they’re *watching* us.”

“Shit. I didn’t even think about that. All this time we’ve been worried about people overhearing us.”

“On the other hand,” I said, “it could just be a mindfuck. Whoever’s been calling us is trying to spook us, trip us up.”

“Could be,” he agreed.

“Damn!” I paced across the redwood. “When is this shit going to end?”

“I don’t know, bro.” He shook his head. “I just don’t know. I hate burdening the whole family with our past. I hate it, especially with Melanie and Jade both being pregnant.”

“They all seem to want to help.”

“Of course they do. But how can we protect them if they’re helping?”

“I don’t know. They’d say they don’t need protection.”

“Whether they do or not isn’t the issue. I want to protect them.”

"I know. They're not even my family, and I want to protect them too."

Marjorie invaded my mind. I'd take a bullet for her, no thought required. Jump into the Grand Canyon if I thought it would keep her safe.

"I love her, you know." The words came out almost by themselves.

"You'd better."

"I tried to stay away because I felt so broken after..."

"You're not broken, man."

"You're right. I'm not. I'm a little fucked up is all. It's all so stupid. I'm not responsible for the sins of my father. Life doesn't work that way. But you know what bothers me the most?"

"What?"

"The memories. I have some really good memories of the time the three of us spent together. Justin Valente aside, and he made us forget that for decades."

"I know, man. I have the same memories. Your dad taught me a lot."

"He taught both of us."

Joe laughed. "My own father refused to teach me how to shoot. Said we were ranchers, and any man who held a gun to an animal—any animal, men included—was an animal himself. He never understood that I didn't want to harm anyone. I just wanted to learn how to handle weapons. I taught Tal and Ryan. My father never knew."

"Brad Steel didn't shoot?" I shook my head. "How did I never know that?"

"He wasn't any kind of pacifist or anything. He owned guns himself. It's just another of the many things about my own father I'll never understand."

"I get that. At least your father didn't..."

"Yeah. He wasn't perfect, but I'll let you win the shitty father award, though you may have to share it with Ruby."

"Mathias was a shitty father to Ruby. That's the thing, man. My father was *good* to me. That's what I'm having a hard time with. It's hard to reconcile, you know?"

"Yeah, I know. My father wasn't who I thought he was either. And before you say it, yes, I know your situation is different. Worse. A lot worse."

"I'm done saying that," I said. "I just wish I didn't feel so guilty about the good memories. I feel like I should erase him from my mind, from my life."

"Have you talked to anyone yet?"

"You mean therapy? No."

"I know a good one. She knows everything now anyway."

"She's your wife, Joe. Your pregnant wife."

"She needs to keep working right now. I know her. This will get into her psyche, and she'll work to keep herself from thinking about it."

"You're saying this could help both of us?"

"Yeah. That's what I'm saying."

I nodded. "Okay. She did wonders for Talon. She's obviously the best."

"That she is."

"What was in your file, anyway?" I asked.

"A lot of nothing. Mostly invoices for farming equipment."

"What would my father be doing with farm equipment?"

Joe chuckled. "You're right. I work a ranch, so I didn't think anything of it. But fuck it all. You're right."

"What kind of equipment?" I asked.

"Let's take a look." We walked back inside.

Again, that eerie feeling that invisible eyes watched me crackled along my skin like tiny gnats.

We walked to the office anyway, and Joe opened the file. "This is for a mini Bobcat."

"What?"

"You know. You can rent them. It's a little excavator. Like a mini bulldozer."

"Why would my— Shit. You don't think he buried Justin himself, do you?"

"I wouldn't put it past him. What did he tell us? He was taking the body to the police, right? He could have just hidden it and come back and disposed of it later."

"Oh my God. The floorboards. I was afraid when we started pulling them up that I'd find..."

"But you didn't."

"No, thank God. But he could be there. Somewhere."

Joe went white. "This isn't our fight. We were kids."

"Then why do I feel so responsible?"

"I don't know." He shook his head. "I feel the same way. Like we were part of it."

"We were," I said, nausea sweeping up my throat. "We brought him there."

CHAPTER THIRTY-FOUR

Marjorie

I was getting ready for bed when my phone buzzed.

Colin Morse.

Not a person I wanted to speak to ever, but he could have information. More likely, though, he'd be bothering me to talk to Jade again.

"What is it, Colin?" I said, a little more harshly than I meant to, into the phone.

"Hey, Marj. You called me, remember?"

Right. I'd forgotten. I'd called and left a voicemail, but I hadn't mentioned Jade. Only that I needed to talk to him.

"You said you wanted to speak to me," he said. "And I want to see you."

"I thought you wanted to talk to Jade."

"I changed my mind. She's pregnant, and I don't want—"

I cut him off. I was so tired of all of this. "What *do* you want?"

"I can't talk over the phone. Can you meet me in town tonight?"

"You're still in Snow Creek?"

"I'm staying at the hotel. You can meet me here."

"And you're not going to insist that I bring Jade along?"

"No. I said I changed my mind about that. It's important."

After our family meeting outside this evening, I wasn't sure I could take anything more. I opened my mouth to tell him I'd see him sometime tomorrow but then thought again. He was willing to talk now. What if he changed *his* mind by tomorrow?

"All right."

"Meet me at the bar in the hotel."

"Sure. Give me a half hour or so. I'll be there." I ran a brush through my hair and pulled it into a high ponytail. Talon and Jade were both home for the evening, so the boys were taken care of. I was free as a bird.

I'd much rather be at the guesthouse with Bryce, but maybe I could finally get some information out of Colin. I knew him almost as well as Jade did, and in fact, I'd known him longer. I met him before my best friend while we were in college.

I should tell Talon and Jade I was leaving.

The thought hovered in my mind. If they noticed I was gone, they'd be concerned. Not that I felt I had to check in with them, but I didn't want them worrying.

Something niggled at me, though. Something I couldn't quite identify. A feeling that I shouldn't tell anyone I was meeting Colin.

Normally I ignored those silly feelings, but tonight I didn't.

Tonight, it was important I keep this under wraps. I had no idea why, but I felt it strongly.

I walked quietly out of the house with no one the wiser.

★ ★ ★

"Hey." I sat down next to Colin at the small bar in the hotel.

"Let's move to a table," he said.

"Not even a 'hi'?" I said.

He didn't respond, so I followed him to a small round table in the corner of the tiny room and sat down on one of the chairs.

"Spit it out, Colin," I said.

"Thanks for coming."

"How etiquette-minded of you. You couldn't say hello, but you say thank you."

He opened his mouth, but I stopped him with a gesture.

"I'm not interested in any explanation. Let's just get to the meat of the matter. Why am I here?"

He cleared his throat. "My therapist suggested I find someone I trust to share this with."

"And you trust me?"

"Well, you and Jade. But she's pregnant, and I don't want to add to her stress. Besides, the beast probably wouldn't have let her come anyway."

"If that's your term for my brother—the one who *didn't* abandon her at the altar, by the way—this conversation will end right now." I stood. "See you."

"No. Wait. I'm sorry."

I sat back down. "You don't sound remotely sorry."

"The guy kicked the tar out of me. I'm not a fan, okay?"

I said nothing, just gave him the evil eye. My brother had overreacted when Colin showed up at our place last summer. He hadn't been in a good place. All my brothers were prone to be hotheads, Joe most of all. I wasn't going to share this with Colin, however.

"I didn't want to leave Jade," he finally said, staring at the table.

"What are you talking about? You mean for the wedding?"

"Yeah. I said I got cold feet."

"A lot of people get cold feet on their wedding day. You took it one step further."

"This isn't coming out right," he said. "What I mean is, it wasn't..."

"Wasn't what? Spit it out, Colin." My voice came out harsh, and I regretted it, but only because of what Colin had been through at Bryce's father's hands.

"It was my father," he said. "My father's idea for me not to marry Jade."

I jerked in surprise. "That's what you wanted to tell me? You said your father called you a coward when you didn't show up."

"He did. But not because I left Jade at the altar."

"All right. Slow down. You're going to have to walk me through this because none of it makes any kind of sense. You left her. That's a fact. Your father called you a coward. Another fact, at least according to you. Now start at the damned beginning."

He stared at the table again.

And I stared at him. His hair had grown back quite a bit, but still I could see a scar on the top of his scalp. A very precise scar, as if he'd had brain surgery.

He hadn't had brain surgery. Tom Simpson had made that scar. I didn't want to know how or why. The top of his left ear was also damaged. Odd that I hadn't noticed before, except that it was more toward the back. Looking at him face-to-face, I wouldn't have seen it. It almost looked like someone had taken a small bite out of the outer shell of his ear.

This man had been brutally abused.

And I was beginning to wonder...

"Your father has controlled you since you were born, hasn't he?" I said.

Colin looked up, meeting my gaze. "No."

"Colin..."

"He *thinks* he controls me. He doesn't."

"How, then, was he able to get you to leave Jade on your wedding day? If indeed he was behind it as you say."

"He didn't think Jade was good enough for me."

"Really? I'm not buying it. Jade was at the top of her class in college and law school, and she's the daughter of a supermodel."

"There were other circumstances."

"Like what?"

"She might be Brooke Bailey's daughter, but she didn't come from money."

"So?"

He let out a soft huff. "You're right. It's all bullshit."

"Yeah. I already knew that. What's really going on? Was your father behind your decision not to marry Jade, and if he was, why does it matter now?"

He looked back down at the table.

For several minutes.

Then, finally, "Do you have anything keeping you here?" Colin asked.

"What?"

"Would it be possible for you to go away for a while? You and Jade?"

"Are you kidding me? Jade is pregnant and just adopted two kids. You think she can just up and leave?"

"I want the two of you safe."

"We *are* safe. Safe at home with Talon." And Bryce, but I didn't want to tell Colin about Bryce and me. I wasn't sure why. It wasn't a secret. It was just too new.

"Marj, things are heating up."

"What things? You come to us and you talk in riddles. If you want our cooperation, you need to start spilling some facts."

"I don't have any facts. I mean, I can't substantiate anything. Not yet, anyway. But I've been looking. My father..." He rubbed his chin. "I don't want to believe everything I'm seeing, you know? Things I'm finding out."

My mentally ill mother was missing, and I was getting nothing from Colin. I'd had enough. "What the hell is this all about?"

He took a drink from the brown liquid in his glass. Probably Scotch. Colin used to drink a lot of Scotch. "My father has been meeting with someone. I don't know who it is."

"Man? Woman? Black? White? You've got to give me something here, Colin."

"It's a man. A white man. He has dark hair."

"Eye color?"

"I haven't seen him close enough to tell."

"Height?"

"Average."

"And why do you think this person has anything to do with us?"

Colin held his drink, swirling the amber liquid in the glass. "It's a feeling."

I shook my head. "You're lying. You wouldn't bring me here and tell me Jade and I have to leave town over a feeling."

He stared at the mahogany wood of the table. "Like I said,

I can't substantiate anything. Not yet. That's all I can say."

"I'm not buying it."

"You don't understand. That's *all* I can say." Without moving his head, he looked to the doorway. Someone had entered.

Someone I knew.

CHAPTER THIRTY-FIVE

Bryce

"We're done here. At least for now." I closed the file and regarded Joe. "I can't deal with this anymore tonight."

"Amen to that." Joe stood. "We can talk tomorrow. Most of these files look like dead ends anyway. I'll let myself out."

I nodded. I tidied up the desk a little and then headed to my bedroom. Big. Big and empty.

I wanted Marjorie. I pulled my phone out of my pocket to call her.

She didn't respond, so I called the landline at the main house. "Yeah?" Talon answered.

"I'm trying to reach Marjorie," I told him.

"Oh? Didn't she answer her phone?"

"No."

"I assume she's in her bedroom. Hold on a minute."

He hadn't asked why I wanted to talk to her. Why should he? We were all adults.

"She's not in her room," Talon said. "Jade hasn't seen her."

Worry boiled in my gut. "It's after nine."

"I know. I don't like this. Not with everything that's going on. I'm going to try texting her."

"I will too."

I hurriedly wrote out a text.

Is everything okay? No one can reach you. Where are you?

I didn't get an answer.

"Anything?" I asked Talon.

"No."

"I'm going out to look for her," I said.

"I'll come along," he said.

"No, you need to stay with Jade and the boys. I'll handle this."

"But—"

"I got this. I'll find her. I promise." I ended the call.

I raced to my car as my phone rang again. I looked at the name. Ted Morse. Seriously?

"What is it, Morse?" I said angrily.

"Hello to you too."

"I don't have time for this bullshit. What do you want now?"

"I know where she is," he said.

My heart nearly stopped. "If you've so much as touched one hair on her head, I swear to God I'll fucking mutilate you."

"Why are you threatening me? I called to help you."

"You have no intention of helping me."

"Why do you think I've been warning you—"

"Shut the fuck up. You know where she is, huh? Where is she, then?"

"In town. At the hotel. With my son."

Jealousy tore into my gut. "At the hotel?"

"Relax. They're in the bar having a drink."

I didn't reply. I ended the call abruptly, got into my car, and raced into town.

★ ★ ★

"Hold it like this, son," my father said.

I smiled from ear to ear. I was holding a pistol. A real pistol. Not the toy cap guns Joe and I played cowboy with.

"Keep your finger off the trigger. Never put it on the trigger until you're ready to shoot."

"Tom, he's awfully young," my mother said, coming out from the cabin.

"A man is never too young to learn how to handle a gun, Evie. I was younger than he is now when I learned."

My mother shook her head. "Whatever you say. Lunch will be ready in a half hour, so don't get too involved." She went back inside.

My father had set up some old soda cans on a big stump several yards ahead. Was he really going to let me shoot?

"You're little yet, son, and you're going to get a lot of kickback."

"I can do it, Dad. I wish Joe were here."

"We'll bring Joe along next time. This time it's just a father-son thing, okay?"

I smiled again. A father-son thing.

I had the best dad in the world. The very best.

★ ★ ★

I jerked as I steered the Mustang back onto the road. I wasn't prone to daydreaming while I was driving. It was well into the evening, and the country roads into Snow Creek were pretty deserted. Good thing. I'd veered across into the opposite lane.

I had the best dad in the world.

Boy, had I been deluded.

I'd first held a pistol when I was seven years old. Pretty damned young. But he'd taught me gun safety, and by the time we were nine, both Joe and I were crack shots.

We were good at it. Damned good at it. Even now my Smith & Wesson was strapped to my ankle. I'd never shot at another person. Never had to.

But I would if life necessitated it.

I would to defend myself or someone I loved.

Absolutely.

Marjorie was at the hotel bar with Colin Morse, if Ted was to be believed. Colin Morse was hardly a threat. Still, I'd come prepared.

What was she doing meeting Colin Morse this late on a weeknight in town? I was pissed off just thinking about it. Colin had already met with her and Jade. Why the hell couldn't he stay away from us?

A half hour later, I'd parked the car in a loading zone and stalked into the hotel bar.

There she was, sitting with him.

Then she looked up.

Straight at me.

I stalked toward her. "Why haven't you been answering your phone?" I demanded.

"I haven't heard my phone," she said. "Who do you think—"

I grabbed her arm and pulled her out of her chair.

"Bryce, what—"

"Come with me." I walked quickly to the front desk. "Give me a room. Now."

"Hello, Bryce," the night manager said. "What can—"

"Whatever you have. Now."

He arched his brow.

"Now," I said, "or I'll come behind the desk and do it myself."

He quickly typed on his computer and then handed me a keycard. "Room twenty-one. Second floor."

This old hotel was small and had no elevators. Once we made it to the staircase, I lifted Marjorie into my arms and carried her up the one flight to the second floor. A few seconds later, we were inside room twenty-one, Marjorie pinned against the wall, our lips smashed together.

I kissed her angrily. Possessively. Without gentleness.

No, tonight I wouldn't be gentle.

She'd scared the shit out of me, and she'd pay for it.

I didn't have to pry her mouth open. Her lips parted quickly, and her velvet tongue met mine. I thrust into her mouth, jabbing, swirling, taking.

I wanted to drug her with this kiss, poison her against anyone but me.

Truly make her mine and only mine.

Never again would I find her in a hotel bar with another man. Never again would she not answer her phone.

Never again.

Mine.

All my thoughts jumbled together into that one word.

Mine.

Mine.

Mine.

Her fingers dug into my shoulders, and I felt her lever her body against mine, attempting to push me away.

No.

I would have her, and I would have her now.

I deepened the kiss, my heart racing and my cock already fully erect inside my jeans. I ground it against her belly, still pushing my tongue farther into her mouth. Her moan vibrated into me, mingling with my own.

Mine.

Mine.

Mine.

When I finally broke the kiss to draw in a deep breath, her brown eyes were glowing with embers. "Bryce."

"No talking. Nothing except me inside you."

She nodded slightly, kicking off her sandals and pulling her jeans and panties off. I freed my cock and shoved it into her heat. She was already slick and ready, and as I sank into her body, my thoughts finally became less jumbled, and my heart found peace.

This was where I belonged. Where she belonged. She sucked me into her body, and with each upward thrust, I became more a part of her—no longer Bryce but Marjorie's Bryce.

"Mine," I groaned as I pushed into her again and again, her back still against the wall, her legs curved around my waist. "Always mine."

I didn't last long. Within seconds, my balls had tightened and the tiny pulses began, flowing through my cock and into my Marjorie.

"Mine," I growled again. "Mine."

When my release finally settled, I eased back, helping her feet hit the floor.

Her eyes were still on fire. She wanted more. She hadn't come yet, and she wanted more. She walked past me toward the queen-size bed, stripping along the way. Her shirt and bra lay on the floor, and she was now naked, lying supine.

I wouldn't let her down. I quickly rid myself of every piece of clothing, including the gun strapped to my ankle, and joined her on the bed. She said nothing, which surprised me. I knew Marjorie Steel. She'd want to know what had brought this on.

But first I'd give her an orgasm that would blow her mind. Maybe two or three.

Her tits were swollen, the nipples erect and beautiful just waiting for my mouth and fingers. I fingered one, squeezing it, while I lowered my head and nipped at the other.

She arched her back and moaned. The texture of the nipple was silky against my tongue, and her skin tasted slightly salty. I inhaled. A lavender fragrance accented her natural apple musk. Her rosy flesh a sharp contrast to my tan hands. She was a feast for all my senses.

I could nibble at her breasts for hours, so beautiful they were, and the raspy sounds from her throat spurred me on further. So lovely. So gorgeous. So perfect.

So *mine*.

Always mine.

I replaced my mouth with my other hand, squeezing her rosy globes as I kissed down her flat abdomen to her luscious pussy.

Her fragrance was ripe and fresh. I inhaled first. I could go slowly now that I'd gotten the edge off my own need. I'd looked before, touched before, tasted before, but now I wanted to truly take my time. Savor her.

She was pink and swollen, her labia engorged and ready. I kissed her first. Kissed her wet opening, swirled my tongue over her slit, and then tugged at her lips. Next I nipped her clit lightly. Just lightly, but she arched her back and moaned, bending her knees and lifting her hips to give me better access. I moved my finger to her canal, teasing the bottom of her slit as I sucked at her hard clit. She tasted like springtime, like perfection, like the perfect storm of love and lust.

The sucking sounds mingled with her moans were a treat to my ears. All my senses were on high alert, and I continued to nibble at her, teasing her with just the tip of my finger.

"Bryce, God! Please!"

I smiled against her wet folds. I'd tease her more, make her wait. In a way, I was punishing her for not answering her phone tonight. For making me crazy.

Now I'd make *her* crazy.

Still just the tip of my finger. Just the lightest of sucking on her clit.

Until I couldn't take it anymore.

I wanted my fingers inside her, wanted to feel the suction of her pussy walls around them as they'd been around my cock only moments before.

I plunged two fingers into her.

And she shattered around me.

"Yeah, sweetheart." I let go of her clit for only a second to watch the pink hue scatter across her flesh. "That's it. Come for me."

Her pussy walls were wet and clamped around my fingers, and every part of me reacted. I was hard again, even after a short time, and I wanted more. I wanted to be inside her again.

Wanted it badly—but even more, I wanted to torture her further.

When her contractions slowed, I went back to her clit and sucked hard.

And she began again.

Again.

And again.

She fisted the comforter as I continued to torment her, pleasure her, make her mine. So sexy, so perfect, so delicious.

She was mine, mine, mine.

Her wetness had doubled, and I slid another finger into her. Three fingers, and she took them. Took them all as I continued to force her into nirvana again and again and again.

"Bryce, please." Her voice was raspy as she panted. "I can't. I can't. No more."

I looked toward her, my lips and chin wet from her honey. "You can," I said. "And you will."

CHAPTER THIRTY-SIX

Marjorie

I lay limp. I couldn't give any more. Couldn't. He'd worn me down. My body was replete. My pussy had no more to give. *I* had no more to give.

Yet still he fucked me hard with his fingers, tormented me with his tongue. Tortured me with his sparkling eyes that looked upon me with raw lust.

"Can't," I said again. "Can't."

He didn't stop, only thrust his fingers harder and harder into me, finding a spot so deep that took me to a new level.

Passion whirled around me, almost visibly cloaking us. And he forced another climax from me.

And then another.

I shivered. I quaked. I sank into the bed and became nothing. Nothing but the pulses of climax after climax. Marjorie Steel was gone. All that was left was her pussy that wouldn't stop pulsating. Would never stop pulsating.

Each pulse pushed outward, taking my whole body with it, sinking me deeper and deeper into something, something, something...

Until the last shred of Marjorie Steel was gone, the light flickered out.

Only Bryce. I was here only for Bryce.

For a moment, I was okay with that.

But only for a moment.

"Stop," I said softly.

I meant it. I couldn't lose myself. Not tonight. Not until we found my mother. She was as innocent as a child—as Talon had been at ten—and she needed me. Needed all of us.

My voice must have resonated the anguish I felt. Bryce finally unclamped his mouth from my pussy and looked up, his lips and chin awash in the shine from my juices.

He said nothing.

"It was wonderful," I said. "Truly wonderful. But I have no business getting lost in you right now. No business getting lost in anything, for that matter."

Again, nothing.

Did he understand? Or was he still full of raging lust? He'd come already, but clearly he was hard again.

Finally—

"You're right," he said.

I gave him a weak smile.

"I went a little crazy when you didn't answer your phone. And then, to see you with Colin..."

"Colin means nothing to me. He isn't any threat to you."

"I know that. But he's dangerous, Marj. He and his father—"

"Colin is not his father. In fact, he was getting ready to tell me some stuff when you stormed in and dragged me off like a pirate's prize."

This time he gave a weak smile. "I won't apologize for that."

"I'm not asking you to. I love it that you want me that much."

"I do. Don't ever scare me like that again. Answer your damned phone."

"I would have if I'd heard it."

"Was it noisy in the bar?"

"Not really. Maybe the phone died. Or maybe I put it on silent by accident. I promise I didn't ignore your call on purpose."

"You wouldn't do that."

"No, I wouldn't. Do you need to...finish?"

He shook his head. "I'm okay. My dick is a lot less important than everything else going on."

I smiled. "Your dick is plenty important, but we have a lifetime for sex."

I hoped I spoke the truth. My mother's disappearance had made me realize what a dangerous situation we might be in. When it was just Ted and Colin and their enigmatic statements, I'd been concerned, but now?

I was frightened. All-out frightened.

Why? Why couldn't our family be left in peace? Hadn't we been through enough?

And why take a mentally ill woman who had no way of defending herself? Preying on children was the worst thing ever, but this was a close second.

We had to find her.

"Tell you what," Bryce said. "Call Colin. Get him back here, and we'll both talk to him."

"It's late."

"So? He didn't mind bothering *you* when it was late."

"Good point. He's staying here at the hotel, so we can go back down to the bar."

"Or we can talk here. Or in his room," he said. "Here would

be better. If he's been staying in his room for more than a day, it could be bugged. No one knew you and I were going to be in this room. It's probably safe."

I rubbed at the invisible creepy-crawlies on my arms. I hated the feeling of being watched, monitored. After knowing members of my family who'd truly been violated physically, I hesitated to call it a violation, but it was.

A violation.

If we were all being watched, we were all being violated.

I felt sick. Really sick.

"Well?" Bryce said.

"Well what?"

"Will you call Colin?"

"Right." I nodded. The creepy-crawlies had clouded my mind for a moment. I quickly dialed Colin.

"Yeah?" he said into my ear.

"Let's finish our conversation," I said. "Come to room twenty-one."

★ ★ ★

"I'd tell you more if I could," Colin said. "I honestly don't know exactly what my dad is up to."

"But it's not anything good," Bryce said, his eyes angry. "Why did you want to talk to Marj in the first place?"

"Because something's coming. I'm not sure what."

"You said your father didn't want you to marry Jade," I said, "but you never elaborated. Why?"

"I told you. He didn't think she was good enough for me."

"Why didn't he make that clear once in the seven years before you actually got to the altar?" I asked. "Seems like there was plenty of time."

"Jade had no contact with the Steels at that time, so this isn't related," Bryce said.

"It wasn't then," Colin said. "But my father's a master manipulator. He twists things. And he covets things. He'll do almost anything to get what he wants. He fucks with people's minds, and he's good at it."

"And you're saying he fucks with yours?" I said.

"He has since I was born. The whole thing with Jade was a test, I think. He told me I should call it off, but when I did, he called me a coward."

"How was that a test?"

"He wanted to see how far I'd go to please him, but in the end, he had less respect for me."

Bryce regarded Colin sternly but said nothing.

Silence for a few minutes that seemed like hours, until—

"Who's watching us?" Bryce asked, though it came out more like a statement than a question.

"I don't know."

"Your father called me tonight," Bryce continued. "He told me where Marjorie was, that she was with you. How did he know that?"

He shook his head. "I've given up trying to figure my father out."

"Tell me more about this person your father has been meeting with."

"I told Marj all I know. White guy. Dark hair. Average height."

"What was he wearing?"

"Nothing memorable."

"Not good enough," Bryce said. "Think harder."

Discomfort and unease whirled through me. Bryce was getting angry, and if he was anything like Joe when he was angry—

"Jeans. A hoodie."

A hoodie. That got my attention. "What color was the hoodie?" I asked.

"I don't know. That heather-gray color, I think."

Gray hoodie. Dale had said the guy who spooked him had been wearing a gray hoodie.

"I know what you're thinking," Bryce said to me. "Gray hoodies are a dime a dozen, sweetheart."

Colin's brow lifted ever so slightly at Bryce's endearment, but that was the least of my concerns.

"Did the hoodie have any design? A school name? A team?"

"I don't know. I only saw it from a distance."

"You're sure it was gray?" I asked.

"No, actually I'm not sure. Your boyfriend here asked me to think harder, and I did. That's what I came up with, but like I said, it wasn't anything memorable."

"What does your father want from us?" Bryce said, his voice low and angry.

"Money, probably," Colin replied matter-of-factly.

"He won't get a penny out of the Steels," Bryce said. "They're pissed off now. You don't take someone's mother and then expect—"

"What?" Colin's brows shot up.

"I didn't get around to telling him that," I said. "My mother is missing, Colin. Someone posed as Joe, walked right into her nursing facility, and took her."

"But how? Don't they have security?"

"They do, but there are ways around security," I said. "Usually with money. And your father has money."

"Not Steel money."

"You don't need Steel money to bribe nursing home caregivers," I said. "You know that."

"No. No way," Colin said. "My father couldn't have had anything to do with taking a mentally ill woman. He wouldn't stoop—"

Bryce stood this time and grabbed Colin by the front of his shirt, bringing him to his feet. "Stoop? You mean stoop to blackmailing Jonah Steel by telling you to name him as your rapist?"

Colin's face reddened. He didn't try to break away.

"Bryce..." I began.

"Yeah, I know. You've been through hell, Morse, at the hands of my father. I'm not my father."

Colin shrank into himself. "Your eyes. His eyes. I only saw his eyes."

"Your father was probably wearing a mask," I said. "Talon said all his assailants always wore masks when they..."

"A mask," Colin said. "A mask. Your eyes..."

Bryce let go of Colin, and he sank back into the chair where he'd been sitting.

"I am *not* my father." Bryce curled his hands into fists.

I rose and grabbed one of Bryce's fisted hands. "No one is saying you are."

"He is," Bryce said through gritted teeth.

"He's just saying you have your father's eyes." I paused a few seconds. "And you do."

"And what else have I got that also was my father's? Is that it? You think I could—"

"No," I said, trying to sound as soothing as possible. "No one is saying that."

Colin looked up then. "I'm sorry."

I had no idea what to say. Colin didn't really have anything to apologize about. Bryce *did* have his father's eyes. He was almost an exact physical replica of his father, just like Joe was of mine. It happened. Genetics.

"Colin," I said, "if you have more information for us, we need it. Now."

"I'm trying. Sometimes my thoughts are all a blur."

"I understand." At least I tried to. He'd been through so much at Tom Simpson's hands. He could hardly be expected to—

"Yes," Colin said. "There's something else."

CHAPTER THIRTY-SEVEN

Bryce

Marjorie's touch helped calm me down a little.

But only a little.

"What?" I gritted out. "What else?"

Colin shrank back in his chair again, fear lacing his greenish eyes. I'd scared him, and I felt ambivalent about that. I was not my father, but the fact that I looked like him had to affect Colin. I understood, yet I didn't. I wanted to separate myself from my father, wanted to cut every part of him from me.

At the same time, though, I didn't.

I didn't want to let go of the good times. The pleasant memories. My happiness as a child.

I had the best father in the world.

How many times I'd thought those words as a kid, even as an adult. He'd been so supportive when I brought Henry home, had doted on him, fussed over him.

My God, I'd left my son alone with that man.

Henry was fine. I had no doubt that my father had cared for him as much as he'd cared for me. I knew in my heart that he'd never been inappropriate with my son, as he never had with me.

So much going on in my head. I wanted to jump out of my

skin to escape sometimes. I'd let go. I'd professed my love to Marj and committed myself to a relationship. I hoped I hadn't succumbed too soon.

If I continued down this path of self-destruction and hurt her in the process...

I couldn't.

I absolutely couldn't.

"Start talking," I said, trying to sound calmer than I felt.

"My dad told me something a while ago, right after Joe Steel rescued me."

"What?" Marjorie asked.

"He said this wasn't over. He'd find a way to make someone pay."

"Your assailant is dead," Marj said. "He's already paid the ultimate price."

Colin shook his head vehemently. "That's not what I mean. That's not what he said. He said he'd find a way to make someone pay. *Someone.* Not necessarily my assailant."

"And you think he meant us?" Marj said.

"I don't know what he meant. Honestly? My father blames me for what happened."

"What?" Marjorie's face reddened.

"I know it sounds terrible. But I'm a grown man, and I couldn't fight off"—he looked meekly to me—"your father."

A brick hit my gut. My father had been a big man, like I was, but Colin was hardly small. He was thin now, still recovering from his abuse, but he was six feet tall and, according to Marj, had been strongly built before.

"Are you saying he wants to make *you* pay?" Marjorie asked. "That hardly makes sense."

"I don't know. Maybe. He thinks I'm weak. But that

started long before your father…" He gulped.

"He's manipulating you," I said, more to myself than to Colin or Marj. "He thinks the more he tells you you're weak, the stronger you'll be."

The words echoed in my head. I'd heard them, or some variation of them, before. From my father? No, my father was never unkind to me.

Yet as I said the words and then heard them again in an echo, it was my father's voice that uttered them.

"Bryce?" Marj said. "You okay?"

I cleared my head quickly and nodded. "Yeah."

"I've often wondered," Colin continued, "what my father's childhood was like. He never spoke of it, and his parents were dead before I was born."

"How did they die?" I asked.

He stayed silent.

"A car crash, wasn't it?" Marjorie said. "I think that's what Jade told me."

"Yeah," Colin mumbled.

"So you don't really know much about your father," I said. "What kind of man he is?"

"Oh, I know what kind of man he is. I'm finding out more by the minute. Things I don't want to know. Things that…"

I couldn't quite read the tone of Colin's voice, and for a moment, I felt a kinship with him. He both loved and hated his father.

I could relate.

"In my father's mind," Colin continued, "I should have been strong enough to escape…or better yet, to not be in the position in the first place."

"Are you and he close?" I asked.

"In some ways. We were, anyway. Not anymore. Not the more..."

"The more what?"

"Nothing," he said. "No, I'd say we're no longer close."

"What does this have to do with anything?" Marj queried.

"It has everything to do with everything," I said. "His feelings about his father are going to color what he tells us."

"You mean whether he tells us everything?"

"Yes. Exactly."

"I only want to help," Colin said. "I don't want to see Jade or her family go through anything more."

"What about me? Do you blame me for what my father did to you?"

"Of course not."

"Your words are empty," I said. "I can hear it in your tone. Part of you does blame me, and I can't even fault you for that."

"I don't *want* to blame you," Colin said.

"But you do." I curled my hands into fists once more. "We're in similar situations, you and I."

"How so?"

"Your father is not the man you want him to be. Mine wasn't either. Granted, mine was probably a thousand times worse than yours is, but still, he was my father. I wouldn't exist but for him, and sometimes that's very hard to deal with. Hard to reconcile."

He looked at me then, met my gaze with understanding.

He and I actually had something in common.

"So I get it," I continued. "I do. But if you ever cared about Jade, you need to accept your father for who he is and be completely honest with us. We can protect Jade, but only if we're armed with everything you know."

He nodded. "I know that. Why do you think I'm here?"

"Then you've told us all you know?"

"I have."

"You're lying, Colin," Marj said. "You said there was stuff you couldn't substantiate."

"When I can substantiate it, I'll tell you." He looked down. "He's still my father."

As much as I didn't want to, I understood. My father was still my father. Blood ran deep.

I cleared my throat. "When you can substantiate anything else, you'll come to us?"

"I will. I'll do anything for Jade. Part of me still loves her very much."

Marjorie smiled then, and her smile put me at ease. Well, a little.

"Thank you, Colin," she said. "Is there anything we can do for you?"

"No. I don't need anything."

She nodded. "All right."

Colin stood. "I *am* really sorry. Sorry this all started. Honestly, if I hadn't abandoned Jade the day of our wedding, none of this would have happened."

"I know you've been through hell," Marj said, "but don't think of it that way. My brother needed Jade. She saved him. I'm not discounting what you've been through, but Talon went through the same at the hands of not one but three men, and he was an innocent child of ten. He lived with what occurred for over twenty years. It was Jade who helped him through it, gave him a reason to heal. In a way, you helped that happen."

He inhaled deeply. "All because I was a coward and listened to my father. I think that might have been a turning point for my father and me. I think..."

I looked to Marjorie, hoping she would say something. She didn't.

"Now you know who your father is," I said. "That counts for something."

"I don't understand," Colin said. "I never understood."

Again I spoke more to myself than to Colin. "You never will."

CHAPTER THIRTY-EIGHT

Marjorie

Talon and Jade went into the city early for Jade's checkup and the boys were at school, so I was alone in the main house. Bryce was at work, of course, only his second full day on the job. His first full day had gone well into the night. It was after midnight by the time we'd gotten home from the hotel. Though I'd been tempted to stay with him at the guesthouse, I'd come back to the main house and slept in my own bed. I didn't want to cause any more unnecessary upheaval. My phone had died, I'd discovered, which was why I hadn't heard Bryce's call.

The last thing my family needed was to worry about me. We had two pregnant women, two troubled boys, and Joe and Bryce dealing with a repressed memory of Bryce's father killing a young friend of theirs.

I was not about to add to the mix.

The image of my scar popped into my mind. At the moment, the cutting seemed ridiculous. I had everything. Fucking everything. I'd been born to great privilege, and having enough time to dwell on what was wrong in my life was simply another aspect of that privilege. Rumination leading to self-mutilation was a luxury, one I would now do without.

Again, I would not add to the mix.

Bryce mentioned when he saw me to the door last night that he was going to talk to Mel about his issues. Bryce needed her now, and I wasn't going to waste her time with my self-serving nonsense.

No more cutting.

No more rumination.

No more self-absorption.

I was so done.

My father's strength flowed every bit as strong through my veins as it did my brothers', and I wouldn't let anyone down. Out of everyone in my family—including Bryce, who I now considered family—I'd been through the least.

Time to let it go and concentrate on ending this nightmare once and for all.

My phone buzzed, knocking me out of my long-coming epiphany. Not a number I recognized. "Hello?"

"Ms. Steel?"

"Yes?"

"This is Carrie Umbrage, principal at Snow Creek School. Your brother asked that I call you."

"How can I help you?"

"Dale is upset again. He thinks he saw the same stranger lurking around before school this morning. Mr. and Mrs. Steel are at a doctor's appointment in the city and figured you could get here before they could."

"Of course. I'm on my way. Is Dale all right?"

"He's okay. The nurse says his heart rate is elevated, but that's from fright. He's lucid and doesn't have any problem answering questions."

"What about Donny?"

"Donny's fine. He's in class."

"All right. I'll be there as soon as I can."

Then I quickly dialed another number.

★ ★ ★

"Your mom and dad will be here as soon as they can," I told a quiet Dale. "Your mom had a doctor's appointment in the city."

"I don't want to be a bother to them."

"You're never a bother to any of us, sweetie. We love you." I turned to the principal. "Have you called the police?"

"They've already been and gone. He answered all their questions."

"Good for you," I said to Dale.

I looked up when a knock sounded on the door.

"Come in," the principal said.

The doorknob twisted, and in walked Ruby Lee Steel, Ryan's wife. I'd called her and asked her to meet me here as soon as she could get away.

"Thanks for coming." I stood and hugged her. "This is my sister-in-law, Ruby Steel. She's a former police detective. I wanted her to come and look around."

"Nice to meet you," the principal said. "Feel free to do what you need to do. I'll be happy to help any way I can."

Ruby shook Ms. Umbrage's hand. "I appreciate it. I'd like to have a look around the playground. Is that where you saw the man this morning, Dale?"

"Yeah."

"Outside the fence, like last time?" I asked.

He nodded.

"Can you show me where he was?" Ruby asked.

He nodded again and stood. "Can I go now?"

"Show your aunts where you saw the man," the principal said. "After that, they can take you home if you'd like."

"No. I want to stay at school."

"Are you sure?" I asked.

"Yeah. Talon says it's important to be strong and that I'm safe here."

"You are," the principal said. "We have an on-site police officer, as you know. School is safe."

I hoped she was right. I didn't feel great about leaving Dale, but I agreed with Talon. Dale and Donny both needed to learn that they were safe now, but we couldn't shelter them and never allow them to leave the house. They'd grow up agoraphobic.

My brother was a smart man. Having been through what the boys had been through, he knew what was necessary for their healing.

"Okay, Dale. Let's take Aunt Ruby outside and show her where you saw the man."

He led us out the back door of the school to the enclosed playground. A ten-foot-tall chain link fence encased the large play area, which was covered in pea gravel.

"This way." He pointed to the far end of the area, where two sides of the fence met in one corner.

Once we got there, Ruby put on some blue rubber gloves, knelt, and examined the ground. "Definitely some indentation on the other side, which could mean footprints. I'm going to go around and have a look."

"Do you want to go along?" I asked Dale.

He swallowed. "Yes, I do. I want to face my fears."

More words of wisdom that had come from Talon. I was sure of it.

"Are you sure?" This time from Ruby.

"I'm sure."

He seemed a little less spooked than he had been the first time. We walked all the way back and then around to the other side. Green parkland surrounded the back of the school. A baseball diamond and football field were overgrown with weeds and grass. A shame.

Ruby knelt again when we came to the spot where Dale had seen the strange figure. "Someone has definitely been here. I can't really tell much else." She picked up what appeared to be a cigarette butt. "Was the man smoking a cigarette, Dale?"

"I don't think so."

"Okay." She put the butt in a zippered plastic bag anyway and began raking her fingers through the soft dirt. "I'm afraid I'm not finding—" She pulled something from the ground. "Well, what do you know?"

"What?" I asked.

"A cufflink. A gold cufflink." She held it up.

"Why would a guy in a hoodie have a cufflink?" I asked.

"Good question. We don't know for sure that it's his, but why would anyone hanging around a schoolyard be carrying a cufflink?" She examined it. "It's engraved with initials. CM."

CM. Oh, God. "Colin Morse?"

"That's the only CM I know who has anything to do with any of this."

"But Colin..." I shook my head. "It's a plant. It's got to be."

"That's my first instinct as well. You ever thought about becoming a cop, Marj?"

I chuckled. "The cooking cop? No, not for me."

"There are a lot of people with the initials CM," Ruby said. "Not a lot of people hanging around schoolyards with gold cufflinks, though. So yeah, probably a plant." She placed the trinket in another zippered bag and sifted through the dirt again.

"This reminds me of something," I said. "When Mills and Johnson were searching Jade's room after that rose got left in there, they found one of Colin's business cards shoved under the wall-to-wall carpeting. Obviously a plant."

"If this belongs to Colin, someone out there wants him involved in this. But why?"

"I guess that's what we have to find out. I can ask Colin if this is his, if you want."

"I want to keep it, but you can certainly ask him if he's lost an initialed cufflink. That would help."

"Will do."

Ruby searched the ground for a few more minutes.

"I don't see anything else," I said.

Dale turned to me. "I do."

CHAPTER THIRTY-NINE

Bryce

Nothing like sneaking out with the boss on your second day of work. Joe and I arrived at my father's cabin complete with shovels...and armed.

He followed me to the bedroom we used to share, the place where Marj and I had found my mother's jewels along with the firearms and file folders.

"There could be more," I said. "We'll have to pull up all the floorboards."

"Why would he put this stuff in the room we used to sleep in?" Joe asked. "Wouldn't it make more sense for him to hide them in a place only he goes into?"

"Like his room?" I nodded. "I had that same thought, which probably means..." The remaining words clogged my throat.

"...what's in his room is worse," Joe finished for me.

I nodded. "Yup."

"You want to start there?" Joe asked.

"I don't want to start anywhere, but we don't have a choice."

"We have a choice," he said. "We can leave right now and hire someone to do this."

"Then we have to put our trust in someone else."

"True, and I'm not overly comfortable with that."

"Neither am I," I said. "Let's do it."

"It's odd that the Feds didn't already dig this stuff up. This was your dad's cabin, after all."

"Except that it's owned by the Tamajor Corporation, and we still have no idea what that's about."

"The PIs are on it. Surely the Feds checked this place out," Joe said.

"They might have, but they probably didn't pull up floorboards. Obviously they didn't, or they'd have found this stuff already."

"Maybe they didn't come here," Joe said. "When was the last time your father used it?"

"I have no idea. He kept Colin at that Fleming Corp house."

"Maybe this place didn't appear anywhere in your dad's papers. Maybe the Tamajor Corporation was something he kept entirely to himself."

"There has to be a person behind every corporation."

"But it doesn't have to be your dad."

"True. I'll have to ask my mom if she mentioned the cabin to the Feds when they talked to her. I never mentioned it. Honestly, I never even thought about it."

"All this stuff was so long ago," Joe said, his voice echoing of memory.

"It was." I cleared my throat. "Let's look in my father's room. We'll have to face it eventually. I'd just as soon get it over with."

"I hear you." Joe followed me out of the small bedroom and into the larger one where my father had slept during our many camping trips.

It looked the same.

An eerie feeling of unease swept over me. Ghosts lived here. My father's presence was unmistakable in this room. No, I didn't believe in ghosts, but this room reeked of Tom Simpson. I inhaled. It even smelled like him. Cigar smoke, sweat, and woodsy cologne. My mother hated cigars, and when we were at the cabin without her, my father had never failed to indulge.

Years and years had passed, and my father still existed in this room.

"You okay?" Joe asked.

"Fine."

"You looked a little off for a minute. Like you were somewhere else."

"I was. I can smell him here, Joe. It's like it was all yesterday."

"You're imagining things."

"Maybe. You didn't live with him twenty-four-seven. I did. I know his scent. I know the feeling of being around him. I'm feeling that now."

Joe didn't reply. He no doubt thought I was crazy, and perhaps I was. As far as I knew, my father hadn't been here in years, and definitely not recently since he was dead.

Still...

Joe pulled the area rug off the wooden floor. "I don't see anything that indicates a loose board. I guess we just pull it all up?"

"Maybe it's under the bed," I said. "If there's something huge to hide, he'd probably have put it there."

"Let's check."

We moved the bed, the sound of it sliding across the wood

like fingernails on a chalkboard. It shouldn't have been, but it was.

"I still don't see anything that looks out of place," I said.

"I guess we pull everything up, then," Joe said. "Leave no stone unturned."

I nodded, slipping the crowbar under a board.

★ ★ ★

Nothing.

Three hours of moving all the furniture out of the cabin and then prying up every board in the bedroom...

And nothing.

"Okay," Joe said. "That was a dead end."

"Why in our bedroom? Why not in his? We could have found that stuff at any time. Little boys are curious creatures."

"We're not thinking like your father," Joe said.

"That's a good thing, from where I'm standing."

"I agree."

"You're right, though. My father hid in plain sight all those years. He hid behind his career as a lawyer and then mayor of Snow Creek. He was a pillar of the community, and no one suspected anything. He went out of town? There was always a reason." I let out a sarcastic chuckle and shook my head. "We just played right into his game."

"We did. Any logical person would assume he'd hide stuff in his bedroom. Maybe we've already uncovered everything there is."

"Maybe," I said, "but I doubt it. If he hides in plain sight, what's more in plain sight than our bedroom?"

"The living area. The kitchen."

"Right. No stone unturned." I grabbed the tools and walked out of my father's bedroom.

Joe followed me.

"Let's finish our bedroom first," I said. "We're already halfway there."

He nodded. We each took a side of the first bed, hoisted it up, and carried it out of the cabin.

"Looks like we're setting up house out here," Joe commented.

My father's bed, nightstand, and dresser sat on the ground, as though waiting for some fairy folk to make it home.

I didn't reply to Joe. I didn't want to think about anything other than the task at hand. If I allowed my mind to wander—even to fairy folk, which I didn't believe in, of course—I might think about all the horrible things we could uncover.

I didn't need the help of imagination. The horror would make itself known soon enough. I could only hope it would be less evil than my mind was already assuming it would be.

Once all the furniture was hauled out, we tackled the remaining floor in the second bedroom. We uncovered some more of my mother's jewels and more manila files. No more guns, at least not that we found.

More and more boards, until we were walking over joists. Nothing more...until—

"Got something," Joe said, holding up a small wooden box.

"What is it?"

"I don't know. You want to open it, or should I?"

"Go for it." I had no desire to be the one who unearthed more of my father's horrors.

Joe slowly lifted the lid. "It's a gold cufflink."

"A gold cufflink? My father never wore cufflinks."

"Yeah, he did," Joe said. "Remember? Talon recalled seeing a cufflink with the initials TS at the place where he was kept?"

"You never told me that."

"Didn't I? It came up in one of his guided hypnosis sessions with Melanie."

"All I can say is I don't remember ever seeing my dad wearing cufflinks."

"No one *wears* cufflinks," Joe said, "but a lot of men own them. Did he have any?"

"I don't know. Do you think this is the cufflink Talon saw?"

"I don't know. There's only one here." Joe lifted it out of the box and examined it. "Except the initials aren't TS. They're CM."

CHAPTER FORTY

Marjorie

"What do you see?" Ruby asked.

Dale picked up a rock. "This," he said. "It doesn't belong here."

A polished stone of some sort. It had clearly been through a rock tumbler. It was black and white and easily blended in with the other stones and dark dirt of the ground.

"May I see?" Ruby asked.

Dale handed her the stone.

"Wow, good eye, Dale," she said. "You're right. It doesn't belong here."

"Wait," Dale said. "Let me see it again."

Ruby handed it back to him.

"Sometimes people carry stones for good luck. That's what my mom used to tell me when I collected them." He turned the stone over.

"You collected rocks?" I asked.

"I used to. I don't know what happened to my collection." He examined the rock more closely. "This is obsidian. Snowflake obsidian."

"Are you sure?" I asked.

"Yeah. I had one just like it."

I dropped my mouth open, and Ruby glanced at me,

shaking her head ever so slightly. I understood. We had to keep him calm so he'd continue to talk. So far, he hadn't freaked at finding something that reminded him of his past.

"What happened to your rock collection, Dale?" Ruby asked, her voice even.

"I don't know. I assume it's back in my house." He swallowed. "My old house."

Words wanted to tumble off my tongue, but I took Ruby's advice to stay quiet. I didn't want to upset Dale. Talon and Jade had packed up everything from the boys' room at the house they'd lived in with their mother, along with anything else of value they might want someday. No rock collection had been among those things, as far as I knew. Dale had never mentioned them until now. Clearly he'd had a lot more on his mind.

What had happened to Dale's rock collection? And why would a similar rock be here, where he allegedly saw a strange man he thought he recognized?

Ruby put the rock in a zippered bag and smiled. "May I keep this? Just for now. I'll give it back to you soon if you'd like."

He nodded.

"Thank you. You'll make a good detective someday, Dale," she said. "Seeing things that don't belong is a big part of it."

Dale smiled.

A big smile.

Which made me smile.

Had I ever seen him smile like that before? No, I hadn't.

The rock might turn out to be nothing. But he had found it. He had helped Ruby. He had helped himself.

This was *huge*.

Huger, though, was the fact that Dale's rock collection was missing, and a similar piece was *here*. Why would anyone want a little boy's collection? And why would someone leave a polished rock here?

Ruby knelt again. "Just want to give this one more look. After all, sometimes things hide in plain sight." She moved her gloved hands over the dirt. "Nothing that I can see. Let's walk around a little. If there was a slight breeze, something could have blown away."

Dale and I followed her as she scanned the area. Every other step or so, she'd stop and look at something. I had no idea what she was looking at, but she was the expert. Finally she zeroed in on what appeared to be a small piece of paper. She knelt down and picked it up, staring.

"What is it?" I asked.

"A baseball card," she replied. "I don't follow baseball. Do you?"

"No."

"Do you, Dale?"

"Not really. I like it and all, but I don't know the players."

Ruby sealed the card in a zippered bag. "Could be nothing again, but I want to cover everything." She continued walking around the area. Finally, after about fifteen more minutes, she stopped. "I think we've seen everything there is here. The cops would have stopped a half hour ago."

"What are you going to do with that stuff?" I asked.

"Take it to a friend of mine for analysis. It's a long shot, but you never know."

A cigarette butt, a gold cufflink that was probably planted, a polished piece of snowflake obsidian, and a baseball card.

Not a lot to go on, but more than we had before.

I ushered Dale back to class.

He was still smiling.

★ ★ ★

"I don't know what you did, Marj, but Dale has been more animated today than he's ever been," Jade said in the kitchen while I prepared dinner.

"All because he found that stone," I said. "I think that's the thing. He found it. He took some initiative in his own healing."

"Because he found a rock?"

"Well...yeah. He found it and saw that it didn't belong there. Of course anyone could have dropped a piece of obsidian on the ground, and it's probably nothing. But Dale found it. He took action. He helped Ruby, and that made him feel like less of a victim."

"Oh, yeah." Jade nodded. "He was helping."

"Helping yourself goes a long way," I said, echoing words I'd heard from Mel more than once. "It doesn't matter that it's probably nothing. What matters is he found it and saw that it was out of place."

Jade smiled. "I can't get over the smile on his face. All because of a rock."

"Did you know Dale used to collect rocks?" I said.

"No. He never mentioned it. Then again, he never mentions much of anything."

"Apparently he had quite a collection, but they didn't make their way from his old house to here."

"Why not?"

"I don't know. I thought you and Tal brought everything from their room."

"We did. There wasn't a collection of rocks."

"That's strange. Maybe Dale kept it hidden."

"Maybe... If it meant that much to him, would he have—" She shook her head. "No, he probably wouldn't have said anything. He didn't say anything at all until now."

"Right."

"You don't think..." Jade bit her lip.

"Think what?"

"That you actually found one of Dale's rocks? That someone took his collection because they're after him?"

"Why would anyone steal worthless rocks?" I asked.

"I don't know. Whoever this guy is has spooked Dale more than once now. I don't like it."

"None of us do, Jade."

"I'll talk to Dale. See if he left the rocks somewhere hidden."

"Okay." I finished up the chicken breasts I was frying. "Call in the boys for dinner. It's ready."

CHAPTER FORTY-ONE

Bryce

CM? Colin Morse? He was Marj's age. Why would he have cufflinks, and why—

"This is Colin's," I said. "It has to be."

"But you said your father didn't come here after we grew up."

"That I knew of. But who else could it belong to?"

"Well...anyone with the initials CM. There's probably more than one."

"He held Colin captive," I said.

"Not here," Joe retorted.

"Does that matter? He kept this cufflink for some reason. Put it in a wooden box and hid it. There has to be a reason."

"Does there? Maybe the cufflink is part of the stuff your mom inherited."

"The jewelry belonged to an aunt, not an uncle."

"So?"

"Would you quit disagreeing with everything I say? If there's one thing I've come to terms with about my father, it's that he had a reason for everything he did. He wasn't stupid. How did he get away with it for so long? Because he covered his tracks by hiding in plain sight. No one ever suspected that the esteemed mayor of Snow Creek could ever do anything wrong. He was calculating and manipulative. So if he kept this cufflink, he had a reason."

"Okay, that makes sense. What reason would he have for keeping a cufflink belonging to one of his victims? If it indeed belonged to one of them."

"Colin was his last victim," I said, "that we know of. It's probably a trophy."

Joe nodded. "Then he most likely kept trophies of other victims as well. Which means there's a lot to dig up here."

I was afraid of that. I didn't want to do any more digging. But that was why we'd come here.

"There's the living room," Joe said, "and the kitchen."

"And outside. A lot could be buried outside."

Joe looked at his watch. "It's getting toward dinnertime. Melanie will be expecting me. You want to meet here later? Around eight?"

"We need light to dig."

"No, we don't. We can search inside the cabin during the day, but we're safer working outside under the veil of night. It was a warm day. The ground won't be too hard."

He had a point. "Eight o'clock, then."

★ ★ ★

I'd jammed my shovel into the ground outside the cabin, ready to step on it and push it farther down, when my skin chilled. Headlights glared in the distance. Someone was coming up the narrow driveway.

I looked to Joe. "Shit."

"You said it." He glanced around. "You armed?"

"Absolutely."

The car stopped several yards away from us, and a figure stepped out. Joe shined his flashlight.

I sighed as both relief and fear welled in me.

"You really think someone wouldn't follow you two?" Marjorie said, walking toward us quickly.

"You can't be here, Sis," Joe said.

"I agree. It's not safe."

"The two of you are here. I think my big, bad boyfriend and my big, bad brother can protect me."

We both glared at her.

"Come on. I want to help. This involves all of us. Look around. We're alone out here. If anyone was watching this place, he'd have shown up by now."

"I don't want you in any danger," I said.

"Do I look in danger to you?"

"We're digging up God knows what tonight," Joe said. "Just how can you help?"

"I can dig."

"It's hard work, Sis. Work that will blister your manicured hands."

"That's why I brought leather work gloves." She waved a pair in our faces.

"I can't talk you out of this, can I?" Joe said.

"Nope." She turned to me. "And neither can you, so don't even try."

I sighed in defeat. "Just stay where I can see you."

"I'm not a child. You don't have to tell me not to wander off." She covered her pretty hands with the work gloves and then grabbed an extra shovel lying on the ground. "Let's party." She shoved the blade into the dirt.

I couldn't help but smile.

"I did as much work around the ranch as any of my brothers."

"She did," Joe said. "She was a major pain in the ass, too. She was my apprentice on the beef ranch when she was a teen."

I well remembered. Marjorie Steel as a teen had been something I hadn't allowed myself to think about. I cleared my mind of the image. Marjorie Steel as a young woman I *did* think about, and she was so much more beautiful than she'd been as a teen.

"How much digging did you do on a cattle ranch?" I asked, knowing well my tone was a bit smartass.

"Don't get smart with me," she said. "I helped plant seedlings in the orchard."

"We'll be digging a lot deeper than you would to plant a young tree," I said. "You sure you're up for it?"

"I can do anything a man can do," she said tartly, one hand holding the shovel, the other whipped to her hip indignantly.

"Why don't the two of you stop this ridiculous banter and start digging?" Joe said.

I let out a breath slowly. I was already turned on by her very presence. Her brother's presence should have been an antidote, but God, she drove me insane. I shoved the blade into the ground.

Two hours later, we'd uncovered a lot of nothing. So much for this idea. I was sore, and even wearing leather gloves, my hands were aching and starting to blister.

Joe sighed. "Let's call it a night. We'll start again tomorrow."

"What about work?" I said. "You guys are paying me an awful lot to not be there on my second and third days."

"Work will still be there," Joe said. "Talon and Ry are with us on this. We have to figure it all out."

"Who's going to mind the finances, then?"

"Well, your staff of ten people, probably," Joe said. "We trust them."

I scoffed. "Then what do you need me for?"

Marjorie moved toward me and touched my forearm. "We need you," she said softly.

"Of course we need you," Joe said. "But this trumps everything right now. My brothers and I took a ton of time off dealing with this shit last year, and things rolled smoothly. We have good people working for us. That doesn't mean we don't need your leadership. The company is in good shape, Bryce. If you're not there every hour, it will still run."

I sighed. "If you say so. I just feel—"

"Stop it," Joe said. "We've been through this. You're not a charity case. Not by a long shot."

Marjorie squeezed my forearm but didn't say anything.

I leaned my shovel against the cabin. "All right. I need a shower anyway." I kissed Marjorie's cheek, got into my car, and drove back to the guesthouse.

★ ★ ★

Marjorie followed me all the way home. When I expected her to turn off to the main house, she didn't. I got out of the car and waited for her to do the same.

"What are you doing here?" I asked her.

"What do you think I'm doing here?"

"We need a shower."

"Last time I checked, you have one."

Exhaustion weighed on me, but still my body quivered at

her nearness. "Come on in."

The house was so empty without my mother and Henry, though they'd have been in bed by now anyway. I looked at Marjorie. Her ponytail sagged, and several wisps of dark hair had escaped their confinement. Her cheeks were flushed red, and sooty dirt marred her face.

She'd never looked more beautiful.

More than that, she looked more content than I'd seen her in a while, which didn't jibe.

"Something good happened today," I said.

"Yeah. Sort of."

"What?"

I listened as she told me about Dale and Ruby and what they'd found at the school.

"A baseball card?" I asked.

"Yeah. Ruby's going to check everything out, but that's not the main thing. Dale seemed different after he found the rock. Like he'd done something to help himself. It seemed to mean something to him."

"He's been doing a lot to help himself," I said. "Through therapy and all."

"No, this was different. Someone else is there with therapy. This was something *he* found. He took an active role and noticed something didn't belong in the space. It probably has nothing to do with anything, but it helped him. I talked to Mel about it on the phone before dinner. She thinks this could be huge and that maybe we should let him take a more active role in what's going on."

"He's ten."

"I know, and Talon and Jade would probably never allow it, but Mel thinks it could bring him out of his shell. It already has, sort of. He smiled today, Bryce. He actually *smiled*."

Marjorie's grin lit up her whole face. Warmth surged through me. Those poor boys—Dale especially, who'd taken the brunt of the abuse to spare his little brother. Had my father done anything to them? I had no way of knowing. He'd died before the boys had been found, and as far as I knew, he hadn't been in the Caribbean during that time.

I'd never know.

All I knew was that we had to put an end to this once and for all. For all our sakes, especially the boys'.

"What can Dale possibly do to help?"

"Little things, Mel says. We can ask his opinion on stuff. Obviously no one wants to put him in any danger, but he needs to feel like he's a part of this, and today he did."

I smiled. "You're amazing, you know that?"

"Me? It's Mel's idea."

"I mean with Dale. You're just as much a parent to him right now as Talon and Jade are. You're going to be..."

An amazing mother someday. She would be. She could be to Henry. She and I loved each other, so why hadn't I been able to say the words?

"I'm going to be what?"

I gazed into her chocolate eyes. "You're going to be well and thoroughly used before this night is over."

I lifted her in my arms and carried her to my bedroom. Then I walked into the attached bath and turned on the shower. We undressed quickly and stepped in, letting the pelting warm water soothe the aches from digging.

She closed her eyes as she pulled the band out of her ponytail and set it on one of the shower shelves. "Man, that feels good."

I inhaled, letting the steam from the shower infuse me. Yes, it felt good. Amazingly good. I pulled her to me, our slick bodies sliding together. Her height made her the perfect fit against me, the perfect yin to my yang. I didn't kiss her, didn't try to fuck her, though my dick was more than ready. Just held her, felt her warmth against me, inhaled the steam, and relaxed.

Relaxed.

How long we stood there, I couldn't say. The water gradually morphed to lukewarm, and I grabbed a shower pouf and lathered both of us with my woodsy gel. When we were thoroughly clean, I turned off the water and handed her a dry towel.

"That was amazing," she said.

"Nothing like a shower when you're sore and dirty," I agreed.

"No. I mean, yeah. But I was talking about just holding each other, you know?"

I smiled. "I know."

"Not that I didn't want more."

"I did too, but we have all night in a clean, dry bed for that."

"Last one there's a rotten egg." She threw the towel on the bathroom floor and ran into the bedroom.

I laughed. "You used to say that when you were little."

She returned my laughter. "I never stopped!" She leaped onto the bed, her dark tresses a tangled disarray around her shoulders and chest.

She looked beautiful.

I joined her on the bed, and she snuggled into my shoulder.

"I love you, Bryce," she said softly.

"I love you too, Marjorie. So much."

CHAPTER FORTY-TWO

Marjorie

The first rays of sunlight streamed into the strange bedroom as I awoke to Bryce tugging on one of my hard nipples with his lips and teeth.

My hair was a dry and stringy mess pasted to my cheeks and shoulders, and I needed to rise soon to see to the boys and their breakfast.

Oh, but his sweet mouth on my nipple. His thumb and middle finger played with the other one, and for a moment I couldn't decide which felt better, his mouth or his fingers, and then I stopped thinking altogether. What did it matter? It all felt amazing.

My hips began rotating of their own accord, and the lips of my pussy tingled as the tickle inside grew in its intensity.

I bit my lip and let out a soft sigh. So, so good.

I arched my back, pushing my chest closer to Bryce, instinctively wanting more tugging, more biting, more pinching on those ultrasensitive nipples.

He groaned against my skin, a soft hum that I felt as well as heard. His intensity matched my own. Without words, he knew when I wanted a stronger pinch, a harsher suck.

Until he trailed his hand over my thigh and between my legs...

"Oh!"

He thrust two fingers into my soaking-wet pussy, flicking his thumb over my clit.

Both nipples, clit, and pussy... If only he had another pair of lips to kiss me with, I'd have everything.

I missed his tongue in my mouth, his lips sliding against mine, but I couldn't bear to have his lips leave my nipple. He kissed it, licked it, sucked it, nibbled at it. And with every tiny nip, I got wetter, wanted him more.

The rhythmic movement of his thumb over my clit sent need barreling through me, and soon I found myself on the precipice. I was going to come. I was going to come hard, and I wanted that hard cock in me, slicing through me as I shattered.

"Bryce, please. Inside me."

He dropped my nipple from his lips and crawled forward—

"Yes!" I cried when he thrust into me.

His cock was thick, hard, and he rammed it into me just as I wanted. My nipples were chafed from his attentions, and his chest hair abraded them as he pumped.

He grunted against my neck, nipping at my flesh with his firm lips. Emotion swirled through me in a rapturous kaleidoscope. Bryce, inside me. Always inside me. Every part of me taking in every part of him, as if we were now one being. The perfect pleasure—to have my emptiness filled, filled by the man I loved.

All was right in the world.

At least for now.

My pussy contracted around him, and one orgasm led to another, and then another. I quivered, running my hands up and down his slick back. I loved the feel of his skin underneath my fingertips. Loved the sandy hair on his chest torturing my nipples. Loved his big hard cock inside me.

If perfection existed in the world, Bryce and I together were it.

He thrust harder, harder, harder until he grunted against me, releasing. So in tune with him was I that I felt every pulse of his cock as he emptied into me.

For a moment, I let myself think about making a baby with him. About the future.

We hadn't talked about it, and I didn't want to bring it up with all we were dealing with.

I brushed the thought away from my mind, let myself revel simply in his orgasm and mine, as we released together in perfect harmony.

We lay there then in each other's arms. Finally, I couldn't help giggling.

He kissed the top of my head. "What?"

"I guess I'll let you off the hook."

"Off the hook for what?"

"Did you or did you not say to me that I would be well and thoroughly used before last night was over?"

He chuckled into my hair. "I guess I did."

"And then, Bryce Simpson, you fell asleep."

"I seem to recall you falling asleep as well."

"At any rate, you're forgiven."

He pounced then, rolling over to his side and flipping me over. He landed a sharp smack on my ass.

"Ow!" The pain lanced through me, making me shudder. Was it pain I felt? Or was it pleasure? No one had spanked me before. Not as a kid for punishment, and not as an adult during sex.

I wasn't sure how I felt about it.

"What was that for?" I demanded.

"That was for being a little brat," he teased. "And trust me. There's a lot more where that came from." His palm came down on my ass again.

I could tell him to stop. He would if I asked. But the words lodged in my throat. I wanted to try this. I really wanted to try this.

"Your ass is gorgeous, sweetheart. Especially now, with my red handprint on it."

His words sent a spike of pleasure through me. He'd marked me, in a way. But a handprint wouldn't last forever.

Was he even ready for forever?

Before I could think again, he smacked me once more, this time easing the sting with his lips on my ass cheek. Tiny kisses chasing away the sharpness and leaving only loving pleasure.

I sighed softly, burying my head in his pillow. Soon, instead of his lips and hands, I felt his hard cock between my ass cheeks. He slid it downward, through the juices of my pussy, and then back between my cheeks. Was he going to...?

"No," he said in answer to my silent question. "Not today. Not until we're both ready."

I looked over my shoulder. "Have you ever?"

"No. But I want to. With you."

"I want to," I said, only now knowing the truth of the words.

"We will. But right now, I need that hot little pussy of yours." He thrust into me.

I was tight from my orgasms, and the burn of his cock tunneling into me was good. So good. I didn't care about coming. All I wanted was to feel him inside me, taking me, marking me, making me his forever.

CHAPTER FORTY-THREE

Bryce

So complete. So perfectly complete. Every time I entered her felt better than the last. Every time her walls sank around my cock was a more perfect fit. Just when I thought it could never be any better...it was.

It so was.

I fucked her this time. I needed a hard, fast fuck after spanking her gorgeous ass. I loved this woman so much, and I adored making slow, sweet love to her.

But sometimes, I just wanted a fuck. A good, hard fuck. A meeting of cock and pussy and all the raw beauty of it.

So I fucked her. I fucked her hard and fast and with everything in me. And when my body became my cock and balls and released into her, I felt more than lust and love and wonder.

I felt peace.

The pure peace that can only come from the physical. Endorphins drifted around us, through us, almost visible to me as I emptied every last drop of myself into her.

I needed peace in my life. We both did.

I collapsed on top of her, holding my weight so as not to crush her. Then I rolled over and gathered her into my arms, kissing her moist forehead. "I hate to say this, but I have to get up."

"Me too." She lifted her head and kissed my lips. "I need to make breakfast for the boys and get them off to school."

"I thought Jade was feeling better."

"She is, but I like doing it. It's nice to be needed."

"Hey," I teased. "I need you. I think I just proved that."

She laughed. "I need you too, but we both have obligations."

"True enough." I sat up and stretched, the sun's rays making me squint. "Another sunny day."

"Good old Colorado." She rose from the bed. "I'm going to take a quick shower. And don't you dare come in and join me, or we'll never get moving."

My cock twitched as I thought of making love to her in the shower, but she was right. We both had stuff to do. I quickly texted Joe to see if he wanted to go back to the cabin or if he wanted me in the office this morning. Then I wrapped a robe around myself and went to the kitchen to start a pot of coffee.

The manila folders we'd uncovered yesterday afternoon lay on the kitchen table. I hadn't opened them yet. I let my fingers hover over one for a moment while the coffee brewed. Why was I so hesitant? The other files hadn't yielded anything too scary. Farm equipment, yes, but so far we hadn't found anything buried near the cabin. We'd hardly exhausted the area, though.

I peeled one edge of the folder back—

"Coffee. Excellent." Marjorie walked into the kitchen wearing one of my shirts, her hair wet and her nipples protruding.

My cock responded, of course.

Though the pot was only half full, she poured herself a cup and sat next to me. "What are you looking at?"

"Some more files Joe and I found under the floorboards

in the bedroom at the cabin."

"Oh?"

I nodded. "I haven't opened them yet."

"Why not?"

"No reason." I opened the first folder.

And my heart dropped into my stomach.

Three words stood out from the rest, as if they were pulsing in time with my heart.

Henry Thomas Simpson.

Henry Thomas Simpson.

Henry Thomas Simpson.

This document concerned my son.

Marjorie stroked my hand. "Bryce?"

I jolted back to reality. This was a contract. A fucking contract.

Tom Simpson had paid off Henry's mother to relinquish her parental rights.

My fucked-up father had bought my son.

CHAPTER FORTY-FOUR

Marjorie

Bryce went pale.

"What is it?"

He said nothing, just scanned the document, his eyes moving rapidly.

"Babe?"

"I can't believe this," he said.

"What?"

"My father. My fucking nutjob of a father."

"What did he do now?"

He thrust the piece of paper at me. "See for yourself."

I rapidly read the document. "Francine Stokes. Is that your ex? Henry's mom, right?"

He nodded.

"She—" I gasped. "What? He paid her a hundred thousand dollars to give up her rights to Henry?"

"It sure looks that way."

"Oh my God."

"She called me last week," Bryce said. "She wanted to see Henry. I told her no. I always figured she'd given up her rights voluntarily, so why should I let her come near my son? What kind of mother does that?"

"A mother who gets a hundred grand, apparently," I said.

"There's more to it than that," he said.

"What do you mean?"

"Well, you're not a mother, but let me ask you this anyway. How much money would it take for you to give up your own child?"

My mouth dropped open. He was right. I wasn't a mother, but I had two little boys I loved, and I'd never give either of them up for any amount of money.

Which was exactly his point.

"Somehow she found out my father is dead now, so she wants to see Henry."

"Are you going to allow it?"

"I wasn't, but now everything's different."

"She still gave him up for money, no matter how you look at it."

"Yeah, she did, but my father didn't play fair. You can bet on it."

"You mean he held a gun to her head?"

"In a manner of speaking. It might have been a metaphorical gun. A mindfuck. Apparently my father was good at that."

"Bryce, you can't lose Henry." My heart nearly stopped. That little boy was everything to Bryce.

"No, I can't. I *won't*."

"She gave up her rights. Whether it was voluntarily or not shouldn't matter." Even I didn't believe what I was saying.

"She was so adamant when she called. She sounded desperate," Bryce said, his eyes tormented. "I treated her like shit."

"You can't blame yourself. You thought she'd given him up."

"I should have been able to foresee this. This has my father's stench all over it."

"You're not a mind reader, Bryce."

"Why didn't she say anything?" Bryce queried, more to himself than to me.

"Maybe it didn't happen the way you think. Maybe it was a simple exchange for money and that's all, which makes her a shitty mother."

He shook his head. "Nothing my father ever did was simple. This is just another piece of a puzzle that seems never-ending."

"You don't have to deal with everything today."

"But I do. I have to exorcize that bastard from my life."

"Why would he have done such a thing? Get rid of Henry's mother?"

"Why did my father ever do anything? If I could get into his head and figure it all out, I'd be as psychopathic as he was. I'd rather not."

"Maybe he did it for you. He got your son for you so you'd have him full-time. He knew that would make you happy."

He didn't reply, just stared at the agreement, his forehead wrinkled.

"Bryce?"

"I *was* happy," he said, his tone anything but. "I was always happy...until I found out who my father truly was."

"You're not happy now?"

He turned to me, his eyes overflowing with emotion. "Honey, I am. You make me deliriously happy, but I have so many unanswered questions. So much I still need to deal with."

"When are you going to talk to Mel?"

"God only knows. Between the new job, which I haven't

given a hundred percent to yet, and trying to uncover the mystery of Justin and Colin Morse and now Frankie—"

"Frankie?"

"Francine. She went by Frankie."

"Oh." Cute. Kind of. I felt bad for her if Tom had forced her into giving up her son, but she was still Bryce's ex. I wasn't going to like her. "Let's take things one at a time. We don't know whether Frankie is innocent here. She may have been happy to take the money."

"Marj..."

"Why did you leave her in the first place?"

"I caught her cheating."

"With whom?"

His mouth curved up on one side. "A pizza delivery guy."

I couldn't help myself. I laughed out loud.

"Marj..." he said again.

"Come on. This was a woman who cheated on you with a pizza delivery guy, for God's sake. Hardly a paragon of virtue."

That got a smile out of him—this time from both sides of his mouth.

"Look. Henry is safe with your mom in Florida. Frankie has no idea where he is. This isn't something you need to worry about right now. Documents have been filed with the court showing that she gave up her rights. If she tries anything, she doesn't have a leg to stand on."

"But is it right for me to keep Henry from his mother?"

"For now. Until we know for sure whether there were extenuating circumstances."

"This is my father, Marj. There *were* extenuating circumstances."

He knew both Tom and Francine better than I did, so I

didn't argue the point further. I stood and kissed his cheek. "I have to get home and see to the boys. Call me later."

"I will. Love you."

"Love you too."

As soon as I got into my car, I pulled out my phone to make a call.

"Colin," I said to his voicemail. "We need to talk."

CHAPTER FORTY-FIVE

Bryce

"I've never shot a gun before," Justin said to me.

"You don't have to. You can just watch Joe and me. We're both really good at it, but my dad's the best. He never misses the bull's-eye."

Justin's skin was an olive tan, but I swore he went pale when I showed him the guns at the cabin. Dad had gone outside to do some stuff. Joe and I liked to look at the guns when he was gone. He never let us touch them without him being around.

"Thanks for bringing me here," Justin said.

"No problem," Joe said. "Why do you let those jerks bother you, anyway?"

"It's hard. I'm always the new kid."

"How come?"

"We move a lot. I don't really know why."

"Taylor Johns is an asshole," I said. "I'd love to crush his skull."

If possible, Justin went a little bit whiter.

"He'll get what's coming to him one way or another," Joe said.

I'd heard Joe's father utter those same words many times. Given enough rope, he'll eventually hang himself. Joe's dad said that a lot too. I didn't really understand what it meant. More rope meant more slack, which made hanging yourself impossible.

But I didn't worry about what it meant. I was just raring to get outside and start shooting. I loved the feeling of holding a gun, of pulling the trigger and shooting it. It gave me power over those empty soda cans. Power over the bull's-eye in the middle of the paper target.

Power.

I liked power.

My father tramped through the front door of the cabin. "All right, boys. Ready for some target practice?"

"Yes!" Joe and I both shouted.

Justin said nothing.

"Come on, Justin," Dad said. "There's nothing to it."

"I'm not sure I want to, Mr. Simpson."

"You don't have to, son. You can just watch." My father clamped his arm around Justin's shoulder. "But learning how to shoot is part of becoming a man. Just watch Bryce and Joe. You'll see."

We went outside where my dad had set up the targets. I always liked to start with the cans. I loved the sound of the aluminum clanging as the entire pyramid came tumbling down with one shot.

"You watch Bryce, son. He'll go first."

The pistols lay out on a small picnic table. I chose Clark, my favorite. Joe and I had named all the guns. This one was named after Clark Kent.

"Shooting is an art," my father was saying to Justin as I loaded the weapon. "Every man should know how to do it and to do it well."

"Why, sir?" Justin asked.

"You might need to defend yourself someday. Or you might

have to protect someone you love. Or you might need to buy someone's silence."

Buy someone's silence? The words went in my ears and then out again. How could you buy silence? Silence wasn't something you found at the store. You didn't pick up a box of quiet at the market. If you could do that, my teacher would be buying it all the time. That made me laugh. I must have misheard because I was focused on getting ready to shoot.

In the background, more words from my father's mouth.

"Money buys silence for a time, son, but a bullet buys it forever."

★ ★ ★

I jerked out of my daydream. I sat at the table, my cup of coffee full in front of me.

Money buys silence for a time, son, but a bullet buys it forever.

Had my father actually said that to a scared little boy? To Justin? Had he ever said those words to Joe and me?

The whole weekend with Justin was still a blur, thanks to the drugs my father had undoubtedly given Joe and me. Maybe I'd made this up.

But the words were crisp and clear in my head.

I heard them in my father's voice. That "I'm your father" tone he used when he wanted to make a point and didn't want any argument.

I squeezed my eyes shut, trying desperately to find the image in my mind. Outside the cabin. Target practice. Where was Joe? Had he heard my father? I scanned the picture in my mind's eye. I couldn't find Joe. Where had he gone? Probably went to take a piss in the woods. We were little boys, after all. We'd thought it great fun to pee anywhere we wanted.

Yes, I could still hear the words in my father's authoritative voice. I wasn't certain he'd ever said the same to me or to Joe. I'd ask Joe, but I already knew the answer.

He hadn't said those words to us. Only Justin, as if in some kind of foreshadowing.

Justin wasn't going home.

Justin would be silenced forever.

My father had already decided.

Chills skittered down my back and through my legs. What kind of maniac could say something like that to a nine-year-old kid, especially a kid who'd been bullied relentlessly?

Unless...

I gulped. Oh my God.

We'd found Justin's body, but...

I squeezed my eyes closed harder, trying, trying, trying...

Justin was olive-skinned. Probably another reason why I'd thought he had a Spanish surname. I'd seen him go paler when we were showing him the guns, but when we found his body beside the river...

It wasn't pale. He looked normal. His lips looked normal.

If he were dead, his lips would have been blue.

Was it possible?

Had Justin survived?

And if he had, where was he now?

I frantically dialed Joe.

★ ★ ★

"What the hell do you two want?" Larry Wade said.

I'd accompanied Joe to the prison to see his half uncle. He didn't look good.

"Get into a fight?" Joe asked.

"What the fuck do you care?"

"I don't. Serves you right, and it's still not even a down payment on what you did to my brother and those other kids. I imagine child molesters aren't looked too favorably upon by other prisoners."

Larry said nothing.

"Today, Uncle Larry," Joe said, "you're going to tell us the names of those other two abductors."

He shook his head. "Nope. I'm afraid I'm not."

"What the hell do you care? The DA is offering a good deal. And you're already getting your ass kicked in prison. Look at you."

Still, he shook his head. "I can't. And I won't."

"What if we're willing to sweeten the pot a little?" I asked.

"With what? If I walked away from the Steels' money, what makes you think you have anything to offer me?"

"My father's the mayor of Snow Creek. He can talk to the governor. Maybe get you a pardon."

Joe turned to me. "What the fuck?" he said through clenched teeth.

"What's the problem?" I said. "You want to find out who did this, don't you?"

"Not at the expense of letting this asshole free. Hell, no."

Larry chuckled. "I can guarantee you one thing, son. Your father won't do shit for me."

"How can you say that?" I asked. "He appointed you as a city attorney when you needed a job."

"There were special circumstances there."

"Like what?"

"Confidential special circumstances."

"Just as well," Joe interjected. "Because, Bryce, we're not letting this asshole out. I don't care if the president himself wants to pardon him. I will not let it fucking happen. Absolutely not."

"Calm down, Joe," I said. "I didn't know you would freak out this way."

"This scumbag molested my brother. This scumbag molested and killed your cousin."

Larry started to speak, but Joe silenced him with a gesture.

"How could you possibly think I would be okay with getting him pardoned? Not only does he deserve to be in prison for life, but also, what if he got a pardon and then he got out and molested another kid? Maybe your kid?"

I went cold. "Okay. It was just a thought. My father probably wouldn't do it anyway." My dad was a good man. He'd never pardon anyone who didn't deserve it.

"That's for damn sure," Larry said.

"Just what in the hell do you have against my father?" I demanded. "He's been the mayor for over ten years. Before that, he was a prominent attorney in Snow Creek."

Silence for a minute. Neither Joe nor Larry responded to me.

Finally, Joe said, "I have a name, Uncle. Was one of the men Nico Kostas?"

"No," he said.

"Just tell us," I pleaded. "It will be worth your while. You'll get a lighter sentence. And Joe has already offered you money for a lawyer."

Larry looked intently at me. "Why is it so important for you to learn the truth?"

"Because Luke Walker was my cousin. Because Talon is Joe's brother. Because I have a son of my own now, and I would die inside if anything like this ever happened to him. So I want to know the truth. I want to know who those fuckers are so we can get them off the street and they'll never again hurt innocent children like my son."

Larry regarded me, his face stern but unreadable. "Look, I've got nothing against you, kid—"

"Kid? I'm thirty-eight," I said.

"To me, you're a kid." Larry coughed. "I'm not going to tell you who they are."

I stood. "Then Joe and I will find them on our own."

Larry curled his lips into a sleazy half smile. "Keep looking if you want to, kid, but let me give you a piece of advice. The truth is overrated. Once you open the door to that dark room, getting out is damn near impossible."

★ ★ ★

"Yeah, I was probably pissing in the woods," Joe said after I'd relayed my memory to him. "I don't recall any of that."

"Let your mind relax."

"You sound like Melanie."

"All I can say is that's when I found it. I was sitting at the kitchen table this morning, staring into space, and the memory just came to me."

"I'm not real good at forcing my mind to relax," he said.

"I'm not either. It kind of happened by accident, like it did the other time in the hot tub."

"Then what makes you think I can do it on demand?"

"I'm not saying you can. If you don't remember, you don't

remember. Like you said, you were probably pissing in the woods somewhere."

"Why would your dad say that to a kid?"

"Because he was my dad, Joe. He was fucked up. He probably didn't think I could hear him. And even if he did, if we're right and he drugged us, that whole weekend would be lost or fuzzy, which it is."

"You think Justin might be alive."

"I don't know. Maybe he was drugged, and my dad left him by the river to retrieve him later, only we found him first."

"Why would your dad keep him alive, if he..."

"I don't know. Maybe he didn't touch him after all. Damn!" I shoved my hand over my forehead and my fingers through my hair. "I want to get into his head, but I don't want to just as badly."

"I know. I get it. But if it helps us to think like he does, we need to try."

"Fine for you. You're not his flesh and blood."

"Just because you're his flesh and blood doesn't make you him. Remember that."

I nodded. I knew that. I truly did.

Still, getting into his mind scared me. I didn't want to get into his mind...and then find I understood him.

Find I was like him.

No. Just no.

My phone buzzed, a welcome respite from this line of thinking. Marjorie.

CHAPTER FORTY-SIX

Marjorie

I sat on a park bench next to Colin Morse. Neither of us felt comfortable talking on the phone or inside any building. So the park it was.

"There's no easy way to say this," I began. "Bryce and Joe found a cufflink at Tom's cabin. A gold cufflink, with the initials CM on it."

Colin lifted his brow.

"We think it's yours. It has to be."

"Except I never wore those cufflinks."

"So you do have gold cufflinks?"

He nodded. "They were a high school graduation gift, but I've never worn them. They're in my top dresser drawer in my parents' home in Denver."

"Are you sure? Have you seen them recently?"

"Well...no."

"Then it could be yours, right?"

"I'd say no, except..."

Silence again. I was getting damned tired of this routine.

Then, "I'm sorry about your mom."

Had I told him? Maybe. I couldn't recall. Everything was a jumble in my mind since my mother had disappeared. I couldn't think too much about her or I'd go crazy. I had to compartmentalize, or I'd give in.

I couldn't go to the dark place, no matter how enticing it was. I owed my family more than that.

I simply nodded. "Thanks."

Silence again.

I was done with this. I faced him, grabbing his shoulders and forcing him to meet my gaze. "Describe the cufflinks, Colin."

"I haven't looked at them in ages. Small gold ovals. Engraved with my initials in block lettering."

Sounded like a match, though he'd also just described every other pair of cufflinks I'd ever seen, minus the initials.

"Anything else you want to tell me?" I asked.

He looked down. Classic tell. Yeah, there was more.

"Spit it out, then. This time, you're going to level with me."

"I can't substantiate—"

I resisted the urge to shake him. "I don't give a damn! What's going on?"

"This is hard to say. I don't want to believe it. Not about anyone, and especially not about my own father."

I finally let go of his shoulders. "Tell me. Please. A lot of lives might depend on it."

"Only mine," he said.

"Tell me anyway."

He finally met my gaze, his eyes clouded. "I've found evidence that leads me to believe..."

"What, Colin? What?"

He sighed, cleared his throat, fidgeted, and then sighed again. "That my father was behind my abduction. That he"—again with the throat clear—"sold me to Tom Simpson."

★ ★ ★

"Hi, sweetheart," Bryce said when I called him.

"Hey, I need to talk to you and Joe."

"We're outside the office building. I can put you on speaker if you want, but I'm not sure we should be—"

"Sorry. I know you don't want to talk on any of our phones, but this can't wait. This is big. Put me on speaker. Can anyone hear you where you are?"

"Only the steers. It's Marj," he said, presumably to Joe. "She wants to talk to both of us."

"What is it, Sis?" Joe asked.

"I just talked to Colin."

"Where are you?" Joe asked. "We should speak in person."

"No," I said adamantly. "At this point, I don't care if anyone hears us. Colin *did* have a pair of gold cufflinks. They were a gift for high school graduation. He described them, and they sound like they could be a match to the ones we found at the cabin and outside the school playground. Only one problem."

"Yeah?" Joe said.

"He never wore them. They were always in the top drawer of his dresser at his parents' house."

"Are they there now?"

"He doesn't know. He'd have to go to Denver to find out."

"Then he needs to go to Denver."

"He refuses."

"Why?"

"Because"—I paused a minute—"he thinks..."

"He thinks what, Marj? At this point, we don't have to tiptoe around this. What does he think?"

"He's been doing more research. Apparently he had a

feeling, but he didn't tell us that night at the hotel. Not until he had proof. And he didn't want to find proof... In fact, he still can't quite substantiate..."

"Sis, come on," Joe said. "What are you getting at?"

I cleared my throat. "He didn't want to tell me this, but I pushed. I pushed hard, and he finally buckled."

"What? What did he tell you?" Bryce asked.

"This is so awful."

"What, Marjorie?"

"He found some documents. They weren't overly clear, but he's pretty sure—"

Nausea crawled up my throat in an acidic trail. I didn't want to tell Bryce. Didn't want to tell him his father was even more of a monster.

"—that his father sold him. To *your* father."

Stark silence on the other end of the line. Neither Bryce nor my brother spoke.

I cleared my throat. "I told him that probably wasn't the case."

Still silence.

"I mean, your father and the others never dealt in men, right? Just children"—I bit back the gagging in my throat—"and women. Right?"

Still nothing.

"You guys okay?"

But of course they weren't. Especially Bryce. In one day, Bryce had found out his father had bought his son for him and a young stud plaything for himself. If what Colin said was true, it wasn't hard to believe. If Tom Simpson could buy his own grandchild, he could certainly buy a grown man.

"Come on," I said. "You're scaring me now."

Bryce, then, "I'm sorry."

"Yeah. Sorry, Sis."

"It's okay. I'm pretty sick about it myself." And if *I* felt sick, I could only imagine how Bryce was feeling.

"I wish we knew how all of this fits together," Bryce said. "My dad. Colin. Ted Morse. Justin. The guy in the gray hoodie at the school."

"Don't forget the Spider," Joe said. "He's still missing."

"And the rock and the baseball card and the cufflink. Ruby thinks the cufflink was a plant."

"I trust her instincts," Joe said.

"I do too," I said. "But someone wants us to think Colin was where gray hoodie guy was."

"You don't think—" Bryce began.

"God, no! Colin is a shadow of his former self. He's not going to go skulking around a school playground. What would he have against Dale and Donny or *any* kids? Also, Dale thought he recognized the guy. We know Colin wasn't anywhere on that Caribbean compound."

"Whoever the gray hoodie guy is, he somehow got his hands on Colin's cufflink," Joe said.

"Or one that's identical to it," Bryce added.

I walked away from the bench where Colin and I had sat, and—

CHAPTER FORTY-SEVEN

Bryce

Silence on the other end of the line.

"Did you hear us?" I asked. "About the cufflink?"

Nothing. Maybe her battery had gone dead. If it had... Was someone listening in? Had someone...?

My heart hammered into itself, my chest heaving. "Marjorie? Sweetheart?"

"Sis," Joe said, his tone panicked. "What's going on?"

"Marj! Marj!" Franticness strangled me like a noose of fire.

Something was wrong. Very wrong.

"Did she say where she was?" Joe asked.

"No. I just assumed she was home. But now I'm not sure."

"Fuck," Joe said, pulling out his phone. "Keep that line open. I'm calling the cops."

"Marj!" I shouted again into the phone. "Marjorie! Talk to me! Damn it!"

"The cops are on the way," Joe said. "Keep that line open, whatever you do."

He didn't have to make the demand. No way was I severing my only line to the woman I loved.

No fucking way.

"We're coming, baby," I said into the phone, hoping

she could still hear me. "We're coming for you. I love you, Marjorie. Be strong. I love you."

EPILOGUE

Now I have what I need.

CONTINUE THE STEEL BROTHERS SAGA WITH BOOK TWELVE

Coming January 28, 2020

MESSAGE FROM HELEN HARDT

Dear Reader,

Thank you for reading *Ravenous*. If you want to find out about my current backlist and future releases, please like my Facebook page and join my mailing list. I often do giveaways. If you're a fan and would like to join my street team to help spread the word about my books. I regularly do awesome giveaways for my street team members.

If you enjoyed the story, please take the time to leave a review on a site like Amazon or Goodreads. I welcome all feedback. I wish you all the best!

Helen

Facebook
Facebook.com/HelenHardt

Newsletter
HelenHardt.com/SignUp

Street Team
Facebook.com/Groups/HardtAndSoul

ALSO BY HELEN HARDT

The Steel Brothers Saga:
Craving
Obsession
Possession
Melt
Burn
Surrender
Shattered
Twisted
Unraveled
Breathless
Ravenous
Insatiable (Coming Soon)

Blood Bond Saga:
Unchained
Unhinged
Undaunted
Unmasked
Undefeated

Misadventures Series:
Misadventures with a Rock Star
Misadventures of a Good Wife (with Meredith Wild)

The Temptation Saga:
Tempting Dusty
Teasing Annie
Taking Catie
Taming Angelina
Treasuring Amber
Trusting Sydney
Tantalizing Maria

The Sex and the Season Series:
Lily and the Duke
Rose in Bloom
Lady Alexandra's Lover
Sophie's Voice

Daughters of the Prairie:
The Outlaw's Angel
Lessons of the Heart
Song of the Raven

Cougar Chronicles:
The Cowboy and the Cougar
Calendar Boy

ACKNOWLEDGMENTS

Thank you for reading *Ravenous*! Things are heating up, and you know I can't resist a cliffhanger. All will be revealed in *Insatiable*!

Huge thanks to the following individuals whose effort and belief made this book shine: Jennifer Becker, Audrey Bobak, Haley Byrd, Yvonne Ellis, Martha Frantz, Jesse Kench, Robyn Lee, Jon Mac, Amber Maxwell, Dave McInerney, Michele Hamner Moore, Keli Jo Nida, Jenny Rarden, Chrissie Saunders, Scott Saunders, Celina Summers, Kurt Vachon, and Meredith Wild.

Thanks also to the women and men of Hardt and Soul. Your endless and unwavering support keeps me going.

To my family and friends, thank you for your encouragement.

And most importantly, thanks so much to my readers. None of this matters without all of you.

ABOUT THE AUTHOR

#1 *New York Times,* #1 *USA Today,* and #1 *Wall Street Journal* bestselling author Helen Hardt's passion for the written word began with the books her mother read to her at bedtime. She wrote her first story at age six and hasn't stopped since. In addition to being an award-winning author of romantic fiction, she's a mother, an attorney, a black belt in Taekwondo, a grammar geek, an appreciator of fine red wine, and a lover of Ben and Jerry's ice cream. She writes from her home in Colorado, where she lives with her family. Helen loves to hear from readers.

Visit her at HelenHardt.com